Into the Darkness

V.C. Andrews® Books

The Dollanganger Family Series
Flowers in the Attic
Petals on the Wind
If There Be Thorns
Seeds of Yesterday
Garden of Shadows

The Casteel Family Series
Heaven
Dark Angel
Fallen Hearts
Gates of Paradise
Web of Dreams

The Cutler Family Series
Dawn
Secrets of the Morning
Twilight's Child
Midnight Whispers
Darkest Hour

The Landry Family Series
Ruby
Pearl in the Mist
All That Glitters
Hidden Jewel
Tarnished Gold

The Logan Family Series
Melody
Heart Song
Unfinished Symphony
Music of the Night
Olivia

The Orphans Miniseries
Butterfly
Crystal
Brooke
Raven
Runaways (full-length novel)

The Wildflowers Miniseries
Misty
Star
Jade
Cat
Into the Garden (full-length novel)

My Sweet Audrina
(does not belong to a series)

The Hudson Family Series
Rain
Lightning Strikes
Eye of the Storm
The End of the Rainbow

The Shooting Stars Series
Cinnamon
Ice
Rose
Honey
Falling Stars

The De Beers Family Series
Willow
Wicked Forest
Twisted Roots
Into the Woods
Hidden Leaves

The Broken Wings Series
Broken Wings
Midnight Flight

The Gemini Series
Celeste
Black Cat
Child of Darkness

The Shadows Series
April Shadows
Girl in the Shadows

The Early Spring Series
Broken Flower
Scattered Leaves

The Secrets Series
Secrets in the Attic
Secrets in the Shadows

The Delia Series
Delia's Crossing
Delia's Heart
Delia's Gift

The Heavenstone Series
The Heavenstone Secrets
Secret Whispers

The March Family Series
Family Storms
Cloudburst

Daughter of Darkness

V.C. ANDREWS®

Into the Darkness

GALLERY BOOKS
New York   London   Toronto   Sydney   New Delhi

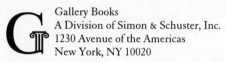

Gallery Books
A Division of Simon & Schuster, Inc.
1230 Avenue of the Americas
New York, NY 10020

Following the death of Virginia Andrews, the Andrews family worked with a carefully selected writer to organize and complete Virginia Andrews' stories and to create additional novels, of which this is one, inspired by her storytelling genius.

First Gallery Books hardcover edition March 2012

V. C. ANDREWS® and VIRGINIA ANDREWS® are registered trademarks of the Vanda General Partnership

GALLERY BOOKS and colophon are registered trademarks of Simon & Schuster, Inc.

For information about special discounts for bulk purchases, please contact Simon & Schuster Special Sales at
1-866-506-1949 or business@simonandschuster.com.

The Simon & Schuster Speakers Bureau can bring authors to your live event. For more information or to book an event contact the Simon & Schuster Speakers Bureau at
1-866-248-3049 or visit our website at www.simonspeakers.com.

Design by Esther Paradelo

Manufactured in the United States of America

10 9 8 7 6 5 4 3 2 1

Library of Congress Cataloging-in-Publication Data
Andrews, V. C. (Virginia C.)
  Into the darkness / V.C. Andrews. — 1st Pocket Books paperback ed.
    p. cm.
  I. Title.
  PS3551.N454I54 2012
  813'.54—dc23
                        2011029905

ISBN 978-1-4516-6430-0
ISBN 978-1-4516-5095-2 (ebook)

Into the Darkness

Prologue

He was looking at me from between the full evergreen hedges that separated our houses and properties. I don't know why he thought I wouldn't see him. Although it was what Mom called a crown jewels day because there were no clouds and the bright sunshine made everything glimmer and glisten, even dull rocks and old cars with faded paint, scratches, nicks and dents. The sun was behind me, so I wasn't blinded by its brilliance. In fact, it was like a spotlight reflecting off his twenty-four-karat-gold hair.

Even from where I was standing on our front porch, I could see he had blue-sapphire eyes. He had a very fair complexion, close to South Sea pearl, in fact, so that his face seemed to have a hazy, soft glow, which contrasted dramatically with the rich, deep green leaves of the hedges.

My first thought was that there must be something mentally wrong with him. Why else would he stand there gaping at someone unashamedly? When someone stares at you and doesn't care that you see him doing so, you're certainly ill at ease, even fearful. You might be angry, but nowadays, especially, you don't go picking fights with strangers. He wasn't a complete stranger, of course. I knew he was our new neighbor.

I had no idea whether he had been spying on me from the very first day that his family had moved into their house, but this was the first time I had caught him doing so. Because the hedges were easily five and a half feet high and he was crouching a little, I estimated that he was at least five feet ten inches tall. He was wearing dark blue jeans and a long-sleeved khaki shirt with epaulets, the sort of shirt that you might find in a store selling military paraphernalia and uniforms.

For a few moments, I pretended not to have noticed him. I looked away and then sat on the wide moonstone blue porch railing and leaned back against the post as if I were posing for a sexy dramatic shot in a film. I closed my eyes and took a deep breath like when the doctor tells you to breathe in and hold it while he moves his stethoscope over your back. My breasts lifted against my thin, light jade-green sweater, and I held the air in my lungs for nearly thirty seconds. Then, as if some film director were telling me to look more relaxed and more seductive for the shot, I released my breath and brought my right hand up to fluff my thick, black-opal shoulder-length hair.

For as long as I could remember, my family always described most colors in terms of jewels. My parents owned a jewelry store that had been established by my paternal grandparents in Echo Lake, Oregon, more than forty years ago. My grandfather taught my father how to make original jewelry, and most people who saw them said that he created beautiful pieces. My mother ran the business end of our store and was the main salesperson. Dad called her his personal CFO. I helped out from the day I could handle credit-card sales. Rings, necklaces, bracelets, earrings, and pendants found their way into almost any conversation at our dinner table. Nothing was just good in our world; it was as good as gold. Many things had a silver lining, and if something glittered, it glittered like diamonds.

Mom said my hair was truly opal because it was just as unique as the jewel. The color and the pattern of opals could change with the angle of view, and she claimed that the same was true for my hair.

"No one that I know has hair that changes color as subtly as yours does, Amber, especially in the sunlight." She took a deep breath and shook her head softly. "I swear, sweetheart, sometimes when I'm looking for you and see you from behind, I'm not sure it's you. Just as I am about to call out to you, your name gets caught in my mouth as if my tongue had second thoughts."

Dad wasn't as dramatic about it, but he didn't disagree. Mom was often histrionic. She had a bit of a Southern drawl and was a beautiful platinum-brown-haired woman who had once gone for a screen test at Screen Gems Studios in Wilmington, North Carolina, when she was still in high school because a young assistant producer had convinced her she could be the next Natalie Wood. She didn't get hired, but it was her moment in the sun. Dad was proud of her head shots and kept four of them on his desk at home.

I wondered if the boy next door would notice how my hair color subtly changed when I sat up and then walked slowly off the porch and into the sunlight. No one but my parents had ever mentioned it, although people did compliment me on the richness of my hair. I kept my arms folded just below my breasts and walked with my head down like someone in very deep thought, someone who was oblivious to anything and everything going on around her. I was barefoot and wore an ankle-length light blue cotton skirt and a gold ankle bracelet with tiny rubies. I was taking every step pensively as if the weight of a major decision were wrapped over my shoulders like a shawl full of great and desperate concerns. I guess I was always in some pose or another because I lived so much in my imagination. Dad always said I lived in my own movie.

"You're just like all you kids nowadays, always in one sort of performance or another," he said. "I watch the girls walking home from school. You could see every one is glancing around to see 'Who is looking at me?' Those girls with green, blue, and orange hair and rings in their noses drive me nuts."

"Don't knock the nose rings, Gregory Taylor. We sell them," Mom told him.

"Whatever happened to the au naturel look, the Ingrid Bergman look?" Dad cried, throwing up his arms. He had an artist's long, muscular fingers and arms that would have no trouble grabbing the golden ring on a merry-go-round. He was six feet two, slim, with what Mom called a Clark Gable mustache and jet-black hair with thin smoky gray strands leaking along his temples. He was rarely out in the sunlight during the summer to get a tan, but he had a natural dark complexion that brought out the jade blue in his eyes.

"Ingrid who?" I asked. I knew who she was. Both Mom and I just liked teasing him and suggesting that he was showing his age.

At that point, he would shake his head and either sit and pout or leave the room, and Mom and I would laugh like two conspirators. He wasn't really that angry, but it was part of the game we all liked to play. Dad was always claiming to be outnumbered and outvoted in his own home, whether it was a discussion of new furniture, dishes, drapes, or even cars. That comment would bring smiles but inevitably remind us that four years after I was born, Mom had miscarried in her seventh month. I would have had a brother. They seemed to have given up after that.

It was great having my parents' full attention, but I would have liked to have had a brother or a sister. I told myself I wouldn't fight with either or be jealous or be anything like most of the girls I knew when it came to their siblings. Their stories made it sound as if their homes rocked with screams and wails about unfair treatment or one being favored over the other. I could only wail or complain about myself to myself. It was like living in an echo chamber.

From what I could tell, the boy next door probably was an only child, too. I was certainly not spying on him and his parents, but my bedroom window looked out over the hedges at his house, and I couldn't help but see the goings-on. Days before, I was in my bedroom reading one of the books on my summer requirement list when I heard the truck arrive and saw the men begin to unload cartons. I had never really been in the house since the last people living there had left, but I recalled Dad saying they had left furniture.

Seeing new neighbors suddenly move in was a great surprise. My parents had never mentioned the neighboring house being sold or rented. No one had, in fact, and news like that in a community as small as ours usually made headlines. There were just too many busybodies to let a tidbit like that go unrevealed.

At first, I didn't even see that the neighbors had a son. His parents appeared along with the truck and the men. I didn't get that good a look at them, but the woman looked tall and very thin. She kept her opened left hand over the left side of her face, like someone who didn't want to be recognized, and hurried into the house as if she were caught in a cold downpour of rain and hail. Her husband was about the same height, balding, and I thought a little chubby, with an agate-brown goatee and glasses with frames as thick as silver dollars that caught the sunlight. He walked more slowly, moving like someone in deep thought. I wondered when they had first come around to look at the house. It had to have been a very quick decision.

After the movers began to bring things into the house, the boy suddenly appeared, as if he had been pouting in the backseat like someone who had been forced to come along. I didn't get that good a look at him, either. He had his head down and also walked quickly, but my first thought was that he was probably a spoiled only child, pouting, angry about having to leave his school and friends. Of course, he could have an older sister who was either at a college summer session or perhaps studying abroad.

I watched on and off as the move-in continued, the men carrying in clothing and some small appliances. It didn't take them very long. I waited to see more of the neighbors. No one emerged, and I didn't see the boy again until this day. As a matter of fact, I didn't see any of them. It was as if they had been swallowed up by the house. The moving men came out and drove off only an hour or so later. Immediately, it grew as quiet as it had been. None of the windows was opened, and no lights were turned on. One might think they had gone in the front door and out the back, never to be seen or heard from again.

Right now, I knelt down on my bright green lawn pretending to look for a four-leaf clover, but out of the corner of my eye, I was watching to see whether he would move away from the hedges or continue to spy on me. He never changed expression or turned his head away for an instant. Finally, I stood up abruptly and, with my heart racing, said, "Can I help you?"

I remained far enough away that I could quickly retreat to my house and lock the door behind me if need be.

He smiled. "What did you have in mind?" he replied.

"I'm not the one peeping," I said. "Maybe I should say 'gawking.'"

"Maybe you're not at this moment, but I've seen you looking for minutes at a time in my direction out your bedroom window between the curtains."

"That's different," I said, smothering my embarrassment. I had thought I was inconspicuous in my curiosity. And when had he seen me? I never caught sight of him or any of them looking out a window toward our house.

"And that's different because?"

"I was just . . . interested in who were to be our new neighbors. Who wouldn't be?"

"And I'm just curious about you. Who wouldn't be once he saw how pretty you are?" he asked.

I felt myself blush. Dad always said I didn't blush red so much as a cross between the translucent golden yellow of a bangle and a touch of a pink coral bead. Mom said he was color-blind for a jeweler and that I had more of a classic deep red ruby tint in my cheeks when I blushed. Both agreed that I normally had a light pink Akoya pearl complexion with a face that was truly a cameo because of my perfect diminutive features, especially my slightly almond-shaped eyes and soft Cupid's bow lips, all of which I had inherited from Mom.

"Well, you don't have to spy on me through the hedges," I said in a less belligerent tone. "You could have just come by to say hello and introduce yourself properly."

Although my parents and their friends always lavished great compliments on me, I was never sure of myself when it came to responding to one. A simple "Thank you" seemed to be too little. Not saying anything seemed to be arrogant, as if I was thinking my beauty was obvious or I was too stuck-up to respond. And pretending to be surprised and falsely modest always came off as phony, at least when I saw other girls and even boys doing that. I didn't deny to myself that I was attractive. I just didn't know whether I should rejoice in my blessings or be concerned about the responsibilities they brought along with them.

I know none of my girlfriends at school would understand how being attractive brought responsibilities, but I always felt obligated to make sure that I didn't flaunt myself or take anything anyone said for granted. I also felt I had to be careful about whom I showed any interest in, even looked at twice. People, especially older men, were always telling me I would be a heartbreaker. To me, that didn't sound very nice. I envisioned a trail of men with shattered emotions threatening to commit suicide everywhere I went.

"You're absolutely right," the new boy said. He stepped between the hedges and approached. I was right about his height. He was at least five feet ten, if not five feet eleven. With the palms of both hands and his fingers stiffly extended, he brushed back his hair. Uneven strands still fell over his forehead and his eyes. His hair was almost as long as mine and certainly looked as thick and as rich. He had perfectly shaped facial features like those of Greek and Roman statues. I thought he had a remarkable complexion, not a blemish, not a dark spot or anything to spoil the softness and smoothness. For a moment, I wondered if he wore makeup. He wasn't heavily built, but he looked athletic, like a swimmer or a tennis player.

"I apologize for, as you say, gawking at you. I didn't intend to make you feel uncomfortable. Although," he added with an impish smile, "you didn't quite look uncomfortable. Matter of fact, you looked like you were enjoying it."

Before I could respond, he performed a dramatic stage bow and added, "I'm Brayden Matthews." He extended his hand awkwardly, as if he wasn't sure it was something he should do.

"Amber Taylor. And I wasn't enjoying it. I was uncomfortable seeing someone staring at me like that. Actually, I tried to ignore you."

He kept holding his hand out.

"I'm glad you couldn't," he said.

I offered my hand. He closed his fingers around it very gently, watching his fingers fold around mine as if he was amazed that his could bend or he was afraid that he might break mine. Then he smiled like someone who had felt something very satisfying, as if shaking someone's hand was a significant accomplishment. He tightened his grip a little and didn't let go.

"Can I have my hand back?"

"So soon?" he replied. He let go and then looked up at our house. "Your house is one of the older houses on the street, right? Not that it looks run-down or anything. Matter of fact, it looks quite well cared for."

"It's the oldest on the street," I said as modestly as I could. My father was always bragging about it. "It's been in our family for a little more than eighty-five years," I said. "Of course, there have been many renovations, but the first fireplace still stands just the way it was. The floors are the same, as are the window casings. My father treats it more like a historical site."

"I bet. There was a time when things were built to last," he said.

"Really? How old are you, ninety, a hundred?"

He softly laughed, flashed me an amused look, and then gazed at my house again, concentrating, I thought, on my bedroom windows. "I bet you can see the lake from your window." He turned to look at his own roof. "Your house looks to be about ten feet taller than ours."

"Yes, I can," I said. "At least the bay. This time of the year, the trees are so full they block out most of it."

The lake was only a little more than a half-mile from our street, but it was a privately owned lake anyway. Because our homes weren't lake homes, we weren't shareholders in the Echo Lake Corporation. Most everyone who didn't belong thought the people who did were snobby about their property and their rights, but I thought these people were simply jealous. It was true that no one without lake rights could swim, row, or fish there. You had to be invited by a member, but what would be the point of having a private lake and expensive lakeside property otherwise? We had been invited from time to time. Most recently, the Mallens had invited us for a picnic on the lake. George Mallen was president of the Echo Lake bank, and Dad always gave him good deals on the jewelry that he bought for his wife and two older daughters, both married and living in Portland.

"So I guess you've lived here all your life," he said.

"Yes, that's a safe assumption to make."

He laughed again. I could see that he really enjoyed talking to me. It was like sparring with words.

"Where are you from?" I asked.

"Oh, somewhere out there," he replied, waving his right hand over his shoulder. "We've lived in so many different places that the U.S. Postal Service has declared us undesirables. They're still trying to deliver mail sent to us ten years ago."

"Very funny, but you had to be born somewhere, right?"

"I think it was on a jet crossing the Indian Ocean," he replied. "Luckily, we were in first class. I'm a sea baby, or more of an air baby. Yes, that's it. I'm from the international air above the Taj Mahal."

"Sure. Your parents are Americans, aren't they?" I asked, not so sure.

"Yes."

"Then you're an American."

"Very constitutional of you."

He looked at my window again. "My bedroom faces yours, you know. Yours is about six inches higher but diametrically opposite."

"Thanks for the warning, now that I know you're a Peeping Tom."

He laughed.

"I wasn't peeping, really, as much as I was wondering if you would see me."

"I'd have to have been either blind or terribly oblivious not to."

"Well, I'm glad you're not either."

"Why was it so important to test me about that?"

He looked stymied as to an answer. "I'm sorry. You're right. It was juvenile and not the best way to make a new friend." He looked afraid that I would end the conversation or continue to take him to task.

"Apology accepted," I said.

"Whew." He wiped his forehead. I couldn't help but smile at his exaggerated action.

"Okay, we don't know where you're from, but what made your parents decide to move here of all places?"

"Why? Is it that bad here? You make it sound like the last stop on the train or the edge of the world."

"No, it's far from bad here. I just wondered. We don't get that many new families these days."

"I think my father put a map on the wall, blindfolded himself, and threw a dart. It hit Echo Lake, Oregon."

"You're kidding, right?"

He nodded and smiled. "It's what he tells people. My father has a dry sense of humor."

"Brayden," we heard. It was a woman's voice, but she sounded very far-off. "Bray . . . den." In fact, it seemed she was calling from inside a tunnel, and she sounded a little desperate, almost in a panic.

His smile evaporated. "Gotta go," he said. "It's been nice talking to you, and I apologize again for being a Gawking Tom."

"I'll settle for Peeping Tom. Who's calling you?"

"My mother. We're still moving in. Lots to do. Help with unpacking, setting things up, rearranging and cleaning up the furniture that was there, and organizing the kitchen," he listed quickly. He leaned toward me to whisper, "My dad's not too handy around the house." He pointed to his temple. "Intellectual type, you know. Thinks a screwdriver is only a glass of orange juice and vodka."

"I'm sure he's not that bad. What does he do?"

"He's a member of a brain trust. Meets with other geniuses to discuss and solve world economic problems.

All quite hush-hush, top-secret stuff, so secret that he doesn't know what he's talking about."

"What?"

He laughed again. "I wasn't kidding about our living in many places. Often we go on family trips to foreign countries and around the country—when he's going to be away for a prolonged time, that is."

"Do you have any brothers or sisters?"

"None that I know of," he replied with a sly smile. "You're an only child, too, I take it, and your parents own a jewelry store on Main Street, a jewelry store that has been in your family for decades."

"You did some homework?"

"I've scouted the neighborhood. A few interesting people live on this block, especially that elderly lady who hangs her clothes on a line at the side of her house, visible to anyone walking in the street."

"Mrs. Carden. What about her? What makes her so interesting? Many people like to hang out their clothes in the fresh air. Mrs. Carden's not unique."

Mrs. Carden was an eighty-something retired grade-school teacher who had lived for ten years as a widow and never had any children of her own. She would smile and nod at me when I walked by, but I didn't think I had spoken a dozen words to her in the past five years. I was curious about why someone new would find her interesting.

"Oh, I think she is quite unique," he insisted.

"Why?"

"She whispers to her clothes as if they were errant children, scolding a blouse for being too wrinkled or a skirt for shrinking. I think she put a pair of stockings in the corner, sort of a time-out for wearing too thin or something. Maybe that's something a grade-school teacher would do, but I've always found people who hold discussions with inanimate objects unique, don't you?"

"Errant children?"

"Hang around with me. I'll build your vocabulary," he said, winking.

"If she was whispering, how did you hear her? Were you spying on her, too?"

"A little, but I have twenty-twenty hearing," he kidded. "So watch what you whisper about me."

"Bray . . . den," I heard again. It sounded the same, a strange, thin call, like a voice riding on the wind.

"Gotta go," he repeated, backing away as though something very strong was pulling him despite his resistance. He spun around to slip home through the hedges and then paused and turned back to me. "Can you come out for a walk tonight?"

"A walk?" I smiled with a little incredulity. "A walk?"

"Too simple an invitation?" he asked, and looked around. "It's going to be a very pleasant evening. Haven't you ever read Thoreau? 'He who sits still in a house all the time may be the greatest vagrant of all.' Are you afraid of walking? I don't mean a trek of miles or anything. No backpacks required."

"I'm not afraid of walking," I shot back. "And I love Thoreau."

He lifted his arms to say, *So?* And then he waited for my response.

"Okay, I'll go for a walk. When?"

"Just come out. I'll know."

"Why? Are you going to hover between the hedges watching and waiting?"

He laughed. "Just come out. A walk might not sound like very much to you, but I've got to start somewhere," he said.

"Start? Start what?"

"Our romance. I can't ask you to marry me right away."

"What?"

He laughed again and then slipped through the bushes. I stepped up to them to look through and watch him go into his house, but he was gone so quickly I didn't even hear a door open and close.

How could he be gone so fast? I leaned in farther and looked at his house, a house that had been empty and uninteresting for so long it was as if it wasn't there. I felt silly doing what he had been doing, gawking in between the hedges, studying his house, checking all the windows, listening for any conversations. It's the very thing I criticized him for doing, I thought, and I stepped away as if I had been caught just as I had caught him.

He was very good-looking, but there was something quirky about him. Nevertheless, it didn't put me off. In fact, it made him more appealing, a lot more alluring than the other boys my age that I knew. No matter how hard most of them tried, there was a commonality about them, about the way they dressed and talked. As Dad would say whenever the topic of young romance came up, "I guess no one has yet set the diamonds in your eyes glittering, Amber Light." That was his nickname for me, Amber Light.

No, none of the boys in my school had set the diamonds in my eyes glittering, I thought, and which one of
them even would think to mention Henry David Thoreau as a way of enticing me to do something with him?

Looking around, I agreed that it truly would be a
beautiful late June night. I laughed to myself. Almost any
other boy I knew would have asked me to go to the movies
or go for a burger or pizza or simply hang out at the mall
as a first date. But just go for a walk? I didn't think so.

I started back to my house. I thought I might finish
some summer required reading and then help Mom with
dinner. It was Friday night, and Dad kept the store open
an hour or so later than usual.

I was almost to the porch steps when I stopped and
looked around. There was something odd about the day.
What was it?

It was too quiet, I realized. And there were no birds
flying around or calling, just a strangely silent crow
settled on the roof of Brayden's house.

We lived on a cul-de-sac, so not having any traffic
wasn't unusual, and it wasn't unusual to see no people
outside their homes for long periods of time. Yet the
stillness felt different. I didn't even hear the sounds of
far-off traffic or an airplane or anything. It was as if I had
stepped out of the world for a few moments and was now
working my way back in.

And despite the brilliant sunshine, I felt a chill surge
through my body. I embraced myself and hurried up the
stairs. I paused on the porch and looked at the house next
door. Up in what I now knew was Brayden's bedroom
window, the curtains parted.

But I didn't see him.

I didn't see anyone.

And then a large cloud blocked out the sun, dropping a shroud of darkness over the entire property. It happened so quickly it was as if someone had flipped a light switch. Under the shroud of shadows, the neighboring house looked even more tired and worn. The new residents hadn't done anything yet to turn it from a house into a home. It doesn't take all that long for a house to take on the personalities and identities of the people living in it, but this house looked just the way it had before I saw the Matthewses move into it.

It was as if the whole thing, including my conversation with Brayden, was another one of my fantasies, another movie Dad thought I lived in. I could hear him laughing about it and then doing his imitation of me walking like someone in a daze, oblivious but content.

All of this from a short conversation with a new neighbor who made me realize how different I was from any of the girls I knew. None would have agreed to go for a walk with a stranger so quickly, especially at night. Why had I? Where was my sensible fear of new boys, especially one who talked and behaved as he had? I could just hear my friends when and if I told them. *You agreed to go for a walk with a stranger who was spying on you like that? Crazy.*

Maybe I was.

But when I looked at my reflection in the window, I thought I saw diamonds glittering in my eyes.

1

New Neighbor

"I met one of our new neighbors," I said when my parents and I sat at the long, dark oak dining-room table for dinner.

The dining room was almost as large as our living room. Grandpa Taylor had had the wall between it and the kitchen removed to accommodate this handmade table. Grandpa had been a lot more political and involved with the local government than Dad. Dad said there had been many important business dinners held there with other important families. It had been my mother's idea to take out the two small windows and have one big window made. We had a view of the woods and the field on this side of the house. My favorite time was autumn, when the colors of the leaves rivaled those of all the jewelry in our store. My mother once whispered to me that although my grandfather believed I was named after amber jewelry, I was really named after the amber leaves.

Tonight Mom and I had prepared one of Dad's favorite meals, chicken piccata with Israeli couscous. I did the salad and heated the bread. Dad opened a bottle of Chardonnay and poured each of us a glass. Ever since I was fourteen, my parents had permitted me to have wine with them at dinner. Dad was proud of his knowledge of wines and never lost an opportunity to talk about them, either with us or with customers at the store. Tonight we were having a California Chardonnay from Sonoma. He described it as just a touch dry but with a nice clarity.

Neither of my parents had mentioned the new neighbors since I had told them about someone new coming to the street. There was never a For Rent or For Sale sign in front of the house after the previous occupants had sold it. Someone came periodically to cut the lawn and trim the bushes, but other than that, nothing much was done. The paint was still chipped on the porch railings and the window frames, and the steps on the front stoop looked as if they needed some reinforcement, if not outright replacement.

I suppose it wasn't all that unusual for us not to know that the house was going to have new tenants or owners. We had grown accustomed to seeing it unoccupied. No one on the street bothered to talk much about it anymore. It hadn't fallen enough into ill repair to warrant the city taking any action. It was easier for everyone simply to ignore it. My parents were very busy at the jewelry store with tourists from Canada and the States pouring into the area. I had been the only one at home when the truck had appeared and the men had begun carrying in things. My parents had been at the store doing an inventory. Dad wanted enough raw materials for him to work up his unique bracelets and pendants.

"You met one of the new neighbors?" Mom repeated.

Dad was still standing with the bottle of wine in his

hand as if he had forgotten to pour someone a glass and was trying to figure out who that was.

"I was beginning to think that house would remain vacant forever. What's it been, four years since the Sloans moved to Dallas?" he asked, then put the bottle on the table and sat.

"More like five," Mom said. She tasted the dressing I had prepared for the salad and smiled. "You're getting very good at this, Amber. We should open a restaurant."

"Thanks, but no thanks," Dad said. "I see how Von Richards has aged. The man's only a year older than I am and could be mistaken for my father. He was quite an athlete in high school, too. But that restaurant is a vampire, draining him. He's always complaining about his help and the price of food, not to mention the picky customers he has to serve. Soon he'll set the place on fire."

"Oh, it's not that bad," Mom said. "But I agree that there is a lot more stress with a restaurant than there is with a jewelry store."

"Speak for yourself when it comes to measuring the stress," Dad said, and laughed before she could slam back a retort. Both of us could see it coming. He winked at me. I knew he was just teasing her. I wondered how many girls in my class were as synchronized with their fathers as I was with mine. "So, whom did you meet, Amber Light? I don't even know their names. Do you know their names, Noreen?" Dad asked.

Mom shook her head. "Been too busy to get involved with neighbors. I know that's not nice, but who told them to move in at the start of our busy season?"

"Right," Dad said, raising his glass. "Anyway, to the new neighbors, whoever they are, as long as they don't have an annoying barking dog or something."

Mom lifted her wineglass. I lifted mine, too.

"Their last name is Matthews," I said after we all had taken a sip.

"Oh?" Dad began his salad. "This is a good dressing."

"I didn't meet the husband and wife, just their son."

"What's his name?"

"Brayden."

"Brayden. That's an unusual name," Dad said. "Interesting."

"Which fits him," I said.

"Why?"

"He seems unusual."

"In a good or bad way?" Dad quickly followed up.

I thought a moment and shrugged. "Good."

"How old is he?" Mom asked, suddenly looking suspicious at the way I had responded to my father's question.

"About my age, maybe a little older," I said.

"Sooooo," she said, raising her eyebrows and looking at Dad, who broadened his smile. "Good-looking? On a scale of one to ten," she added, fixing her gaze on Dad. "If men can do it, rate women all the time the way some people rate diamonds . . ."

Dad put up his hands. "Who has time to rate women?"

"Yes, like it takes time," Mom said. She turned to me. "Well?"

I shrugged. "Eleven, I guess," I said, and they both went into stop action. That made me laugh. "We just spoke for a few minutes. Apparently, they travel a great deal. His father is some kind of genius who works in something called a brain trust."

"Is that so? What do they study?" Dad asked.

"Economics . . . world economics, top-secret stuff, he said."

"Good. Maybe he'll help me find a way to lower my insurance costs."

"I got the feeling he works mainly in theories and not . . ."

"Mundane, everyday stuff like me," Dad said.

"What do you mean, you? I think that description fits my job description more than yours," Mom said.

Dad raised his hands again. "Well rebuked. I admit it. I had trouble with simple multiplication and division. Your mother is an absolute whiz with numbers. If it weren't for her, we'd be bankrupt."

"Flattery will get you everywhere," Mom said.

"I'm not looking to go anywhere else," Dad said. Mom laughed and then began to serve our main dish.

I suppose I should say I was blessed having parents like mine. For one thing, they seemed continually in love. I knew everyone's mother and father were supposed to be in love, but when I met any of them or spent time with any of them, I had the feeling that, yes, maybe they had fallen in love once, but somehow life had put a sort of crust around their feelings. I think they had gotten too used to each other and took everything for granted, even smiles and laughter. For my parents, almost everything one of them said still seemed surprising to the other. I could see the delight on their faces.

Maybe it was corny, but to me, they seemed never to grow tired of looking at each other with what I had come to understand was pure desire. They wanted to be together, to go out together, and to go on trips together. It seemed so important that any discovery either one made be immediately shared, and anything they could discover together was always extra special.

If any of her female friends asked her why it was so important they always do so much together, Mom loved to quote Dante Gabriel Rossetti's line, "Beauty without the beloved is like a sword through the heart."

Some of her friends nodded and smiled; some looked completely puzzled but were obviously afraid to ask for a further explanation.

"Tell us more about him," Mom said. "This eleven, Brayden Matthews."

"I don't know all that much yet. In fact," I said, "I don't know anything except that he likes reading Thoreau."

"Thoreau?" Dad shook his head. "'Time is but the stream I go a-fishing in.'"

"Why, Gregory Taylor, the only things I ever hear you quote these days are prices on rings and bracelets," Mom teased.

"Is that so? I want you both to know that I won the English award at high school graduation. I used to dream of living the life Thoreau proposed. If we all did, there would be fewer heart attacks, strokes, and nervous breakdowns," he said, waving his extended right forefinger like some soap-box orator.

"Big shot," Mom said, pointing her fork at him. She turned to me. "This is the man who wants us to get a new television set because ours isn't high-definition. That's not very Thoreau-like, Mr. Taylor."

"Well, if we're going to work ourselves to the bone . . ." Dad paused and thought a moment. "I said I dreamed of living like Thoreau. I also remember dreaming of being Superman."

We both laughed.

"So, why was this eleven talking about Thoreau?" Mom asked.

"He asked me to take a walk, and when I hesitated, he quoted Thoreau to emphasize how important it was to get out of the house and into nature."

"Now, there's a new approach," Dad said. "Quoting famous authors to win over a young maiden's heart."

"Really? As I recall, you quoted poetry when we first met, Gregory Taylor," Mom said. She sat back and narrowed her eyes in a pose of faux suspicion. "Was it just a slick come-on or did you mean it?"

Dad tugged his left earlobe as if he was hoping to shake the right response out of his brain. "It happened to be spontaneous. The moment I set eyes on you, I thought, 'Shall I compare thee to a summer's day? Thou art more lovely and more temperate . . .'"

"That wasn't the quote," Mom said.

"It wasn't?"

"No. You were a John Denver fan."

"Oh, right." Dad smiled. "'You're so beautiful, I can't believe my eyes each time I see you again.'"

"I thought he had made it up until he played the

song for me," Mom told me. "Of course, I wondered how many girls he used that line on, but he swore I was the first," she added, looking at him suspiciously again.

"You were—the first and only, Noreen, and always will be."

Mom's eyes glittered like the eyes of diamonds that Dad anticipated I would someday have for a certain special man.

In fact, if someone really wanted to know why I was so hard to please when it came to boyfriends, he or she simply had to spend a few minutes with my parents. The man I fell in love with would have to have eyes full of me the way my father's eyes were full of my mother, I thought. I'd never be some man's stopover on his way to finding someone he believed was right for him. Maybe that was my problem. I was adamant about it. I had seen too many of my girlfriends devastated by boys they had thought were special. Of course, the same was very true for boys who thought that of girls. Sometimes, I thought, it was all just too complex. *Think less, feel more,* I told myself, but I didn't listen to myself, at least not right then.

"So, are you going on this walk?" Mom asked.

"I guess. It's just a walk."

"Nothing is *just* anything," Dad said, assuming the role of elder statesman in our house. "Everything leads to something else, young lady. Shall I review history, the causes of the First World War, the . . ."

"Spare us, Gregory. Besides, did you ever think that's what she's hoping for, something leading to something? Don't throw cold water."

I felt myself blush. "No. Really. It's just a walk. I

don't even know if I like him or anything. I just spoke to him for a few minutes. I mean, I hardly . . ."

I struggled to find the right words. Both of them laughed.

I felt as embarrassed as a little girl who had stumbled on something very sophisticated, like the time I asked how women without husbands could still make babies.

"Oh, we're just funning you," Mom said, reaching for my hand. "You just go and enjoy yourself."

"I don't know," Dad said. "Eleven or not, I should meet this boy first. He might be a young Jack the Ripper. Rumor was that Jack the Ripper was a handsome man who could easily tempt the young women."

"Stop it, Gregory," Mom snapped. "She doesn't need to be frightened off." Her eyes could widen and flame with such fury that I was sure anyone she targeted, including Dad, would cower like a frightened puppy. I knew why she was a little upset. They were both worried about my not having much of a social life. Sometimes I thought they worried about it a lot more than I did or should.

Parents could be so confusing, so filled with contradictions. On one hand, they would be full of great concern and warning, suspicious of everything you did and anyone you knew, but on the other hand, they wanted you to participate, to have a so-called normal youth. Secretly, they dreaded the day the first boy came to take you out, drive you off, because now they would be nervous and concerned, watch the clocks, and fear ringing phones. But then there was the pride in their eyes when you dressed up and looked older.

"She knows I'm just kidding," Dad said, winking at me again. "Right, Amber Light? Besides, he's right next door. I know where to go if you're not back in four or five days."

Mom relaxed with a slight smile. We both had that gentle, almost habitual softening in our lips and eyes. More times than I could count, people had remarked to me how my mother was always so up, so friendly and pleasant to talk to. I think some people stopped in the store to do just that and in passing might pick up a small gift for a relative's or friend's birthday.

She turned to me. "Don't worry about the dishes tonight, Amber. Go for your walk. Get to know the neighbors, and find out all the dirt on them before Risa Donald does and burns up a few cell phones spreading stories."

Dad laughed.

"What are you laughing about, Gregory Morton Taylor? She was the first to spread that rumor that we were in economic trouble during the recession, and all those people who had orders with us were worried about their deposits."

"I go with Katharine Hepburn," Dad said. "I don't care what they say about me as long as it isn't true."

"Who's Katharine Hepburn?" I asked.

"Who's . . ." Dad's smile started to fade until Mom and I laughed. "You be careful, young lady," he said, waving his right forefinger at me again, "or I'll force you to watch a Turner Classic Movie marathon."

After dinner, I went upstairs and checked my hair and my lipstick and did Mom's favorite little trick:

spraying the air with her cologne and then walking into it. I looked at myself in the mirror and fiddled with some strands and then debated putting on some eyeliner. Some men, like my father, were put off by a woman who wore too much makeup. Dad always compared this one or that one to Mrs. Hassler, an eighty-four-year-old widow who had her face so caked that Dad said she had it done by Michael Tooey, the funeral director, just so she wouldn't look much different in the coffin.

"Why are you carrying on so much about your hair and your makeup, Amber Taylor?" I asked my mirror image. "You just spoke to this boy for five minutes, if that. You didn't get this concerned when you went on dates with boys you've known almost all your life. Get hold of yourself."

I stared at my image and then suddenly saw a little rage flow into my eyes.

"I don't feel like getting hold of myself," I said with defiance. "I feel like loosening those reins I keep on myself. Tonight I'd like to gallop," I added, and then smiled at one of my pretend multiple personalities. Moments later, I was bouncing down the stairs as if it was my sixteenth birthday again and I was looking forward to wonderful presents. My parents couldn't help but hear me.

"I'll be back in a little while," I shouted. "Don't call Sherlock Holmes if I'm gone more than a half hour."

"You know who Sherlock Holmes is?" Dad returned.

"I saw the remake," I replied.

"Oh. Well, watch out for Risa Donald," Dad continued from the living room. "Word has it she's hiding in the bushes with binoculars and just waiting for new gossip."

I heard Mom's laugh as I went out the front door. For a few moments, I just stood there, wondering what to do next. How would Brayden know I was coming out of the house unless he had been waiting and watching my front door for the last hour? I didn't have to wonder long. He was there in the street, just vaguely visible in the glow of the moonlight through some hazy clouds. Our street had no lights. No one in the neighborhood wanted them. They were willing to sacrifice the feeling of security for a more natural northwestern sky, often dazzling with shooting stars.

He raised his hand, and I walked slowly to our front gate. He didn't come forward. He waited for me to reach him, with a look of self-satisfaction on his face. I thought, *That's a bit arrogant.* I certainly didn't like being taken for granted, certainly not by someone I had just met. He hadn't even changed his clothes, whereas I had agonized over what would be attractive to wear on a walk.

"What were you doing? Waiting out here for a few hours?" I asked.

"Nope."

"You weren't being a Peeping Tom again, were you?" I asked, now suspicious. Had he planted himself at one of our windows and therefore known when we had finished dinner and when I had gone upstairs to get ready? Or maybe he had been watching my bedroom and seen me make all those preparations, fussing about. I couldn't remember now if my curtains were fully closed, but if he had seen that, I would be almost as embarrassed as I would had he seen me naked.

"Absolutely not," he said, raising his hand to imitate someone on the witness stand in a courtroom. "I learned my lesson about gawking and peeping."

I looked at his house. There were barely any lights on. The entire downstairs was dark.

"Are your parents at home?"

"My father's gone on a trip somewhere in the Middle East. My mother is upstairs, painting." He turned around and started down the street.

I walked quickly to catch up. It was as if he were going with me or without me. I thought that was rude, too, but I didn't complain or turn back. It would be a long time before I would decide for sure whether it was good or bad that I had continued. So many things we do in our lives seem right or wrong at the time but take on a different meaning when years pass and wisdom and experience change our views.

"Painting? What do you mean, painting the house inside?"

"No, hardly," he said, continuing what I thought was a rather fast pace for a get-to-know-you walk. Why was he in such a rush to get away from his house? "My mother is an artist. Some of her work has been in MoMA."

"MoMA?"

"The Museum of Modern Art in New York. And other places, especially art magazines. She goes by the name Saraswati."

"Sara what?"

He laughed. "It's her little joke, I think. Saraswati is the Hindu goddess of all the creative arts. Most people just think it's her real name."

"Is your mother Hindu?"

He finally slowed down but showed no signs of being out of breath. He looked back at his house. Had he just left without telling his mother? Would she be annoyed or something? Whether he knew it or not, he was making me feel uncomfortable.

"Well?" I said when he didn't respond.

"Not exactly, but she does believe in reincarnation, one of the main Hindu beliefs."

"She believes you can have more than one life?"

"Absolutely. If you're good, you come back as something or someone better. If you're bad, just the opposite."

"So, were you good or bad in your previous life?"

"I'm still deciding," he said. "And so is she," he added, but he dropped his voice until it was close to a whisper.

"Most of the parents I know think their children are God's gift," I said, and he laughed.

"Ain't that the truth." He paused and looked toward the lake. "I found a path that will take us to the lake quickly. Want to try it?"

"There are No Trespassing signs everywhere around Echo Lake. It has no public access."

"I don't think they have armed guards watching, do you? Besides, I can't believe you're so law-abiding. I bet you jaywalk."

"Most of the year, there's not enough traffic here for it to matter."

"Rationalization," he said. "Well? Want to risk going to prison with me?"

I looked in the direction he wanted us to head. It

went through thick woods. Even with the moonlight, it was quite dark. I had expected that when he suggested a walk, he meant a walk to the village, maybe to have a soda or something. Why did I spend so much time on my face and my hair if I was going to walk in the darkness?

"Are you afraid of being in the dark with me?" he asked when I continued to hesitate.

"It's not just you being a stranger. You just moved here days ago. How do you know how to navigate through the woods and all? I certainly don't and I've been here all my life."

"Oh, I have radar like bats. I haven't been sitting inside the house. I've been exploring. Trust me," he said. "It's worth the walk."

"If I ruin these shoes . . ." I'd had no idea that he wanted to go off the road. I was wearing a relatively new pair of soft buck leather comfort shoes.

"We come to any puddles or mud, I carry you across. Guaranteed. Well?"

There was something about the way his eyes picked up the moonlight when it sidestepped the clouds. They didn't reflect it; they absorbed it. They seemed to grow larger, brighter. Maybe he did have radar. I was a little annoyed at the way he smiled at me as I considered where he wanted us to go, but I was also quite intrigued. It was more like a challenge, as if he expected that I would back away and run home or something, and yet he looked as if he was really enjoying the debate I was having within myself.

"What are we going to see?"

"No way to describe it," he said. "But I'll bet it's a view of the lake you've never experienced."

"How could you know that? You haven't been here long enough to know more than I do about my hometown and what I've seen and not seen of the lake."

"If I'm wrong, I'll apologize," he said.

Was this crazy? Was I about to go deep into the darkest part of the woods in our village with a boy I had just met literally hours ago and with whom I had spent no more than fifteen minutes? All I knew about him was that he had a mother who was an artist who believed in reincarnation and a father who was gone most of the time doing top-secret economic research or something. Their house looked barely inhabited, and he wouldn't even tell me exactly where he was from. Daddy's joke about Jack the Ripper came tumbling back through my mind.

But then he reached for my hand and took it so gently I stopped thinking bad thoughts instantly.

"Okay?"

"Yes," I said. For a moment, I felt hypnotized. During that moment, it was as if I would follow him anywhere, even through a raging fire.

He held on to my hand, and we crossed in between the Knottses' and the Littlefields' houses. We could hear the televisions going in both, since both families had their windows open. It was a cool summer night, the kind of night when you at least wanted the air flowing through your home, if you didn't go out for a walk or something as we were doing.

"I bet if you could check, you would be hard-pressed to find a house in this village or any town or city where young people our age aren't planted in front of a TV set or a computer screen right now."

"So?" I said.

"So? So, it's a Facebook world where no one sees himself or herself anymore. They look into the new mirrors of our world, and instead of discovering who they really are, they see who they dream of being."

He nodded at the Littlefield house and continued.

"They swim in illusions and disappointments. The sound of someone's voice, the feel of her hands in yours, the scent of her hair, and the electricity of her very life in her eyes is diffused and filtered until what was once warm and human is now a matter of megabytes. I have seen best friends trapped in flash drives."

I stood there, mesmerized. "You don't have a computer?"

"With a father like mine, how could I not have a computer? He had a laptop in the delivery room."

I laughed, but I felt energized, inspired. How bright was he? "What grade are you in?" I asked.

"When I left, I was in the eleventh. You're going to be a senior this year."

"I don't remember telling you that."

"Just like for a walk in the woods, I research first," he replied.

"So we could have classes together?"

"I don't know how long I'll be here."

"What?" I paused. "I don't understand. Your parents rented the house?"

"Sorta."

"How can you sort of rent a house?" I asked.

He started us walking again. We sidestepped a ditch and stepped through a patch of blueberry bushes.

"So?"

"It's like a test run."

"Test run? You mean, to see if you like it, like living here?"

"Yes, exactly. We've done that before—many times before, actually."

"Oh. I guess that makes sense. When you say 'many times before,' what do you mean? How many?"

"Ten, twelve."

"I don't know what it must be like to move so much. I've lived only in one place, one house."

"Believe me, you're lucky," he said. "No matter what you think of your hometown."

"I don't think badly of my hometown. I know I'm supposed to. I'm supposed to be like everyone else and talk incessantly about when I'll finally get out. Some of them make it sound like we're in a prison."

"We're all in one sort of prison or another," he said. "Wait until they get to live in big urban centers and feel the indifference. Nothing makes you feel insignificant as much as walking down a street with about five thousand other people. They'll wish they were back here."

"You talk like you've lived for centuries."

"It's not how long you live; it's what you live, where you've been, what you've done. Life's like a glass you can fill with either water or wine."

I realized how interesting, even exciting, it would be to have someone like him in my school, in my classes—actually, in my life.

"Well, in case you do stay on and attend our school, you know we have a summer reading list with reports to make and . . ."

"I'm sure I've read everything you've been assigned," he said, not with disdain as much as with self-confidence.

"How can you be so sure of that without seeing the list?"

"Watch it!" he cried instead of answering, and then tugged me a little more toward him to avoid a large dip in the ground. For a moment, he wrapped his right arm around my shoulders. I didn't pull away, but he released me. "Sorry, if I was too rough, but I was worried about those shoes."

"No, it was fine. Thanks."

He stared at the gaping hole. It was about two feet wide.

"It looks like a mini-sinkhole," he said. "I saw some enormous ones two years ago when we were in Israel. They were at the Dead Sea. Could easily swallow up a house when the ground collapsed."

"You've been to Israel?"

"One of my father's conferences. Something to do with technology and satellites."

"Where else have you been?" I asked as we continued walking carefully.

"Italy, France, Germany, England, and yes, Greece, but I was pretty young for most of those trips and probably got little more out of them than I would have from Disneyland. We just go between those two tall pine trees," he said, nodding ahead. It was obvious that he did know exactly where he was going and how to get there.

"When were you here? When did you make this fantastic discovery?"

"Last night," he said. "There's a lot of pine up here, and nothing is cooler than being in a pine forest in the summer. Oh, I forgot Switzerland. My father had a major conference in Zurich. My mother and I took a train to Paris and visited the Louvre. I was in seventh grade then, so I remember all of that well. It's where you can see the Venus de Milo," he added.

"I've been to Los Angeles and to New York twice. That's where my father's sister, my aunt May, lives. She's married to a surgeon who works at Sloan-Kettering. I have two cousins on my father's side, Eden and Keith. Keith is a senior at Columbia planning to be a doctor also, and Eden is attending William and Mary. She plans on becoming an international journalist. If it weren't for the Internet, I wouldn't have much to do with them. They're so far away, and they never seem to have time to come here. My aunt wasn't happy living here. She says she felt out of touch with everything going on in the world. We're too rural for her, and she didn't want any part of our family's jewelry business. Look at me," I said, pausing. "Running off at the mouth. I hate the way I sound."

"Why? You have a beautiful voice. I loved every syllable," Brayden said. "You don't have any relatives on your mother's side?"

"She was an only child, like me."

"And me," Brayden said. "We should form a club. We can call it the Club for Those Smarter Than Their Brothers or Sisters."

"Ha ha."

We paused, and then he nodded at the path in the woods.

"Just walk right behind me. It is kind of dark through here," he said.

How could he see so well? I wondered. The moon was blocked again, and the forest looked more like a solid dark wall.

"Maybe we went far enough?"

"You'll see we didn't in a few minutes," he promised.

I stayed right behind him, almost walking on his feet at times, but just as he predicted, we came out at a place on the lake I had never been. It was a small lagoon. How could he have known, made such a discovery so quickly? Why hadn't I ever seen it?

As the moon broke free again, the water glistened, and we could see about a dozen Canadian geese floating just a few feet from shore. I turned at the call of a Northern goshawk looking down at us as if we had intruded in his space. Off to the left were about a half-dozen Great Blue herons.

"Look," Brayden said, pointing toward the cattails and reeds in the water. "Two yellow-headed blackbirds. Aren't they beautiful?"

In all the years I had lived in Echo Lake, I had never seen so many different varieties of birds gathered in one area. Like most everyone my age I knew, I took it all for granted. Unless we were assigned some science project involving birds, I didn't pay them as much attention as they obviously deserved.

It wasn't only the birds and the surprise opening on

the shore that gave us a wide view of the lake, with the moonlight and stars making the water dazzling, that impressed and delighted me. It was the unique silence when so many beautiful things seemed asleep or even, I should say, meditating. Never before had I felt so much a part of it all. It was as if I had suddenly come to appreciate my own home. I felt like someone who had been wearing blinders all her life and suddenly had them removed.

"I can't believe you've been here only a matter of days and you found this spot so quickly," I said, my voice barely above a whisper. I didn't want to disturb even a water bug.

He said nothing. He just stared out with what was now a soft smile set in a face framed with such longing I felt my own heart ache.

"Anything wrong?" I asked.

"What? No. Am I forgiven for making you trek through the bushes and woods?"

"Absolutely. I wonder what it's like here in the daytime."

"It's pretty, but it's not the same. Darkness always adds something special. Ironically, it's as though the light blinds us, washes away important things that are right next to us or right in front of us."

"Is that why your family keeps the lights so low?"

He looked at me strangely. I thought there was some anger in his eyes, anger and annoyance.

"I was just curious," I said.

He looked out at the lake again and was silent so long I thought he would say no more. I was about to suggest that we start back when he turned to me again and said, "My mother is not well."

"Oh. I'm sorry. What's wrong?"

"She suffers from severe depression. Because of that, she sleeps most of the day and retreats to her art studio for most of the night. It's not uncommon to see the light on in the attic and nowhere else, no other room lit, so don't be surprised. And don't be surprised if you rarely see her outside during the daytime. My father has arranged for things to be delivered regularly. She doesn't like shopping."

"How sad. Especially when you think of her being in a strange new place without any friends. I mean, you don't know anyone here, do you?"

"No, but that's not so unusual for us. Or it hasn't been, and now, with the way she is, it might not matter."

"I'm sorry," I said again. "Can't someone help her?"

"I do what I can."

"No, I mean, well, your father, of course, but doctors?"

"She's seen doctors. She's on some medication and is seeing a therapist now. My father . . . my father is more comfortable with statistics than with people. He's not much help when it comes to something like this."

"I'm sorry," I said. I hated repeating myself, but what else could I say? As it was, I felt I had stumbled into more information than he wanted to give, but I also knew how hard it would be for him to live in a town as small as Echo Lake and keep people from knowing what his family life was like. I suspected that most of the boys and even most of the girls, despite his good looks, would be turned off.

"I'd rather, if you can avoid it, you not talk about us with your friends," he said, as if he could read my thoughts. "It would be horrible for my mother if people came around to gawk or something. That's mainly why my father wanted to move here. He thought it was far enough away from . . . that it was innocuous. Do you understand what I mean?"

"Of course."

"I knew you would."

"I hate gossip. My mother hates it the most. My father acts indifferent about it, but it bothers him, too. I can tell you this for sure, my phone rings the least of any of my classmates'. They know that if they tell me something, it dies with me, and that's no fun."

"No boys scratching at the doors and windows?"

"None I care to let in at the moment," I said, and he finally smiled again.

Then he nodded to the right. "Someone once lived out here."

"What do you mean?"

"There's a small, very old cabin about a thousand yards farther down. It's hidden by the overgrowth. None of your friends knows about it?"

"We don't hang out on lake property much. They have regular lake patrols, and the Echo Lake police will jump if someone in the Echo Lake Corporation calls. The properties around the lake are the most expensive and owned by very influential people."

"No one seems to be doing anything with this area," he said.

"I'll find out why not. I'm sure whoever owns it is

just keeping it to wait for a better price or something."

"Whatever. It's my favorite place, so don't talk too much about it and suddenly have dozens of your friends sneaking onto the property to have little private parties."

"This is your favorite place? How can you have a favorite place? You haven't seen very much of the town, have you?"

"Enough to know that this place is special."

I said nothing. We stood looking out at the water, drawing from its energy and beauty. I felt his hand find mine in the darkness.

"Maybe we should go back," he said, turning. "I'm sure you told your parents you were taking a walk with the strange new neighbor who was gawking at you through the hedges. They're probably sitting on pins and needles."

"I didn't mention the gawking, and I didn't say you were strange. My father wouldn't have let me out of the house," I replied, following him.

He paused. "You really don't find me strange?"

"Not strange—different."

"Different works," he said, nodding. We walked on silently for a while until we were out of the woods and he could reach for my hand again. I gave it to him without hesitation this time.

"Are you going to try to get a job or something for the summer?" I asked.

"No. I have to take care of my mother. You might not see that much of me."

"If there's anything I can do to help . . ."

"That's nice of you. No, there's nothing, but if you're around when I'm around, and you don't mind doing simple things with me occasionally . . ."

"Thoreau things?"

"Exactly."

"I don't mind," I said.

We passed between the Knottses' and the Littlefields' again. The TVs were still going, but now we could hear music from upstairs in the Littlefields' house. Angie Littlefield surely had some of her friends over. She was a year behind me but more popular than most of the girls in my class when it came to the boys in my class.

Brayden caught me looking up at her bedroom windows.

"Why are you really so uninterested in doing things with kids your age, Amber?"

"How do you know that's true?"

"Isn't it?"

"Maybe."

He nodded.

"What?"

"Something frightens you," he said.

"Frightens me? Okay, what, Dr. Phil?"

He hesitated, staring at me.

"So?"

"The same thing that frightens me now."

"And what's that, oh, wise know-it-all?"

He didn't laugh. He walked on, cloaked in those same moments of silence that just as before made me think he would not answer. As we drew closer to his house, he paused and looked at me.

"You're frightened about revealing too much about yourself."

"Like what?"

"Things you won't even admit to yourself," he replied. He nodded at the now dark house. "Gotta go. See you," he said, and headed toward the front door. "Oh," he added, pausing to look back. "Thanks for walking with me."

"I enjoyed it. I think," I said. "It was like walking with Socrates or someone."

He laughed.

"Maybe you were. Remember," he said, "reincarnation."

He laughed again, and then I thought I heard his mother calling for him the way she had when I first met him, her voice sounding so far-off and thin.

Or maybe it was just the breeze strengthening and weaving its way over rain gutters, over wires, and through trees. I looked up and then back toward town.

When I turned to look back at him, he was gone, and again, I hadn't even heard him open the front door. Maybe he had to tiptoe around her, I thought. Maybe he was forced to live in the same world of silence.

What had he said about prisons? We all lived in one sort or another.

Having a mother like his put him in a sort of prison for sure, I thought.

How sad for him, and yet he didn't seem depressed. He just seemed more thoughtful, like someone who had been forced to put away childish things.

A part of me envied him for that, but another, perhaps stronger, part pitied him, too.

One thing I knew for sure from just this short time I had spent with him. He didn't like being pitied.

He didn't want sympathy.

"What does he want?" I whispered to myself.

The sound of his mother calling his name lingered like a dream that would never be forgotten.

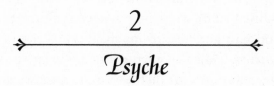

2

Psyche

"And the judge's decision?" Dad called from the living room when he heard me enter the house.

I really didn't know what I was going to say, but I stepped into the living room anyway. Both of them were reading, my mother a novel and my father the newest book about World War I.

My father was a self-appointed authority on the First World War, because my great-great-grandfather on his side had fought in and survived the Battle of the Somme, in 1916. Local residents and other store owners would often stop in the store to ask my father a question or settle a debate about it. My great-great-grandfather was only eighteen at the time but earned the British War Medal and the Victory Medal, both of which were now framed and hanging in our living room beside the dark oak bookcase. There was a picture of him in uniform, too. When I was little, I would study it to see if I could find resemblances to my father. I thought I saw them in my great-great-grandfather's nose and mouth. I knew Dad was happy to hear it.

When my great-great-grandfather was in his late

1

twenties, he married and immigrated to America. It was my grandfather who eventually moved the family to Oregon and started the jewelry store, because my grandmother's father was in the jewelry business in New York and had gotten him involved when my grandparents married. Dad had pictures of his relatives in three good-size albums. Our pictures of my aunt May and her family weren't up-to-date, however. It had been almost two years now since I had seen my cousins. Like me, Dad tried to stay in touch with his sister with phone calls and e-mails, but there was always the sense that they were drifting further and further apart. There was only a four-year separation in ages, Aunt May being younger. Whenever her husband could take time off for a vacation, however, they preferred to go to Europe or the Caribbean rather than visit us.

"The judge's decision about what?" I asked, even though I knew what he meant.

Both of them looked up from their books.

"What else? The boy next door. Wait a minute," Dad said to Mom. "Wasn't there a song called 'The Boy Next Door'?"

"In a famous movie, *Meet Me in St. Louis*."

"Right. Sung by . . ." Dad pretended to be struggling to remember. Mom looked at me and winked. "Oh, yeah, Judy Garland," he said.

"Judy who?" Mom and I said simultaneously.

Dad shook his head. "So?"

"He's interesting."

"Noreen, please translate what she said into man talk," Dad asked her.

"'Interesting' means she would like to get to know him more before she makes any decisions about him," she said, and looked to me for confirmation. Dad did, too.

"That's right," I said. "There is some sad news, however," I continued, and told them what Brayden had said about his mother, how poorly his father was handling it all, and how she spent her time. I told them about her paintings in museums and the name she used.

"So she's an artist, too," Mom said. "Well," she added, looking at Dad, "artists can be moody. It's not easy living with them."

"I beg your pardon. When have I been moody?"

Mom smiled. "There's not enough time left before I go to sleep to list the occasions," she told him. She turned back to me. "However, it sounds like his mother has a far more serious condition. She's under a doctor's care?"

"That's what he said."

I could see the fear in their faces. One way or another, children inherit from or reflect mentally ill parents. I didn't want to tell them about his mother's belief in reincarnation or anything else that would make the Matthewses seem too strange to want to know.

"Brayden is one of the brightest, deepest-thinking boys I've ever met."

Mom nodded. "Well, I'm sorry he has a burden like this at so young an age."

"I'm going up," I said. "Oh," I added, "there's a beautiful spot on the lake where birds, all kinds of birds, gather, a small lagoon. Did you know that?"

They looked at me as if I had begun to speak a

foreign language, and then Dad said, "I didn't know there was any one particular place where they gathered."

"Well, there is," I said.

"And you found it?"

"No, not me. Brayden," I said.

"Someone who has been here only a few days found something on our lake that we've never found in years?"

"We don't exactly spend much time on the lake, Gregory," Mom told him.

"Yeah, but still . . ."

"I told you he was interesting," I said, and then left.

When I entered my room, I remembered that Brayden had told me his bedroom was directly across from mine. My curtains were open slightly. I peeked out and saw that the windows of what would be his bedroom were dark. Perhaps he was with his mother in the attic, I thought. He did seem anxious to get home. I had no idea how I would survive under such pressure. How lucky I was to have the parents I had. I didn't open my curtains any farther, but I didn't close them completely, either. I was curious about when the light from his bedroom would go on and spill into the darkness between us.

After I prepared for bed, I picked up my copy of *Brave New World*, a novel my class had been assigned to read over the summer and about which we were to write a book report. I often liked to read myself to sleep, deciding to close whatever I was reading and put out the lights as soon as I found myself rereading the same lines. Tonight I could barely get started. After every sentence I read, I found myself pausing to think about Brayden, about the way he had walked with me, sometimes seeming to be so lost in his own thoughts that he had forgotten I was with him and then quickly returning to the moment, slowing down and turning to me after something I had said or asked had penetrated the wall that I couldn't help thinking he had fashioned around himself. I thought I must feel the way a prizefighter felt when he couldn't quite figure out his opponent. In this case, the opponent was bobbing and weaving with words, so I couldn't land a blow and discover too much about him.

After all, I still didn't know where he had come from, where he was born, how long his mother had been ill and why, what his likes and dislikes were, whether he would be in our school, or even what he really planned on doing with himself all day. He couldn't just look after his mother.

And then there was the way he looked at me. I couldn't quite put my finger on what it was that disturbed me. I didn't see him gazing at me with that sly, licentious look that could make a girl feel naked, but I did have the feeling that he could see through not only my clothes but any attempt I made to hide something about myself. I concluded that it was the look of someone wise beyond his years, just as I did when I'd said he sounded as if he had lived for centuries. It was as if he knew things about me that I had yet to discover about myself and that would come only from wisdom. Wisdom was different from intelligence. Wisdom came from years of experience. How did someone my age have so much of it?

To be honest, I wasn't sure I liked it. It filled me with a kaleidoscope of emotions. At times, it made me angry, as angry as I would be at anyone who was condescending enough to make me feel dumb, naive, and innocent. Simultaneously, I felt titillated, as aroused as I might be had he run the palm of his hand softly over my breast and rested it on the flat of my stomach. And then again, I was feeling confused, even agitated, and afraid that I would say something silly, unimportant, or downright stupid. No boy I had ever been with had challenged me as much.

I guess that was why I was so undecided about him.

I wasn't so unlike most girls, I thought, at least most girls about my age. Just like them, I was more comfortable with boys who were simpler, boys who were obvious. Most of the time, I could finish the sentences for many of them or think their next thoughts. I never felt threatened or inadequate when I was with them. The truth was, I felt superior. I knew it was arrogant to feel like this, the exact sort of priggishness they accused me of having, but I couldn't help it. I would never tell anyone about these feelings. I hadn't even told Mom. Brayden was so right when he said I was afraid of revealing things about myself, some things I wouldn't even admit to myself.

At the top of that list was my deep and utter craving to be loved. I don't mean loved the way parents love their children, but loved the way my mother loved my father and he loved her. I had always thought that my need for that would come much later in my life. It wasn't just wanting to have sex, to make all the discoveries I read about or heard other girls talk about. I wanted something more. I wanted to love someone so intently that his every word, every gesture, smile, and kiss lingered long into the night and embraced all of my dreams, not the way teenagers could have crushes on each other. No, I wanted something more substantial, something clearly mature, reserved for when you were older and settled. The truth was, I wanted it all now, and that did frighten me, because I realized that I should be more of a teenager than a woman. I didn't know any other girl who was like me, and that wasn't necessarily good.

These should be my carefree days, I thought. My heart and my mind should be full of insignificant little affections. I should be going to parties, dancing beneath crepe-paper ceilings and multicolored balloons, weaving smiles and laughter around lollipop kisses, and writing some boy's name with invisible ink so it could be replaced quickly and easily with another boy's name.

Mom was always telling me just to go and have fun. "Don't take life so seriously. Every boy you date doesn't have to be your soul mate, Amber. It's not a waste of time just to have some innocent fun. Believe me."

I knew what she meant. These would be those delightful little experiences that would fill up my personal yearbook, the one containing all of the ridiculous things that I had said or that were said to me, the pictures of the boys I had crushes on for ten minutes, and the wild predictions my friends and I had made for ourselves on a prophecy page.

But no matter how much or how hard I tried, I couldn't begin to fill that yearbook. I was simply—like Brayden—beyond my years. What had happened to make him that way? I supposed I could blame it on his home life, especially his mother's condition, but what had happened in me that made me the same? Was it just the way we were constructed, something in our genes? Were we living tragic lives because we were losing or had lost our youth too soon? What would I be able to tell my daughter when she was my age if I had never had any of the experiences she was having, experiences that at times she would find a little confusing? Where would my motherly wisdom come from?

I hadn't thought about all of this as intently as I was thinking about it tonight, and I knew it was because of Brayden, because of the thoughtful and serious things he had said. If he could cause this to happen, stir up all these deep thoughts and feelings after the short time we had spent together, what would happen if I did see him again and again?

Was it dangerous to be around someone like him, especially for someone like me who was already too serious?

Was I afraid?

Should I avoid him? Tell myself he was too depressing or weird? That would be easy. My parents would accept it, too, now that they knew something about his family, but would I?

Could I be that dishonest with myself?

I closed my book. *I'm not going to read tonight,* I thought, and rose slowly after I put out the light. In the protection of the darkness, I went to the curtain and peered out at the windows of his bedroom again. It was still quite dark. When did he go to sleep? I looked up to see the attic windows lit, just as he had said they would be. Did he stay there with his mother while she worked? How long did it go on? All night? Nothing else, no other room, looked lit in the entire house. What was her problem? Were her paintings the only window through which she would look at the world? I thought artists had to experience reality to capture something they could paint. Were her paintings all about the chaos within her? That would make it seem more like psychotherapy than art. I was anxious to see one and told myself that I would look her up on the Internet tomorrow.

I was about to close my curtain and go to sleep when I thought I saw a glow in one of Brayden's windows. It was like the reflection of something bright on the glass, something from outside. And then, suddenly, that glow took the form of his face, but his face seemed to be float-ing, as if it were painted on a balloon. He was looking out at me, doing, I guessed, exactly what I was doing, keeping the lights off in his room so he could peer out at mine unseen. I thought he smiled as if he could see me peeping, so I backed up quickly, my heart tapping against my chest like a woodpecker on a tree. I took a deep breath and then closed my curtains.

I stood there thinking and worrying about it. How could he see me in this darkness, anyway? Was that re-ally his face, or did I imagine it? Was it just the glow of someone's light on the street, perhaps the headlights of a car?

I approached the window and peered out between the curtains again. This time, I saw nothing, not even a reflection from the street. I waited and watched and then felt silly about it and returned to bed. How strange it made me feel. *I'll never get to sleep tonight,* I thought, and did toss and turn almost as badly as someone in a cabin of a sailboat on a windy sea. I settled down some when I heard Mom and Dad come up to go to bed. They paused at my bedroom door and then continued to theirs, whispering, their words spoken too softly to be understood but sounding like air escaping from a tire.

I didn't need to hear their words to understand that they were probably worried about me and about the cryptic things I had said about this new neighbor. I was sure my father wasn't kidding all that much when he often turned to my mother for an interpretation of things I had said. At some age, daughters become a mystery for fathers to solve anyway. Understanding what our emotions say is like deciphering a foreign language for them. What I had said about Brayden Matthews and my short but intriguing contact with him was just another speed bump for my father to navigate in his journey to embrace fully this mysterious creature he called his daughter.

This whole situation was just too weird, I thought, and decided that it might be better if I didn't get too involved with Brayden Matthews. After all, he had said himself that they might not be here that long. What did he call it, a test? Well, I didn't want to be part of someone's test, and it would be just my bad luck to grow to like him and find out that he was leaving in a few days to go somewhere else. I was sure that wherever it was, he wouldn't tell me. He was too secretive. Talk about being guarded. Who was more guarded than he was, avoiding the answers to the most basic questions? What were they, a family of spies? It wouldn't be any fun for me to pry the most inconsequential things out of him. Actually, it was already proving to be quite frustrating.

I wrapped my blanket tighter around myself and willed myself to sleep by pushing all of these questions back into some cabinet at the back of my mind, a place that was simply labeled *Later*. There was great logic to Scarlett O'Hara in *Gone With the Wind* saying, "I can't think about that right now. If I do, I'll go crazy. I'll think about that tomorrow."

Tomorrow seemed to come more quickly than usual. It was as if I had only blinked. Dad was always the first one up in the morning. Mom prepared our breakfast, but he liked to find little ways to spoil her, and one of those ways was to turn on the coffee and bring a cup up to her while she was still rubbing the sleep out of her eyes. No matter how many times he had done it, she always acted surprised. I had asked her about that once, and she had thought a moment and said, "When you expect something all the time, take it for granted, it loses its heart. It becomes just something else in your life. I'm almost happy when I do wake up ahead of your father and he can't get me that cup of coffee. I see the disappointment with himself in his face, but I also know he's going to be very pleased the next morning when he beats me to it, and yes, I'll be just as surprised."

Where did older women really get their wisdom? I wondered. Of course, not every woman I had met seemed to be as wise as my mother, but most knew stuff like that. Would I? Was this drag of a teenage life I was having going to ensure that I would not have enough wisdom to fall in love and have someone fall in love with me the way I expected and dreamed?

I rose and took a quick shower, mostly to wake

myself up fully. Even though it had seemed to go by fast, it had not been a good night's sleep, but I didn't want my parents to wonder about it. I dressed and hurried down ahead of them to set the breakfast table. Mom followed. She and Dad had decided to have pancakes with bananas in them. We had wonderful Oregon maple syrup. In minutes, we were side by side working on breakfast. Usually, people didn't go shopping at jewelry stores early in the morning, so we didn't open until ten a.m. Our busiest hours were right before lunch and from midday to five. Most of the time, I remained behind with Dad, and Mom went home to make dinner, but there were many days when business slowed and he closed up himself.

"What's this interesting young man going to do with himself in Echo Lake this summer?" Dad asked when we were all around the table eating our pancakes.

"I told you he said he had to stay close to home, watch over his mother. I imagine he has to do that especially when his father is so far away."

"How sad," Mom said. "That doesn't sound like much of a summer for him. You should introduce him to some of the other boys and girls in your class, invite some people over and introduce him."

"He didn't seem all that interested in meeting anyone else," I said.

"Really?"

I saw them glance at each other.

"Well, give him time," Dad said, finishing up. "You've got to warm up to a new home and a new town, get into it slowly, like a hot bath."

"How would you know that, Gregory, when you've barely slept a week outside of this town?" Mom asked.

"I remember how hard it was that week, too. Wasn't it our honeymoon?"

"Oh, go on with you," she said, shaking her head at him. She turned to me. "Now you can appreciate what it's been like being with the same man day in and day out for twenty-two years."

"Has it been that long?" Dad asked her. She punched him gently on the shoulder, and he pretended to be in pain. Watching them made me wonder what it was like to wake up and face the day surrounded by gloom. From the way he had spoken, Brayden's mornings were rarely anything but depressing. What would he do with himself here? Was he just too ashamed to show how much he really would like to be with others his age?

I was doing just what I had told myself I would stop doing, wondering almost obsessively about him.

My parents started out for the store ahead of me. My job was to stay behind and clean up the breakfast dishes and the kitchen. It was a little less than a mile to the village proper where our store was, and most days in the summer, we all walked. Dad said it was his only chance to get in any meaningful physical exercise. He and Mom went at a good pace, but they still looked as if they were walking mostly to be together as much as possible. Other girls were always telling me about my parents: "Actually still holding hands when they walk!" Most of the girls thought it was cute, but some, especially those like Megan Thomas, thought they were being ostentatious. That was her new word for the year, *ostentatious*.

Everyone but her, it seemed, was too showy and preten-
tious. I knew she said the same things about me.

I, too, liked the walk to the village in the summer.
Unless we had a downpour, there was something delicious about the fresh morning air, the aroma of flowers
and freshly cut grass. I loved the way the sparrows and
robins flitted from tree to tree. There was something so
comforting in the sounds of other families starting their
days, dads and moms getting into their cars, grandparents opening up window curtains, little kids bursting out
into the sunshine as if they had been kept prisoner by the
night, chained to their beds by their sleep. Dogs began
barking, and cats were seen slinking around corners
hunting prey.

When I described all of this in an essay for my English teacher at the time, Mr. Madeo, he said it reminded
him of the play *Our Town*. "You're Echo Lake's Thorn-
ton Wilder," he wrote next to my A plus. We had read
that play in the tenth grade, and then our drama department put it on the following year. Mr. Madeo urged me
to try out for the part of Emily Webb, but I just couldn't
get myself up on the stage.

And yet I was often accused of using our streets as
my private stage. I don't think anyone else, or at least
any other girl in the school, was criticized as much for
the way she walked. They mocked my perfect posture
and self-confidence. Of course Megan said I was being
ostentatious. She didn't understand that if someone
was ostentatious, she had something about her which
she could be.

So I had good posture and I wore a habitual soft

smile on my face—so what? Why was that so annoying not only to her but to some of the other girls?

"It just looks like you're so satisfied with yourself," Barbara Morris whispered to me after I had snapped back at Megan one time at lunch. Megan usually picked on someone at school and did her indictment while she ate and preached to her little cadre of devoted followers. I called them the Gossip Assassins.

"What's wrong with being satisfied with yourself?" I asked Barbara. At least she didn't join in with as much venom as the rest of them.

"Nothing, except . . ."

"Except what?"

"You act like you don't need anyone to give you a compliment. You've given them all to yourself already," she replied.

Her remark got me wondering if that was really the way everyone saw me. Could that be why, especially this past school year, most of the boys were standoffish? I caught them looking at me often, but as soon as I looked back at them, they always looked away, as if they had been caught doing something unethical, if not illegal. That is, all except Shayne Allan, who probably deserved the label of most conceited member of the student body far more than I deserved it.

Yes, he was undeniably very handsome, with his dark brown hair, his soft blue-gray eyes, and his Tom Cruise good looks. He was one of the top athletes in the school, the baseball team's best pitcher and often the high scorer on the basketball team. He dressed better than the other boys but not to the point of looking like a prude. His hair was always well styled and groomed. His father was CEO of the only major industrial enterprise within twenty miles of Echo Lake, Price Manufacturers, a company that sold wood products constructed from Oregon trees. Shayne drove a Porsche from the moment he got his driver's license. The truth was, he looked put together by some Hollywood casting director. To top it off, he was in real contention for valedictorian.

Shayne Allan, Mr. Perfect, also just happened to be the darling of the faculty because of how well he did in his classes, how mature he was in his behavior, and how good he was at making them feel good. When my friends sighed over him and asked me about him, I always said something like, "He's not real; he's a robot. Stick him with a pin, and you'll break the pin."

Ellie Patton, the closest I had to a best friend, had so deep and complete a crush on him that I didn't doubt she would jump into Echo Lake in January naked if he asked her to do it. Nothing infuriated her as much as my apparent indifference to him. Of course, she accused me of putting on an act.

"Don't tell me you don't fantasize about him, Amber. I see the way you look at him sometimes, too."

"I'm just waiting to see if he's going to leak any oil from one of his joints or short out, blow a fuse."

"Right," Ellie said. And then, as difficult as it was for her to tell me, she revealed that most of the kids in our class, especially the girls, thought that Shayne and I would make the perfect couple, the absolute ultimate prom king and queen. After we were married, we would have to have the best-looking children in the world.

A part of me couldn't help but absorb and enjoy the compliment. Even my most envious detractors were forced to admit that they thought I was beautiful. Everyone thought it was only a matter of time until Shayne and I found each other. Until now, he was so enamored of himself that he wouldn't pay much, if any, attention to a girl who didn't reveal how much she would enjoy it. I was careful about giving him a second look and barely said a word to him. I ignored him the few times he said something to me while passing me in the hallway.

"Don't worry about it. There's no room in his heart for anyone else but himself," I told Ellie. "It runs in his family. You know how stuck-up his younger sister, Wendi, is since her parents paid for her new nose. The Allan house must have more mirrors in it than the hall of mirrors in a carnival. Shayne won't walk past a window without glancing at himself. It's a severe case of narcissism."

"That's exactly what most people say about you, Amber," she shot back at me, and the topic popped like a bubble between us, leaving us in a cloud of silence.

Despite the aloof look I wore on my face when I walked to and from the store, I was quite aware of how other people were looking at me, especially men. Even old men, like Mr. Ritter, who ran a small supermarket for so long that Dad jokingly claimed he had sold a half-pound of bacon once to President Woodrow Wilson, and seemed always to be at the doorway of his store when I passed by so he could nod, smile, and wave hello. He wore the sort of smile old men draw out of their youthful memories. When I described it to Mom, she smiled herself and said, "It's all right. You make him feel like a young man again."

"By doing what?"

"Just being there," she said, brushing back my hair and looking at me the way she might look at the biggest diamond with the best clarity in our store ever.

I had to admit that hearing about the way men appreciated me frightened me a little. I never forgot the Greek myth of Cupid and Psyche. The goddess Venus was so jealous of a mortal girl named Psyche that she asked her son Cupid to use his golden arrows while Psyche slept so that when she awoke, she would fall in love with the vile creature Venus had planted there. Cupid approached her, prepared to hit her with the arrow to make her fall in love with the creature, but he fell in love with her instead and wouldn't do it. There was a lot more to the story, but the end always bothered me, because the conclusion was that Psyche was too beautiful to have a mortal man. She ended up with Cupid.

Would I be too beautiful for any mortal man? Was it a sin even to think like that, to worry about it? It haunted me. Everyone has his or her little fears born out of something that happened early in his or her life. This was mine. I'd never tell anyone. I would just smother it as best I could. Here was another example of what Brayden Matthews meant about not revealing inner secrets, I thought. How did he know so much about me after so short a time with me?

When I stepped out of the house this morning, I hesitated, to see if he would suddenly appear the way he had last night, but I didn't see him, nor did I see any sign of life around his house. It still looked no different from how it had when no one was there. Nothing new had been added to dress it up any. There were no new curtains. No one had come to fix the chipped paint on the railings. The windows didn't even look as if they had been washed. An old wheelbarrow was still overturned at the side of the house, and an old garden hose was curled like a pregnant snake beside it.

Brayden did say that his mother slept most of the day, but then, what did he do while she slept? Did he sleep most of the day, too? Had he stayed up all night to keep her company? Was that his burden, the reason he wasn't keen on meeting new people? I walked slowly past his front lawn, keeping an eye on the front door and windows, but I saw no movement, nothing. Disappointed, I continued to the village and to the jewelry store. It was a very busy day, one that kept me going straight to lunch. It was only then that my thoughts returned to Brayden. I wondered if he might stop by or even just step up to our front windows and look at the displays and try to catch my attention.

But I didn't see anything of him, and after lunch, business picked up again. It slowed down a little after four. Mom said we were all going to the diner for dinner. Dad had a craving for liver and onions, and that was the old Echo Lake diner's specialty.

"Why don't you go home first, honey, shower and change, and then drive the car back? We have a lot to do before closing. Then we can drive home and do the same, okay?"

"Sure," I said.

"I know it doesn't sound all that exciting," she said quietly, "but we have to give him his treat. He earned it today."

Dad had had four major adjustments to do on bracelets and necklaces and had put together a beautiful blue sapphire ring in a twenty-four-karat gold setting for Dr. Immerman's wife. He was our family doctor and just recently had bought property at the lake.

"Unless you have something more interesting to do," she added. "I mean, if you'd like, you could invite the new boy over to dinner, make him something."

"No. I don't think so. I don't know him well enough yet. I'm fine. I like the chicken pot pie at the diner," I said, scooping up my purse and heading out for home.

Ellie and Charlotte Watts pulled up to the corner in Charlotte's red BMW convertible just as I reached it and was about to cross the street. Charlotte's father was one of the most successful land developers in and around Echo Lake. She was a very plain-looking girl, about fifteen pounds too heavy for her five-feet-three-inch frame. She kept her popularity by holding parties at her parents' large house just outside the village and treating everyone else to pizza or frozen yogurt. The Wattses owned property on the lake, too, but hadn't developed it. I wondered now if that was the property Brayden and I had visited. I didn't want to ask about it, however. I didn't want them to know I had gone there with him.

"I'm having a July Fourth party tomorrow night," Charlotte announced. "Fireworks and everything. You're invited," she added with the tone of someone who had been forced to apologize. I was sure Ellie had put her up to it.

"It's not July Fourth this weekend. That's next weekend, isn't it?"

"It doesn't matter," she said, visibly annoyed. "This is the weekend my parents are going to Las Vegas. They're leaving tomorrow, and they're taking my brother Julius, so I'm declaring it July Fourth. The maid's off Saturday, so it's perfect. If you don't want to come, don't come."

"They're letting you have the party?"

She looked at Ellie and then turned back to me. "Hello. Figure it out, Prudence Perfect. If you do make the royal decision to come, wear something red, white, or blue or all three. Danny Silver is bringing the fireworks. Everyone's arriving about seven-thirty. I'll have lots of food—catered, of course." She glanced at Ellie again. "By the way, Shayne will be there. He didn't hesitate when I invited him. The invitation was barely out of my mouth."

"Are you coming or not?" Ellie demanded when I didn't burst out with an enthusiastic yes.

"I'll try."

"Try?" Charlotte said. "We know how difficult it is for you to grant an audience to the rest of us mere mortals."

I was thinking so hard about it that I missed her sarcasm.

"What?" Ellie asked, seeing the thoughtful expression on my face.

"Something came to mind. I have a new neighbor. He's going to be in our class this year if his family stays in Echo Lake. I should bring him along so he can meet the mere mortals."

"A new neighbor? He? Is he good-looking?" Charlotte asked quickly.

"Very."

"What do you mean, 'if his family stays'?" Ellie asked.

"They've rented for the summer and are not sure yet about spending the rest of the year or more."

"I wish my parents would have given me that choice," Ellie said.

"Yeah, like any other place would have you," Charlotte told her. She turned to me. "Well, if you bring him to the party and he sees just how much fun we have here, he'll want to stay for sure. Are you bringing him?"

"I'll see. He's a little shy," I said.

"A little shy? You know that much about him already? How come you didn't mention him to me before?" Ellie asked, sounding indignant.

"We just met yesterday. I don't know much about him, but I had that impression."

"Maybe you intimidated him," Ellie said. "You can do that very easily."

"No," I said, refusing to bite. "I think he's just not that outgoing."

"We'll break him out of his shyness, won't we?" Charlotte asked Ellie.

Ellie looked at me suspiciously. "If someone else hasn't done so already or doesn't have plans to do it herself. You met him yesterday? How long have he and his family been here?"

"Only a few days."

"And you never said anything?"

"I told you. I just met him yesterday."

"What did you do?" she asked.

"Do? Nothing. We went for a walk."

"A walk? Where?"

"Just on the street," I said. I wasn't going to tell them about the lake.

They looked at each other as if I had lost my mind.

"Well," I said, "I've got to get home. We're going to dinner tonight."

"We?" Ellie asked.

"My parents and I. No, not my new neighbor—not yet, at least," I added, almost under my breath. I guess it was obvious I wished it were so.

They looked at each other again, and then they both laughed.

"You mean there really is someone you actually deem to be worthy of a date with you?" Charlotte asked me.

Instead of reacting to her sarcasm, I pretended to give it deep thought. "I'm not quite sure yet. I forgot to look to see if he has dirty fingernails. See ya," I tossed at them, and hurried away. When I looked back, they were still parked, laughing.

Brayden wasn't outside his house, and as before, nothing looked touched or changed. The windows were dark, and when I paused, I heard no sounds, no music, no television, nothing going on inside. I had no time to linger. I did look over again, pausing after I had driven out to go get my parents. It was deeper twilight now, and still no lights were on inside his house.

After I brought my parents home, I lingered on the

front porch, watching for some sign of Brayden while they showered and dressed. The look of abandonment actually began to annoy me. How could anyone move into a new home and not want to do anything—change curtains, clean, straighten up the yard, get some flowers planted, whitewash the porch railings, anything? They seemed more like squatters than tenants. And really, what did Brayden do all day? If he had to hang around the house, why couldn't he do any of those things? All of this mystery had become irritating. I told myself that I should never have spoken to him and certainly shouldn't have accepted his invitation to go for a walk. He really was too strange.

I regretted mentioning him to Ellie and Charlotte. *Forget him,* I told myself, and I was very happy when my parents came out and we got into the car to go to the diner.

"You sure you saw one of our neighbors?" Dad asked. "I mean, someone really moved in there? It's so dark. It looks just as deserted as ever."

"Maybe they went out to dinner, Gregory," Mom said.

"And didn't leave a light on for when they returned?"

"Amber told you Mr. Matthews was an economist. He's saving on their electric bill."

She looked to me, but I had nothing to add, no explanation.

Dad shrugged and started the engine. "I haven't heard anyone mention anything about them—except you, of course, Amber," he said as he backed out of the driveway.

"They just moved in," Mom said.

"And Risa Donald hasn't said a word to anyone? That's a first," he replied.

He drove off, and I didn't even look back.

But when we rounded the corner of our cul-de-sac and headed for Main Street and the way out of the village, I was almost sure I caught a glimpse of Brayden looking out from behind the large maple tree on Mrs. Carden's front lawn.

"What is it?" Mom asked when I spun around so abruptly.

If he had been there, he was gone.

"Nothing," I said. "I thought I saw something."

"What?"

"Nothing," I repeated.

"Was it that interesting new boy?" Dad asked. "I suppose we could have asked him to join us for dinner as a way of welcoming him to the neighborhood. That way, we could beat Risa to the gossip headlines."

"No, it wasn't him," I said. I was angry at myself for reacting so dramatically to a possible sighting of him, as if he were a movie star or a singing star.

Mom picked up on the tone in my voice and turned back to Dad. "She told you she wanted to get to know him better first, Gregory."

"Okay, okay," he said. "I'll never mention him again until one of you does."

Under those conditions, I wondered if he ever would.

3
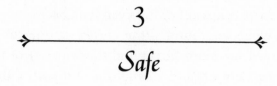

Safe

We all enjoyed our dinner at the old diner. There were many local people there. I thought my father could easily run for mayor. Everyone loved him, wanted to speak with him and say hello to Mom. After all, my family was now one of the oldest families in Echo Lake. I bathed in the glow of my parents' popularity even though I was not very talkative.

I knew my parents sensed that something was bothering me. Sometimes I thought my mother was so tuned in to my moods and feelings that she felt and experienced them as if they were her own. Of course, if anyone should know you inside and out, it should be your mother. At one time, at least for nine months, you were literally a part of her, and what flowed through her veins flowed through yours, and vice versa. There were all sorts of theories about how a mother should behave while she was pregnant and how that behavior would affect and form her child, not only physically but also mentally and emotionally.

Mom once enrolled in a meditation class specifically designed for pregnant women. It was supposed to create an inner harmony between a mother and her child even before the child was born. Dad was a little skeptical until he saw Mom in action after I was born. He saw how quickly she could anticipate my discomfort and unhappiness and how easily she knew how to get me comfortable, satisfied, and happy. I wouldn't say she didn't still have that connection with me, but I did feel that as I grew older, we gradually grew a little further apart. However, it felt natural. I realized that I should be more of my own person, a totally independent being who by definition had to be somewhat unpredictable.

Dad just thought that unpredictability and spontaneous bursts of emotions were the major characteristics of all females. He said that the man who didn't know how to tiptoe around his wife was a husband with many bumps and scars. Mom kidded him about his own peculiar sensitivities, and they would then begin one of their amusing sparring sessions, never ending in anything but laughter.

"You should take more time off," Mom suggested at dinner. "Do more with your school friends, Amber. You've got your summer-school assignments and work at the store," she said, brushing back strands of hair from my forehead. She did that so often when we talked that I thought she would still do it when I was her age and I was doing it to my own daughter or son.

"I'm all right," I said.

"No, you need more time just to relax and have fun," she insisted. "Besides, your father and I have been thinking about giving Millie Williams a little more part-time work. She's been great as a stand-in from time to time and very trustworthy. She could use the extra money since her husband, Fred, died last year."

I shrugged. There wasn't much I was dying to do with any of my school friends, but I also knew that wasn't exactly a normal attitude, especially in today's world, where kids my age were actively looking for ways to avoid work and responsibilities. Nothing was more important than just hanging out, being out from under parents and away from teachers and anything else classified as adult.

"Whatever," I said. My indifference didn't please either of them.

"Well, we'll put Millie on from Friday to Monday. You should at least have your weekends free," Mom insisted.

Her suggestion made me think more about Brayden again, despite my trying to convince myself that he was too unusual for me to have a satisfactory relationship with him. When I thought about it now, especially the way Ellie and Charlotte had reacted to my mentioning him, the prospect of showing him around our community, introducing him to others in our school, and spending some serious time with him was attractive. Maybe I should give it another chance, I thought. I was even thinking of possibly going over to his house to speak to him about Charlotte's party, but when we returned home, I noticed that nothing was different at Brayden's house from the evening before. There were no lights on downstairs. Even the attic was dark.

Dad commented about it as we drove by. It wasn't really very late.

"You're absolutely sure someone moved in there?" he asked me.

"Yes, Dad. I'm sure."

"They go to sleep very early, I imagine," Mom said.

"Yeah, maybe, or they could be vampires," Dad kidded. "Did you check this boy's teeth, Amber Light?"

"Very funny."

"It's not so unusual for people to go to bed early, Gregory. Amber did tell us that the boy's mother was on medication. That often makes people tired," Mom said.

"What, is he taking it, too?" Dad asked, still joking. "I think he needs to get out and about. Who better to help him do that than our Amber Light, huh?"

"I thought you weren't going to mention him again," Mom said, half chastising.

I thought about Charlotte Watts's premature July Fourth party. I hadn't seen most of my classmates since school had broken for the summer. I wasn't dying to see any of them, but I wasn't at the point where I couldn't stand being around them, either. Usually, Ellie was a pretty good friend. She was a very good student and enjoyed most of what I enjoyed.

I mentioned the party when we entered the house.

"Does Stan Watts know about it?" Dad asked.

"How could he not if she's asking so many friends?" Mom replied for me. She thought a moment and then added, "You might think about asking the new boy to go with you, I suppose. It would be an easy way for him to break the ice and get to know people his age."

I shrugged again, even though I was giving it some serious consideration. This time, my reaction bothered her more.

"Don't be so indifferent to everything, Amber. It worries me," she said with a rare show of some irritability. She went upstairs to change into something more comfortable, and Dad went to watch a documentary he had TiVo'd from the History Channel. I thought about going up to start reading again but decided instead to go out and sit on the porch. It was a warm enough night, and if I was going to be honest, I would have to confess that I was hoping to see Brayden despite all of my rationalizations for avoiding him and not caring about him.

I didn't think I wouldn't see him anyway. It was just too quiet around his house. Could it be that he really did go to sleep when his mother did? Maybe she exhausted him. I could only imagine what it might be like caring for someone in so deep a depression that she wanted to shut herself away from people and just work on her paintings.

It was very quiet on our street. Even on beautiful nights like this one, people seemed to roll up their sidewalks and lock their doors to gather around the TV the way I imagined cave people gathered around fires. Anything that shut out the night and the darkness was welcomed. It was as if people no longer wanted just to sit and think. It was more than simply boredom, too. People were afraid of what thoughts they could have.

I sat there for nearly a half hour, wondering and worrying about myself, about the way even my mother was starting to see me. I'd heard the fear in her voice at the diner, and I had certainly heard it when we came home. Had I permitted myself to become dull and indifferent? Was it all really my fault? Why wasn't I as enthusiastic about most of the things girls my age were? Why was I so damn serious about everything and so critical about everything my friends did or said? What other girl my age in this town would just shrug if her parents told her they wanted her to have more freedom, even if it meant just wasting time hanging around and gossiping about silly things with friends? I was aware that my lack of excitement about boys and dates and even sex was creating a wall of distrust between me and the other girls and most of the boys at my school. No one, even Ellie, bothered anymore to tell me about her experiences. It was as if most of the time they believed they would bore me or it was simply a waste of their time.

"Feeling sorry for yourself?" I heard, and nearly leaped out of the front-porch chair. How had he come around to this side of the house and sat himself on the railing without my hearing or sensing him so close?

"You frightened me," I said, holding my right hand over my heart. It felt as if it was rattling more than thumping.

"Sorry, but seeing how deep in thought you were, I didn't think it possible not to."

"You could have just walked up the street and through our front gate instead of sneaking around. I would have had some warning then. What did you do, slip through the hedges again?"

"Something like that." He tsk-tsked his lips like a chastising old biddy. "So touchy tonight? Fight with a boyfriend or something?"

"I don't have a boyfriend," I said.

"That could be your problem."

"What are you, some sort of teenage therapist or something?"

"Something," he said. He smiled that smile that could infuriate and charm me simultaneously. Then he leaned back against the wall and wrapped his arms around his raised knees. For a few long moments, neither of us spoke.

I stared ahead but kept an eye on him, watching the way he seemed to draw in everything around him, looking around as if he could see through darkness. A softer smile lit on his face. He took a deep breath, reminding me of someone who had come up out of a smoggy city to the clear, fresh mountain air. I realized that he was wearing that same military-style shirt he had worn when I first saw him between the hedges. I didn't want to seem as if I was criticizing him about it, so I didn't mention it.

"The nights here are quite spectacular," he finally said. "You rarely get so full a view of the stars, the constellations."

"Better view than the nights in Italy, France, China, India, Spain, Portugal, and Switzerland?" I rattled off, exaggerating.

He laughed. "You forgot Japan." He thought a moment and then added, "I have seen many beautiful things, spectacular things. Most of the time, I was alone or with a maid or a guardian while my parents were off, my father at a meeting and my mother shopping or doing things she thought would bore me. She never missed a single art museum, no matter how unknown the artist.

"Besides," he continued, turning to me, "it's true that seeing beautiful things alone isn't even half as satisfying and wonderful as seeing them with someone you know shares the same appreciation and respect for these things."

"You mean, like a girlfriend?"

"Well, when I was older, a girlfriend. Just a friend would have been nice when I was younger."

"You didn't have any close friends?"

"You can imagine how hard it was to make friends, good friends, for someone whose family was always moving on. I was like what they used to call an army brat, going from one base to another. A good friend is like anything else of value. It takes time. You have to build trust, eventually care about each other."

"What about a girlfriend? You never had one who was something like that?"

"Not like that. I was always on the search for her, of course."

"Was?"

"Well . . . as I said, we moved around too much for me to form any significant relationships. I'm easy to figure out."

"Oh, yeah, easy."

"Now, you, on the other hand, anchored here since birth, should have many close relationships."

He held his gaze on me, and I looked away.

"You don't, do you?" he asked. "Have you ever . . . had anyone like that?"

"That's really none of your business."

"But isn't that what you're sitting here wondering about, why that is?"

"I said, none of your beeswax."

He laughed. "Touchy, touchy."

I felt like pushing him off the railing. "How do you know what I'm thinking about, and how old did you say you were? You sound like someone's wise old grandfather or something, sitting on a pedestal and looking down at me."

"Sorry," he said. "I really don't mean to be condescending."

"Well, you are," I said sharply, so sharply that even my eyes burned.

"*Pardonnez-moi.*"

I fumed for another moment and then calmed. Now I was wondering more about myself. How could he tell that I was thinking and worrying about myself? Was I so obvious that even someone who really didn't know me could sense my thoughts and feelings? If he could, couldn't people who knew me for years do that? Or did he have something special, some older, more mature perception and sensitivity that he had developed because of his mother's condition? Nothing could age and mature you faster than a parent being seriously ill, I thought. I was wrong to be so resentful.

Okay, I told myself. *Behave.* He was the new kid on the block. He was the one who should be vulnerable and afraid, the one looking for a friendly face, listening for a friendly voice. After all, for teenagers especially, moving into a new community and going to a new school were like being thrown into a lake and told to swim or drown. At least, that was the way it was always described in books and the way I viewed new students when they first entered school at Echo Lake.

"Were you in town today?" I asked.

"I passed through, yes."

"Passed through? You could do that in all of five minutes. Why didn't you stop in our store and say hello? I could have shown you around a bit."

"I was on an errand and had to get back home," he said.

"Oh. When's your father returning?"

"That's top secret."

"Well, why would he leave you alone here after just moving into a new house?"

"Duty calls."

"Doesn't his first duty lie here?"

He was silent.

"Sorry. Now I'm putting my nose into your bees-wax."

He stared into the night. I thought to myself, *Go for it, Amber. Shake him out of his darkness.*

"One of the girls in my class is having a July Fourth party Saturday night. Her family is one of the wealthy ones in town. They have a big place, almost what you would call an estate. There's going to be fireworks and great food. She'll spare no expense with her parents' money."

"It's not July Fourth this weekend."

"I know, but her parents are away this weekend."

"Oh, I see. When the cat's away . . ."

"So?"

"I don't think so," he said.

"Why not?"

"I want to wait a while before getting involved with the gang," he said, making *gang* sound juvenile.

"They're not the gang. They're just who might be your classmates if you stay here. What are you, James Dean in *Rebel Without a Cause*?"

He laughed. "Yes, I'm just like James Dean. Thanks for the invite, anyway."

"Well, how about meeting my parents, then? They're just reading and watching television. No big deal. They'd like to meet you and later your parents when they can. It's not every day we get new neighbors."

"No, I'd better get back," he said, now sounding a little frightened and insecure for the first time. "It's not a good time. Thanks."

"Why isn't it a good time?"

He didn't reply. How frustrating he was. *Why am I bothering?* I thought. I looked at his house and then back at him. Was it his mother? Couldn't he leave her longer than he had taken to walk with me?

Before I could ask anything more, he slipped off the railing and was almost absorbed by the darkness when he turned his face away.

"Is your mother doing any better?" I called to him anyway.

He turned back to me, his face glowing in the starlight almost the way I had imagined it in his bedroom window last night. "She's the same," he said.

"She doesn't like it here? What about you?"

"You already know I do. I'd better go." He started and stopped, turning back to me again. "Stop feeling sorry for yourself. You'll be fine," he added, his voice drifting as he stepped away.

Instead of going to the front of the house and down the street, he was heading toward the back and around again.

I rose and went to the railing. "Wait."

He didn't reply as he moved through the light spilling from our windows, speeding up as if he thought the illumination might burn him.

I hurried down the steps of the front porch and around the house to catch up with him, but I didn't see him in the darkness once he had passed through the last bit of light leaking out of our house. I didn't see him behind the house or at the hedges, either, when I got there. I listened for the sound of his feet over the grass, the opening of his front or back door, anything, but I heard nothing.

"Brayden, where are you?" I whispered loudly. I waited but still heard nothing. "Why are you going home this way? Do you have to sneak back into your house? Brayden?"

I walked slowly toward the hedges, listening as hard as I could, but I didn't hear anything other than the distant hum of traffic in town and on the main highway that ran northwest to Portland. The rear of our house had a patio, a built-in barbecue grill, chairs, and tables. Dad was always talking about building a pool, but Mom, the accountant in our family, pointed out how little use we could make of it, especially given that only in the

summer could we use it at all, and therefore what an in-
efficient use of our money it would be. Consequently, we
had a rather big undeveloped backyard.

Our land was almost an acre shaped in a rectangle,
the rear border of which was deep, thick woods. There
was a stream about a mile in, which was fed by the lake
runoff. Freshwater streams flowing from the mountains
and winter snow runoff kept the lake and the stream
healthy. There hadn't been a real drought in our area for
more than fifty years.

I wasn't one to go exploring in the forest. I only
ventured in deeply when I went with Dad, who toyed
with the idea of finding a great place to fish for kokanee
salmon, the version of sockeye salmon that thrived in
lakes. Mom teased him about it because he wasn't that
great a fisherman, often getting more involved in a
history book he was reading. Once he had lost a pole
because a rather big fish bit and dragged it off while he
was absorbed in a detailed description of the battles on
the Gallipoli front during World War I and had rested
his pole on a large rock, thinking he would have time to
seize it if he got a bite.

I smiled at the memory.

Then I looked up at the now lit attic in Brayden's
house. For a minute or so, I saw nothing, and then I was
sure I saw him come to the window and look down in
my direction. How did he get up there so quickly? He
must have run the whole way. I waited to see if he saw
me looking up at him, but he was gone, and soon after,
the light went out, throwing the entire house into darkness. What was that about? Had his mother fallen asleep

up there? How could they navigate through their house in such utter darkness? I waited, but the house remained dark. Why didn't the light go on in his room?

I stared at the attic window for a few moments and then lowered my head and walked back to the porch. I no longer felt like sitting outside and listening to my own thoughts. The truth was, I did so just so I would see or talk to him. Now that he was gone, I decided to go in and go to sleep. My conversation with him had done little more to enlighten me about him. He was still a first-class walking mystery.

"Everything all right?" Dad called when I entered the house.

"Yes."

"Your mother decided to go up and read."

"Okay," I said. "Me, too. Night, Dad."

"Night, Amber Light."

I smiled and hurried up the stairs to look in on Mom. She was comfortably in bed, reading.

"Enjoy your time outside?"

"Yes."

"Did you meet anyone?" she asked with a wry smile.

I thought a moment. "Felt like it, but I can't be sure," I said, and she widened her smile.

"Maybe you need more time to be sure. Do you want more time to be sure?"

We both knew what she meant. Did I?

I nodded. "I guess I will take tomorrow off," I said.

"You have the weekend off, Amber, not just tomorrow, so feel free to make plans. If it should come up," she added with a twinkle in her eyes.

"Okay, Mom. Thanks."

"Great."

I started away, then paused as if I had something more to add. I did, but not in words. I entered the bedroom and kissed her good night.

"Love you," she said.

Do we ever stop kissing our mothers good night? I wondered. Maybe, when we were finally out of the house and in a home of our own, but if she were there for a visit, I was sure that even with children of my own, I would still think of my mother as Mom or Mommy and give her that good-night kiss.

I wondered if Brayden gave his mother a good-night kiss. Somehow, even without meeting her, I thought it might not happen. Someday I would know I had been right, but not for the reasons I thought or could even imagine.

Before I got into bed, my phone rang. It was Ellie, who said she had just gotten home herself. Apparently, meeting me and hearing me talk about a new boy in town had energized her own romantic interests.

"Charlotte and I went to the mall and hung out at the pizza place. Bobby Harris and Tommy Fletcher spent the whole time with us. I know Bobby has a thing for me. I'm just not sure about him. What do you think of him? Should I let him pursue me?"

"He seems safe enough," I said.

"Safe? What's that supposed to mean? I never wondered if a boy was safe or not."

"It could mean a lot of things, Ellie. Sometimes it's not safe getting too involved with someone. He or she could be a bad influence, bring a lot of his own personal baggage that could depress you," I added, thinking of Brayden.

"God, you're getting to talk like Mrs. Fishman, the health teacher. Next thing I know, you'll start talking about peer pressure and all that other garbage we hear from her until it comes pouring out of our ears."

"You asked my opinion, so I'm giving it to you." I paused. Was I was being too curt and lofty? Wasn't this what they were always accusing me of being? Who was I to give anyone romantic advice, anyway? "I haven't heard anything terribly negative about Bobby Harris. But I haven't heard all that much about him, anyway," I added in a softer tone.

"Oh, so now you think he's boring, not unsafe enough. Is that it?"

"What? No," I said, laughing. "A boy doesn't have to be unsafe to be interesting." I thought about my father's joking. "That would make Jack the Ripper an ideal date."

"I asked around about your new neighbors. Nobody knows anything about them. Most were even surprised to hear someone had moved into the house. Tami Spaulding's aunt lives on your street. She was there yesterday, and she said the house looks just as deserted as ever."

"They haven't gotten around to doing much yet," I said. "Mr. Matthews travels on business and is away on an important trip he had to make. They'll probably dress up the place when he returns."

"Oh, so you really are getting to know this someone who is very good-looking," she quickly concluded.

"I've spoken to him a few times, but I'd never claim I've gotten to know him yet."

"What's that mean? You know, you speak more and more in riddles these days, Amber. Everyone says so. Most don't even want to make the effort."

"Sometimes things aren't as clear as we would like," I said. "So they seem like riddles. I don't mean it to sound like that. Look, I've learned he's just very cautious when it comes to meeting new people."

"Cautious? Safe? Can you speak English? Never mind. What's his name? You know that, at least, don't you?"

"Brayden."

"Brayden. I like that. It sounds safe."

"Okay, Ellie."

She laughed. "So? Did you get a chance to ask him to go to Charlotte's party?"

I hesitated, not wanting to give her Brayden's real answer. All that would do would lead to more questions.

"He has a conflict with some family things he has to do," I said.

"Oh, too bad. Well, we'll try to arrange something else soon."

"Yes, good idea."

"Are you coming to the party anyway?"

"I think so."

"Why can't you just say yes? I can pick you up if you want. Well?"

"Okay."

"Or if you'd like, I can arrange for Shayne Allan to pick you up. I'd be glad to do it."

"No, that's fine. I don't need anyone to arrange for me to meet Shayne Allan."

"You're not afraid of him or something, are you? You don't see him as being unsafe? I'm not kidding this time."

"No, I'm not afraid of him. I'm just a fan of letting things happen naturally."

"Huh? Naturally? I swear, I have to work on my foreign-language skills so I can understand you. Anyway, I'll pick you up around seven-fifteen. Don't forget, wear something red, white, or blue or all three."

"Why didn't she just make a party? Why the July Fourth excuse?"

"It will work when her parents find out," Ellie explained. "She'll claim she was just being patriotic."

"Give me a break. They'll believe that?"

"She's just being cautious. That's a new thing for Charlotte to try, caution."

She laughed again, and then we ended the conversation with my reassuring her that I would go to the party.

Ellie did make me think about Shayne Allan. Why was I really avoiding him? I asked myself. Was I afraid of having what everyone thought was the most ideal relationship, the prom king and his queen? Or did I think that because he was so perfect, I would look inferior? Was I really that arrogant? Was I simply just a prude? I overheard the things Ellie and the other girls said about me. I knew they believed that I was afraid of sex. Maybe they were right. Maybe every clever thing I said was simply a way to avoid facing the truth, a rationalization, a smoke screen so no one would be able to see just how frightened I really was to be involved with anyone.

And then it occurred to me that maybe that was Brayden's problem, too. Perhaps what was happening between his own parents caused him to be timid about having any relationship of his own. How could anyone living in a family like his not be suffering from some emotional and psychological issues himself? His bravado and clever talk were his smoke screen. We were more alike than I first thought.

That's why he sensed what I was thinking. He thought about the same things. No matter how cavalier he was about making friends and having relationships, the truth was, he was very lonely. And I had to admit to myself that I was, too.

Perhaps if I helped him break out of his self-inflicted imprisonment, I would help myself do the same. *There. If I needed a reason to keep trying, I found one,* I thought.

I went to my window again, hesitated, and then deliberately opened the curtain wider.

He's watching me, I thought confidently. *Somewhere in the darkness, he's fixed on my lighted windows, drawn to them like a moth to a candle.*

I began to undress, doing my best to pretend to be oblivious, acting as if I had forgotten that someone had moved in next door. Nevertheless, my heart was pounding. I paraded around in my bra and panties and then paused and undid my bra with my back to the window. I slipped it off and down my arms and then tossed it onto a chair as casually as a nightclub stripper. I straightened up with my arms at my sides. I could feel my nipples harden. A tingling began to swirl in my stomach and the insides of my thighs. I felt my breath quicken, my lips moisten. All I had to do was turn around. I started to, but I didn't. It was as if there were invisible hands on my shoulders pressing down firmly to prevent me from doing so. My body calmed. I walked away, put on my nightgown, and turned off the lights.

It was a mean thing to do, I decided. I knew there were all sorts of nasty names for girls who would do something like that. They certainly didn't earn themselves any respect. I could feel my body filling up with guilt and shame. I couldn't imagine my mother ever having done something like that when she was my age, and I knew how disappointed my father would be if he knew about it.

What would Brayden think of me now? Would he pretend that he hadn't seen me? Maybe he hadn't. Perhaps he really had gone to sleep. That was certainly possible. I hoped so. It helped me to feel better, and I was able to fall asleep quickly. But sometime during the night, I woke up, and for a moment, I thought Brayden was standing there, looking down at me and shaking his head disdainfully. I sat up quickly, nearly crying out.

But he wasn't there.

The star glow on the walls made the threads in my pink and white wallpaper sparkle. I could hear the wind weave itself around our house, rush over the roof, and pluck at the rain gutters. I sat for a moment, my hands clasped between my breasts, and then I lowered myself to my soft, oversized pillows. For a while, I was afraid to close my eyes, afraid to fall head over heels down the well of my dreams, but sleep finally seized me again, and I didn't wake until I heard my father coming up the stairs with Mom's cup of coffee.

I sat up and rubbed my eyes, and then I stopped suddenly, actually freezing in place.

The curtains on my windows were closed tightly.

I didn't remember doing that.

4

Child of Circumstance

"Now, don't spend your entire day off sitting in the house reading or doing any of the housework," my mother warned me at breakfast. "That's not why we want you not to come to the store, Amber."

"I won't," I promised, and then told her that I had decided to go to Charlotte's party for sure and that Ellie was picking me up.

"Oh, that's nice," she said. "Did you ask the new boy to go?"

"I did, but he can't go."

"Why not?"

"He doesn't want to leave his mother alone so soon after moving into a new house," I told her. It was probably one of the real reasons for his declining my invitation, I thought, if not the only one.

"Oh, well, I suppose that's very thoughtful and considerate of him." She smiled. "I'm sure you'll have a good time."

I wasn't so sure, but I was also not so sure that everyone else's parents were going to be as overjoyed about them attending a party at Charlotte Watts's house.

Previously, there had been some incidents with binge drinking and drugs. If Charlotte's father wasn't so influential, she would surely have been in more trouble. Her driver's license had already been revoked once, but it was quickly restored. Wealthy, prominent people did seem immune from the consequences everyone else had to face, even in a town as small as ours.

My parents weren't worried about my getting into any trouble, anyway. They had confidence in me. I had never been in any trouble at school, never late for a class or bawled out for talking while the teacher was lecturing. Maybe I was the ideal goody-goody, but if it made my parents happy, it didn't bother me the way I knew it would bother some of my friends.

Think of the words kids my age hate to hear in reference to themselves, I thought. *Decent, well-behaved, obedient,* and *respectful* were a few that some grimaced at hearing next to their names.

My mother was obviously just happy I was getting out, doing any sort of socializing with kids my age. I had no idea how often my parents discussed me and my practically nonexistent social life, but I was confident that it was quite often these days. Daughters of their friends were much more active and even more involved with after-school activities. In their minds, I was surely living the life of a wallflower, always sitting on the sidelines, enviously watching the other girls having the best times of their lives. Here I was, by everyone's standard attractive and polite, responsible and bright. What kept me from at least enjoying as much as someone who was considered plain and average?

Surely they wondered if they were responsible in some way. Were they too restrictive? Had they been demanding too much from me? Was my working in the store discouraging? Was there something they had done that discouraged me from reveling in my youth? It had to puzzle them. They were far from dour people. Yes, they worked hard at our family business, but they weren't severe and dreary and didn't insist that I work as hard as they did. Rarely was either of them stuck in a state of depression. Everyone has down moments, disappointments, and some unhappiness, but my parents were not the kind of people who would dwell on anything unpleasant. In fact, Dad always found something funny in the end, something that made him laugh at himself, and Mom believed in the sunny day ahead.

She had faith that no matter what, morning would bring a change. Whatever the challenge, whether it was something economic, an illness, or an accident, things would get better as soon as the sun came up. They always did get better if you believed they would. No, our house was papered in optimism. We smiled and laughed far more than we scowled and cried. All of the kids my age admired my parents, talked about how young they looked and acted, how easy they were to talk to, and how comfortable my parents made them feel.

Surely my peers believed there was no other reason I could possibly have for being so negative and skeptical except arrogance. Or maybe I was simply too afraid of life, of disappointing my parents or even myself. Few of my friends worried about such things. In fact, being around me was probably a downer for them, because I,

with just my mere presence, would remind them of the
consequences that their misbehaving might bring.

I didn't smoke and always refused to drink hard
liquor, even beer most of the time. I had not taken and
would never take any drugs. Thanks to Ellie, I had just
learned that some of the boys were calling me Prudence
Perfect. Hearing that and how even the girls were doing
it these days, I was honestly surprised that Charlotte
had bothered to invite me to her party. It had to be Ellie's doing, but I thought that my mentioning a new
boy in town had the most to do with her invitation becoming more enthusiastic. Now that I wasn't bringing
him, I had to wonder how she and her friends would
treat me. I was beginning to have second thoughts
about going, but I also knew that it would disappoint
my mother and probably my father if I didn't go. What
could I possibly use as an excuse for changing my mind,
anyway? A headache?

Despite Mom's warning before they left for the
store, I went around the house doing some vacuuming
and furniture polishing. After that, I spent a few hours
straightening up my room and bathroom. Finally, I
put on a bathing suit, grabbed a beach towel to place
on the chaise, and went out back to get some sun and
read. What else was I going to do? No one had called to
ask me to do anything with them lately, although I felt
certain that many of the girls were out together, perhaps
shopping for something new to wear to the party. The
way things were going, I was even surprised to get the
phone call from Ellie and have her volunteer to pick me
up for the party.

Once I had begun working in our store and because of how busy it became during the summer months, I rarely spent a whole day enjoying the weather like this anyway, I told myself when I started to feel sorry for myself for spending my day alone. We had to stay open seven days a week during June, July, and August and half of September. The quaintness of the town, the nearby streams that invited fishermen, and its location along one of the more scenic routes for anyone exploring the Northwest made it a lucrative little stopover community. Dad's specialized jewelry creations had built us a reputation that was spreading because of our Web site. Demand for some of his pieces kept him working longer and harder than he had ever imagined but also permitted him to raise prices. I couldn't help but be as proud of him as Mom was.

What did I have to do to make my life, and therefore theirs, happier? Should I simply overcome my inhibitions, put aside whatever high goals I had set for myself, let go, and be more like the girls who were popular? Who set the height of the bar for misbehavior, anyway? I often overheard my parents' friends, parents of my classmates, laughingly admit to their own indiscretions, remarking on how it was a miracle they hadn't gotten in serious trouble for this or that. How often I had heard one of them say, "I hope my kids never do half of what I did."

What did you do? I wanted to ask. *How did you get away with it? How do you live with it now? How could you condemn your children for doing things that weren't quite as bad then?* Was the whole world a sponge, constantly absorbing hypocrisy and growing fatter and fatter on lies and deceit? We weren't a very religious family, but I couldn't help but wonder about the scale that was used at the door of heaven, the one that weighed all your good deeds against your bad ones, all your charity against your selfishness, all your kindness against your mean-ness, and all your love against all your hate. How rare it must be for the good side to outweigh the bad, I thought. Maybe heaven was still populated only with angels.

I really wasn't worrying about getting into heaven. That wasn't my problem. What was my problem, then? If I asked myself that one more time, I would probably have the record for repeating the same words. I returned to my book, but the words seemed to float off the page, and my eyes flicked from side to side to bring them back.

"Still feeling sorry for yourself?" I heard, and spun around to see Brayden standing behind me on the patio.

"You really enjoy sneaking up on people, don't you?"

He smiled and came forward. "Did you ever notice that when someone thinks no one is around, he or she can't help but be honest?"

"What? I don't understand. Honest to whom if there's no one around?"

"To themselves. They can't help but reveal their thoughts, the truth inside them. As soon as we confront someone, the old defenses go up, the walls rise, the lies get dressed to come onstage, and before long, you're talk-ing to someone else, a costume, an empty suit of armor."

"No, I didn't notice all that," I said dryly. "But I haven't traveled all over the world and met all these sophisticated people, either. Most of all, I don't have the power to read people's minds."

He laughed. "Sure you do."

"Is that right? How come you know more about me than I know about myself?"

"You know it. You haven't admitted it or faced up to it all yet, but you will."

"Don't you get tired of being a prophet?"

"To be honest . . . yes," he said unexpectedly. "Mind?" He sat at the edge of my chaise.

This time, I couldn't help it. I had to ask. "Don't you have more than one shirt to wear? Besides, it's warmer today."

"Oh, it's a fresh shirt. I have about a dozen of these."

"You like dressing the same way every day?"

"Remember Thoreau's warning: 'Beware of all enterprises that require new clothes.'"

"Just dressing differently from day to day isn't a new enterprise."

He widened that impish smile. "I do make slight changes. Today, I left the top two buttons undone. Yesterday, it was only one."

"Very funny."

"Day off?"

"Yes. I don't take them often during the summer, but my parents are employing someone part-time who needs a little financial help, and they didn't need me, too."

"That's quite considerate. I guess they're very nice people."

"You can find out by meeting them."

"I can find out through you. What's that old saying, the apple doesn't fall far from the tree?"

"So, your parents wear the same things every day and sneak around?"

He laughed again and then just looked at me.

"What?" I said.

"I wish we had moved here last year and I had met you then."

"Why?"

"I would have insisted on staying. In fact, I would have chained myself to the door."

I smiled, shook my head, and looked away, because I felt something happening inside me that I had never felt as strongly, a stirring not only in my breasts but deeper, in my heart, a warmth that trickled down my body, into my legs, softening me and in the process waking every cell in my body, giving me the feeling that I was starting to glow inside. I was embarrassed, fearful that he would see it quickly. For some reason, there was also a part of me that wanted to keep this feeling secret for as long as possible. I suppose it was like showing your hand too early and doing what he had described, dropping your defenses and opening yourself up completely. Something always told me that was a dangerous thing to do too soon.

But there was also another feeling here, something I didn't understand. Some sort of an alarm was sounding, but it was a different kind of warning. I wasn't being warned against doing something sexual, or simply revealing too many of the secrets that every girl wants kept sacrosanct. It was a shriller sound, a sound coming from someplace I rarely touched inside myself. It was as if my very life force trembled.

I looked at him. How could he be dangerous to me in any way? He had such a gentle face and spoke so softly. The most aggressive thing he had done so far was reach for my hand in the darkness when we walked. If any-thing, he looked alone and lost and far more vulnerable than I imagined I was.

"Now you're here. Chain yourself to the door. It's not too late, is it?"

"I don't think about it anymore," he said. "I feel . . ."

"What?" I asked, holding my breath. I could sense that he was going to let down his defenses and finally tell me something really important about himself.

"I feel like things are no longer under my control."

He looked out at the woods. I didn't move, didn't utter a sound, and kept holding my breath. Was he re-ally going to start telling me something significant about himself, stop holding back?

"I used to be so confident about myself," he contin-ued, "but it's as if I were vulnerable to any devilish wind. I feel like I'm a sort of surprised victim all the time, a child of circumstance. My choice is either stand still and be pushed or dragged along, or move a little faster than events but not change direction. Can't do that."

"I can understand that," I said.

"Can you?" He turned to me. "Why? What makes you so wise all of a sudden?" He didn't sound offended, just curious.

"Well, look at your life. I mean, you're taking care of your sick mother, and your father, from the way you describe him, seems oblivious to everything. It's as if you have no choices for yourself anymore. All of the responsi-bilities have fallen on you, and you're too young for that to have happened. Despite how wise you pretend to be," I added.

"Very good analysis," he said, sounding like a teacher again. There was no emotion, no appreciation, just a factual reaction. I felt my neck stiffen.

"I'm glad you approve. I expect an A plus."

He laughed. "I can see why most boys would have a hard time with you."

"Oh, really. Why is that?" Now I was really curious. Could he answer the question I kept asking myself?

"Your pride. Did you ever notice how easily most of the girls you know are manipulated? They'll change their clothes, their hairstyles, give up friends, and finally give up whatever morals they once cherished if it all meant having Mr. Perfect. But not Amber Taylor. You don't compromise; you don't make concessions. You're one of those take-me-or-leave-me girls. Rare, I admit, but they're out there. And here," he added, nodding at my house.

"Really," I said dryly. "You ought to be writing a young-romance love column."

"I would, but I fear I would waste my time. Remember, none are so blind as those who will not see."

"You're a walking book of wisdom."

"It's a terrible burden," he said. He didn't smile. Then he looked at the woods again. I thought that the silence that had fallen between us was as solid as a stone wall and that he'd just get up and retreat as usual, but he surprised me. "You have a pretty neat stream about a half mile in."

"You've seen it?"

"First I heard it and then went looking for it. I mean, that's clear, cool water. I think of rivers and streams as being like veins and arteries keeping the earth healthy and alive. So much is getting polluted, so when you see one like the one back here, you can't help but enjoy it. Do you go there often?"

"Hardly ever. My father occasionally fished in it, but he hasn't for some time."

"You want to take a walk now?"

I looked toward his house. "You can get away?"

"Yes, she's asleep. She'll sleep for hours. It's the medication. That's why she's up so much at night."

"It can't go on like this forever, can it?"

"No. And it won't," he said. Then he smiled and stood up. "So, what do you say?"

"I should change."

"Just wrap your towel around yourself," he suggested. "It's not cold, even in the woods."

I nodded and stood up, and we started slowly toward the woods.

"How could you hear that stream from your house? I can't hear it from mine."

"I was just exploring our backyard and went farther and farther until I did hear it. When I found it, there was a beautiful blacktail deer drinking out of it. He looked up at me, flicked his ears, and then finished drinking before sauntering off with total indifference. Maybe we'll see another."

Just as he did the night we went to the lake, he led the way, finding a path through the woods as if he had been living here for years.

"Hear the stream?" he asked after we had walked for about five minutes.

We stopped, and I listened. I did hear it. "Yes."

"Nice sound, isn't it? It's like the sound of . . . life, rich, healthy life, uncluttered, undistorted, pure."

"You sure you're from this planet?"

He laughed. "I was never sure about that."

He walked on. I followed slowly. No one I knew my age or even somewhat older talked the way he did, sounded so wise and *settled*. I think that was the word, the feeling he gave me. It was as if despite the chaos in his life, he had found a comfortable, safe place, a place where he could live without fear and without pain and be as contented as an elderly man rocking on his front porch and reliving the happier memories of his life.

"Were you always into nature like this?" I asked.

"Thoreau and nature? I grew into it, yes. Where else could a loner like me go? Did you ever notice how many animals are really alone? I mean, they're together with their mother for a while, and then, if their mother has done a proper job, they can go off and survive without her, right?" He laughed again.

"What?" I asked.

"My father says that's a major difference between us and lower animals. Our offspring, especially in today's world, cling harder and longer to the nest. We're raising a generation of weaklings, he says." He turned to look at me and my reaction. "What do you think?"

"I don't mean to disagree with your brilliant father, but I don't think you can generalize like that," I offered. "My father clung to his nest and made it bigger and more successful."

"Very good. Oops, sorry. I didn't mean to sound like a teacher again."

"Something tells me you can't help yourself," I said, and he really laughed.

"You've got me pegged right."

"The question is, can I change you?"

He paused and glanced at me. "I wish you could," he said. "I'd like that very much."

"Well, don't hold your breath. I'm no miracle worker."

He had another burst of laughter and then looked up at a tall tree and reached for my hand as if he had eyes in the back of his head. He took my fingers softly and pulled me gently up to him. "Check this out," he whispered, still looking up.

"What?"

"Concentrate. See the nest. Just keep your eyes on it."

I did, and then I thought I saw what looked like a tiny snowball peer over the nest and down at us. "What is it?"

"Bald eagles. Probably a few weeks old. They usually nest near water, feed on fish."

"Oh. I've never seen a bald eagle."

He looked skeptical.

"I mean, maybe I have, but I didn't know it."

"They're still endangered, but up here you should see a few."

"It's really more and more like you're the one who's lived here for years and I've just arrived," I said.

"Some of us just take longer to find home."

"Thanks a lot. Now I'm a slow learner."

"Hardly," he said.

We kept walking until we reached the stream. It looked wider and ran faster than it had the few other times I had been there with my father.

"Don't move," he said as I started a little forward. I froze. "Watch that heavy brush about fifty feet down."

"Why?"

"Just watch," he whispered again, and a few moments later, a small blacktail deer stepped out and up to the stream to drink.

"Oh, how beautiful," I said.

"You live in quite a little wonderland."

"How did you know she would be there?"

"I saw the movement in the brush."

The deer heard us and looked our way. It just stood there for a while and then turned and went back into the woods. Brayden lowered himself to a large boulder and looked up at me. I sat beside him.

"I never much thought about all this," I admitted. "I mean, I've been here, but I don't remember it affecting me as strongly."

"Why did you ever come here, then?"

I described my father's fishing experiences. "He wasn't a big success at it, so he doesn't do it that often anymore."

"I think he was a success," Brayden said.

"Oh? How's that? He lost his pole because he was too relaxed reading and forgot where he was and what he was doing. His friends are always making fun of him."

"They miss the point," Brayden said.

"Okay, Professor, what's the point?"

"Thoreau again. He said, 'Many men go fishing all of their lives without knowing it is not fish they are after.' Your father came out here to relax, get away from it all. The fish were just a minor annoyance."

"I'll tell him," I said, smiling. "He'll like that. I bet he uses it next time he's teased about it. I guess I should go back and read more of Thoreau."

"Maybe you should."

"What brought you to reading so much more of him?"

"I told you. His writing is like a bible for loners," he replied.

"You've always felt alone?"

"Not as much as now," he admitted.

"Then, why not come with me tonight and meet more people? It won't matter if you don't continue living here. At least for now . . ."

"For now, you're as much company as I need. I know I'm not and wouldn't be enough for you, but until you tell me to stay away, I'll keep peeping and appearing."

"You're not exactly a good influence on me. I haven't been the social butterfly, and my parents are worried that I'm too picky about friends, especially boyfriends. How's that for irony? Everyone else's parents are just the opposite, worrying that their children are hanging out too much and with the wrong people."

"When my mother was more stable, she used to say that if you found three good friends in your life, you were fine. The rest would be tolerable acquaintances."

"I haven't found the three yet."

"You will."

"You are so damn certain about everything you say," I replied sharply. "Can you tell me how you know all this? And don't give me that story about traveling so much and being on your own so much. Lots of people do that and know less than I do."

"Well, for one thing, I listen well," he said. He lay back on the rock and put his hands behind his head. I watched him a moment, watched the way his eyes seemed to drink in everything, as if he were going to be blind any moment and wanted to lock as much as possible into his visual memory. No one I knew seemed to seize on sights and sounds as intensely.

I took off my towel and spread it over the rock before lying back beside him.

"What does that mean, 'listen well'?"

"I really listen. Most people look like they're listening, but their minds are off and running down some other street, or they let boredom take over too soon. Maybe most of the world has ADD. I don't know. There are so many reasons most people are deaf to what's around them."

"Okay, what am I missing now," I asked, gazing up at the sky, "O great guru of nature?"

"Sometimes I like to watch clouds gradually change shape. I have a theory that if you could capture all the cloud shapes in the world, you would discover that they're imitating things below."

"Who's imitating things below?"

"The clouds. Like that one off to the right, the one that seems to have broken loose from another bigger cloud. See it? It resembles a big cat; that puffiness is its head. Doesn't it look like it? See what I mean?"

I centered on the cloud and laughed. "Yes, I think it does."

"I knew that if anyone would see it, you would."

"Why?"

He braced himself on his right elbow and sat up to look down at me. "I told you that, too. You have a vision, a kind of extrasensory ability that enables you to see beyond or through what's right in front of you. That's why you're having trouble putting your affections solely in one guy. You see through them too easily. You're waiting for someone more substantial. Don't worry. He'll come along."

"I've said it before, and I'll say it again. I've never heard someone your age talk like you do."

He shrugged. "I am what I am. Anyway, now you know what to listen for."

He leaned back again and looked up at the sky. It was so comfortable, warm, and pleasant. I felt relaxed and closed my eyes. The sound of the stream curling around and over rocks worked like a lullaby. Neither of us spoke. The warm breeze felt like a light blanket. In seconds, it seemed, I fell asleep, or at least I think I did. It seemed as if I had fallen into a dream. In this dream, Brayden was hovering over me again. Then his smile faded as he stared down at me, and I stared up at him, falling into his eyes, already tasting his lips before he slowly brought them to mine.

I was in the ninth grade the first time I kissed a boy on the lips. It was at Ellie's house party. There were three couples. I was the one with the least amount of time logged in as anyone's supposed girlfriend. The boy's name was Reggie Seymour, and he had been in our school only four months. His parents were in a raging divorce, and his mother had taken him and his sister, Pat, away in what was almost a kidnapping. From what all of us eventually learned, she wasn't supposed to leave Washington State with her children. Both Reggie and Pat looked habitually frightened, I thought, always looking toward classroom, cafeteria, and auditorium doorways whenever someone entered. I sensed that they were expecting either their father or a policeman to burst on the scene, someone who would haul them back to Washington.

Reggie was as shy as, if not shier than, I was at the time. We seemed naturally to navigate toward each other with short conversations and quick smiles, and eventually by holding hands. Maybe I liked him or risked liking him because I believed he wasn't going to be with us long. He was cute, about average in class, and not terribly good at any sport. His timidity kept him from being aggressive. I think he was worried that if he got into any trouble, he would make more trouble for his mother and bring about some serious consequences for all of them.

Ellie's party was the first time I had paired off with a specific boy. We all had our little space in the large living room, and when the lights were lowered, the necking began. I was sure that Reggie's and my kissing was the least erotic of any of the kisses going on. Our kiss was more like the snap of a match. We spent most of the time talking, until Ellie finally shouted for us to shut up because we were ruining the mood. We kissed again, both of us trying harder to make it seem like something special, but neither of us came away with any stronger feeling for the other. And then, two weeks later, he and his sister were pulled out of the school, and his mother did return to Washington State. It was one of the more bizarre student memories I had. We all talked about the Seymours for a while, and then they dropped out of conversations and our minds as quickly as a trivial news blurb on CNN.

So, even in this dream, I didn't know what to expect from Brayden's kiss. It was as if his lips settled on mine and formed themselves perfectly to fit my mouth comfortably. It was a kiss filled with expectations but so light and airy that it kept me held to expectations. I fought hard against waking up and losing the moment. It was the longest kiss I had ever experienced, even in a dream, a kiss that finally flowed into me, touching me so deeply that I felt my whole body soften and then become more demanding, trying to draw more and more from it.

When he lifted his lips from mine, they felt naked, aching with disappointment. I lifted my head gently to draw him back, but he moved his lips down over my chin, to my neck instead. I closed my eyes and felt myself grow limp, but willingly. I wanted his hands all over my body, gently caressing and molding it so he could fit his more comfortably against it, turning me toward him, stroking my hair, his lips on mine again, his hands softly moving over my breasts. It felt as though he had somehow gone under my bathing suit top, even though I knew he hadn't.

"You make me feel alive," he whispered, and kissed

my ear and my cheek and then found my lips turned and waiting for his. It was as if he had awakened another me, waiting to be awoken, happy to be awoken. I moaned and welcomed his touch everywhere, my heart beating like a racehorse finally permitted to gallop, to drive every part of itself to the place it was meant to be.

I moaned, raising my lower body so it would press against his. As my excitement grew, I heard him say, "Amber Taylor, meet Amber Taylor."

I cried out at the peak of my passion, and then I felt him easing up, calming me, lowering me softly to my towel, kissing my eyes closed. I didn't move. My breathing slowed. He stroked my hair again, quieting me, relaxing me. His final kiss was softer, a gentle closing of a door. Although he turned away, I still felt a blanket of his warmth over me.

Suddenly, I woke. The river was louder. The sun was lower in the sky and blocked out by trees and leaves. Long, thick shadows seemed to be crawling toward me. I felt no breeze. I heard nothing. The silence surprised me. I sat up, realizing that I was alone.

"Brayden?" I called, looking around. Had he gone for a short walk? Was he down by the water? I called for him again and again, but he didn't respond.

Surprised now, I stood up and wrapped my towel around my waist. I heard some movement in the bushes and turned quickly to my left to see two rabbits. They paused to look at me and then scurried under another bush to disappear.

Where was he? I cupped my hands around my mouth and shouted, "Brayden!"

He didn't reply. There was no sign of him anywhere. What had he done, left me there asleep and dreaming? How long had he been gone? I glanced at my watch. I had slept the better part of an hour. I waited and listened for a few more minutes, and then I hurried around the boulder and started back along the pathway he had shown me. A good ten minutes later, I stepped into my backyard. He was still nowhere in sight. I looked at his house. It was as quiet as before.

How could he just walk away like that? How could he leave me out there?

Fuming, I marched into my house and stomped up the stairs to my room. There I gazed out the window at his room and, as usual, saw nothing. For a few moments, I sat on my bed thinking, and then I shook my head and told myself to stop pouting and caring. Instead, I took a hot shower and, more determined than ever, began to think of what to wear to Charlotte Watts's party.

5

Prudence Perfect

It occurred to me that Brayden had never offered me his telephone number, and, unlike everyone else I knew, he didn't carry a cell phone. I couldn't even call him to complain about his leaving me in the forest, and I didn't want to go banging on his door to see what had happened. I was afraid of disturbing his mother and really getting him angry at me and causing more trouble. As I dressed and prepared for Charlotte's party, I paused occasionally to look out the window, hoping to see him outside his house. The windows of his room were more like mirrors at the moment, so I couldn't see if he was in there.

In fact, everything around the house seemed frozen in time. It was as though any breeze, any wind, avoided it. Not a leaf on any of the trees on the property trembled. Even the clouds above seemed like sails in a dead calm sea, pasted against the blue. And then a crow landed on the roof and settled so completely and so still that it looked more like a decoration.

I decided to go on my computer and look up Brayden's mother. She had her own Web site under her artistic name. There was a list of awards and museums in which her paintings were hung. I thought most of them were very beautiful, interesting, some remarkable pictures of people in street scenes and country scenes. Her work was described as a unique cross between realism and impressionism. There was a biography, describing where she had attended school and such, but no mention of her husband and son.

I looked through the Web site until I heard the phone ringing and then practically lunged for the receiver, hoping, even though I couldn't remember giving him my phone number, that it was Brayden.

It wasn't.

Ellie was calling to remind me what time she would be picking me up, but I think also to confirm that I really was going to the party and hadn't changed my mind. I began to grow a little suspicious about why it was suddenly so important that I go to this party. She had no trouble going anywhere without me. It was as if she had made a bet with Charlotte that she could get me there. Or maybe they had something else planned.

"What are you going to wear?" she asked.

"I'm working on it now."

"Try not to look so . . ."

"What?"

"Safe," she said, and laughed.

"I'm sorry I ever told you that."

"You could try to be sexier, Amber. I know you have the clothes for it."

"I'll try," I said. "But it's not necessary to be so obvious."

"Right, Prudence Perfect." She laughed quickly. "Okay. I'll see you soon."

She could be so infuriating, I thought. Why was I doing this?

My mother called soon after to tell me that she and Dad were going right from the store to Von Richards's restaurant for dinner since I was going out to the party. I had the same sense that she was confirming that I hadn't changed my mind. Was I really this bad about it in their eyes? Did they think I was becoming some sort of a recluse? It was only through the eyes of other people that you saw yourself, I thought. Being oblivious or unconcerned about how other people saw you put you at a great disadvantage. You were blinded by how you wanted people to think of you rather than seeing how they really did. However, you could wrap that cocoon around yourself just so tightly before you were smothered in your own ego.

Ego, however, was what drove me back to the full-length body mirror on the door of my closet at least a half-dozen times because of what Ellie had said. Suddenly, everything I was going to wear did look like something from the wardrobe of Prudence Perfect. I changed five times before settling on a layered look with the tightest black pants I had. I had a dark blue blouse so they wouldn't complain about my not wearing one of the colors, even though this whole thing about July Fourth was a farce. I rearranged my hair twice, deciding to pin it up and back, which made me concentrate more on my earrings. I put on one of the matching turquoise necklaces Daddy had made for me and then redid my makeup three times, adding more than usual before I felt confident enough to step out of my room and head downstairs.

I'll show them who is and who isn't Prudence Perfect, I vowed, gazing at myself in the full-length mirror in our foyer. I wasn't obvious, but I was sexy, and I did feel a little more reckless, a little more excited. Had my dream at the creek woken something inside me, some sleeping feminine side of me that had welcomed being nudged, that had been waiting impatiently?

Once again, I gazed out of windows looking for any Brayden sightings, but he was nowhere to be seen, and the diminishing sunlight put that dismal gray darkness over his house again. From what I could tell, the crow was gone, and no other birds landed on the trees in the yard. Even the leaves looked limp and depressed. How could his father just plant his wife and son in this new home and not arrange for things to be done around the house?

Window curtains were tightly closed, shades drawn down, and the sun wasn't even striking that side of the house anymore. Maybe I could find my way to understanding how or why his mother avoided lights, but what about him? How could he enjoy navigating his new home through shadows? And what about when they ate? Where did they eat? I was not familiar with the house, but I assumed from the size of the windows on the other side that the dining room was there. When I left my house to watch for Ellie's car, I went out to the street and walked far enough to see that there was no light spilling from any windows on that side, either. Did they do everything up in the attic, even eat?

Perhaps he'd had to take his mother somewhere, I

thought. Maybe that was why he had rushed off. He'd remembered an appointment. Or maybe it was some sort of an emergency. He could be at the hospital with her. All sorts of possibilities rained down around me. Perhaps she had taken too much medicine. Was she suicidal? Was that it? That would certainly explain why he hovered around her so much. But why should his father leave her so quickly in a new place and put all of the worry and responsibility on Brayden? How did you do that to your teenage son?

I realized that I should temper my annoyance and anger until I learned his reason for leaving me alone in the woods. I waited out in the street for a few minutes to see if he might see me there and come out, but I heard nothing and saw no one, so I returned to my front porch and waited for Ellie. I saw her car approaching and stepped into the driveway.

"Hi," she said as soon as she pulled up. "Wow, you look great."

"Thanks." I got in.

"Where did you get that top? I never saw you wear it before?"

"I got it months ago but forgot about it."

"How can you forget about clothes? I love your hair like that."

"Thanks."

"Your father made that necklace, I bet. I keep asking my father to buy me one. I told him you'd probably get me a discount."

"I can try," I said. "Let me know."

"Maybe my birthday."

She hesitated, nodding at Brayden's house.

"Did you ask him again?"

"No. I told you he couldn't make it."

"He must have gone somewhere, huh? Doesn't look like anyone's home."

"Right, I don't think so."

She nodded. "Did you meet his parents?"

"No."

"I'd like to see what he looks like," she said, still gazing at the house. "Come on. What's he like, Amber?" She finally started to back out of the driveway.

"I haven't known him long enough to tell you anything more, Ellie."

"You did say he was good-looking."

"So? Rudi Travis is good-looking but has a brain cooked with drugs, and talking to him is like talking to a wind-up doll or something."

She laughed. "He is good-looking. What a shame. What a waste, I should say. I wonder what it would be like to sleep with him anyway. I suppose I could pretend he was someone else."

"Then why bother? Just go with the someone else."

"Yeah, right, except we all can't have what we want—who we want, I mean. You can."

"Don't be so sure."

"I bet this new boy is already bonkers over you."

I didn't say anything.

"He is, isn't he? You can tell pretty fast when that happens, can't you? I mean, I think I can."

"Not everyone is that simple to read, Ellie. And besides, those are usually the most uninteresting guys."

"How come you know so much about men for a
virgin?"

I shook my head.

"Don't tell me you're not a virgin, Amber. We talked
about it a little more than a year ago, and unless you're
doing someone on the side, maybe some older man, I
don't think anything's changed."

"I'm not doing an older man. Don't start spreading
rumors," I said angrily. Sometimes the girls in my school
reminded me of vultures just waiting for some words,
some action, some opportunity to pounce and feed other
vultures. Maybe that was why I was so careful about
what I said and what I did around any of them.

She laughed, but I knew she heard my warning loud
and clear. "Well, I hope this new boy turns out to be nice
as well as good-looking. This town could use some new
blood. Most of the boys are too full of themselves."

She waited for my response, but I was silent, still
thinking about Brayden, the way he had kissed me in my
dream, and my realization that he had left me lying on
a rock in the woods. Her question had made me think
harder about it. How could he take me out there, be so
gentle and interesting, and then desert me like that?
Maybe he was just playing with me. It was depressing to
think that. I couldn't trust anyone anymore.

"You think so, too, right?"

"What?"

"Think the boys in our school are too full of themselves. I just said that. What, are you spaced out already?"

"No. Sorry. Some of them are like that, I suppose."

"Who?"

"I don't know, Ellie. I really don't keep any list in my mind."

"But surely Shayne Allan," she said, nodding. "You still hold that opinion of him, right?"

When I didn't respond, she smirked and was quiet for a while. I just wasn't going to get into the same old argument about him. The truth was, Brayden had washed him right out of my head. Despite what I told Ellie, I used to think about Shayne often. It wasn't something I would ever admit to her or anyone, but since I'd met Brayden, Shayne had rarely entered my mind.

From a half mile or so down the road, we could see that the whole house was lit up. Set on the crest of a hill, it stood out against the dark night sky. Even the stars looked intimidated.

By the time we arrived at Charlotte's family home, there were at least two dozen kids there already. The music was pretty loud. We could hear it as we were approaching. One thing Charlotte didn't have to worry about was neighbors complaining. The nearest ones, because of the amount of land her parents owned, were more than a mile away on either side. Charlotte's father personally had designed their sprawling two-story house, built with natural stone. It had oversize rooms and slate marble floors, and black walnut floors. Mom and Dad had been to a New Year's party there, and they talked about the beautiful mahogany and knotty alder cabinets, the four fireplaces, the very large kitchen with top-of-the-line appliances and slab granite countertops, and all the rich imported furnishings throughout the house. The Wattses had many paintings, both watercolors and oils, but Mom said that Fern Watts chose her art not on the basis of artistic value but for how it fit in with her décor. I wondered if they would ever buy a painting by Brayden's mother. "Can you imagine a Rembrandt reduced to wallpaper?" Mom had asked Dad the morning after that New Year's party.

"Wow. I bet half the school is coming to this party," Ellie said as we got out of the car.

The house had a faux front in the sense that when you came through the front door, you entered a courtyard that had a small pond, some decorative benches, rich-looking grass, and an assortment of flowers. The actual front door was wide open.

The rear wall of the living room consisted of three sliding glass panels that could be drawn apart to open the whole house, so that once we entered, we saw through to the rollicking group of partygoers dancing. All of the lights were on at the rear of the house.

After you crossed the sprawling slate patio that was nearly the width of the house, you came to the large, oval-shaped Pebble Tec pool. It had a diving board and enough chaise longues around it to make it look like the pool at a small hotel. There was a cabana and two fairly large whirlpools at one end of the pool. Charlotte's father had put up lanterns that looked like torches everywhere. Who could not be impressed with it all? I wondered how Brayden would have reacted to all this, although with his worldly travels, he had probably seen far more impressive homes.

Because it was an unusually warm night, the party was being conducted completely outside. That way, Charlotte could at least keep the kids from wandering through the house, and maybe, with a little luck, nothing would be disturbed enough for her parents to get too upset. She and some of the others had set up a few tables for the food she ordered in. From the looks of it, she had gotten something from a few different restaurants. Off to the right, some of the boys were already setting off cherry bombs and firecrackers. Sparklers were everywhere. It did seem like a big July Fourth blowout. To keep up her pretense, she even had a large American flag pinned over the sliding doors leading out from her parents' bedroom.

"Is that really you?" Charlotte asked me when we entered. She looked at Ellie and smiled. "What happened to Prudence Perfect?"

"She couldn't make it," I said. "She had homework left over from last year."

Ellie laughed, but Charlotte just froze her smile and then let it sink into her chubby cheeks. She looked disappointed. I imagined she had invited me to ridicule me with some of her closer friends.

"Shayne Allan isn't here yet," she told me, regaining her impish amusement.

"How will we survive?" I asked, and Ellie laughed again.

"Well, just come in and have a good time," she said. She made it sound like a military order. She stepped back, and Ellie and I continued to the rear of the house.

Maybe Shayne had told her he was coming, I thought, but wouldn't show, or if he did show, it would be quite late. He and his entourage of lackey friends would generously grant their presence, holding back to make a grand entry. Why the other girls in my class weren't put off by his arrogant behavior puzzled me. Many were so obvious when they approached him it nauseated me.

Bobby Harris hurried over to us when we stepped out, yelling to Ellie, but as he approached, his eyes were glued to me. She realized it.

"I'm over here, Bobby," she said when he continued to stand there staring at me and not even looking at her.

"Yeah, sure. Hi, Amber."

"Hello, Bobby." I looked past him. I could see that I was attracting a lot of attention. One boy I did like at school, Curtis Lambert, looked a little lost, so I went right over to him, said hello, and pulled him onto the dance floor. I was just as surprised as he was about how aggressive I was being, but I didn't show it. He was slow to get into it, but I was dancing as if I had been locked up for years. Maybe I had been, but if so, I was my own jailer, I thought. Soon Curtis was moving with as much abandon as he could. Other boys howled, and some of the girls shouted their encouragement and surprise. I'd kill Prudence Perfect tonight or else, I thought.

Even Ellie was shocked at how I was carrying on.

"What's come over you?" she asked with a wide smile. "Did you take something before I picked you up?"

"Yes, vitamin E."

"Huh?"

"Get on the dance floor, and stop making a big deal of it," I told her. Bobby stood next to her with a wide grin on his face. She took one look at him and pulled him away to dance.

It didn't matter whom I was dancing with. I was like everyone else, lost in my own world. I laughed to myself, thinking how Dad would react, claiming that I was in my own movie again or I was getting to be more and more like the girls with nose rings and multicolored hair. I didn't avoid talking to anyone who wanted to talk to me. Whenever I took a break to get something to drink, I had a group of boys around me. I flirted with them all and watched them manipulate themselves to get a chance to dance with me. It really didn't matter to me. I suddenly realized that in my mind, I was dancing with . . . with Brayden.

The face of every boy who stepped in front of me metamorphosed into Brayden's face and wore Brayden's smile. Whether they were as tall as he was or not, they suddenly resembled him. Was I losing my mind? I hadn't drunk anything alcoholic, nor had I accepted any of the pills that were being passed around like candy. I closed and opened my eyes to see if his image would disappear, but it didn't. In fact, he seemed to be everywhere I turned. The vision made me dizzy. I had to stop dancing to get a cold soft drink.

Charlotte and Ellie had spread the word about Brayden, and some of the other girls asked me about him after I came off the dance floor. No one was satisfied with my answers, so the topic died a quick death. I was glad of that. Despite all I was doing to try to distract myself from thinking about him, his kiss, his smile, the way he touched me, and the sound of his voice in my dream, everything about him hovered over me. Maybe I wanted to see his face in the faces of other boys looking at me with such interest. Maybe I wanted it to be his voice when I heard a boy call to me. I wanted it so much that I had made it happen. It was a wild idea.

Thinking about it so hard, I felt as if I had fallen into a trance, despite all of the noise going on. Occasionally, I would realize that someone was talking to me and try to get back into the conversation, but I could see by the way the other person looked at me that he or she thought I was either high on something or ignoring them.

More fireworks were set off. There were a few rockets, too. I thought about mentioning the danger of starting a fire, but I knew no one would be interested in anything that in any way smothered the excitement, and besides, that would be something Prudence Perfect would mention.

"I can see you're having a good time," Ellie said. From the look in her eyes and the way her lip seemed to dip when she spoke, I knew she had taken something. Bobby didn't look much different. It was as if she had thrown a collar around his neck. He was following her that closely.

"Yes. Great party. You look like you're doing just fine, too," I said, nodding at Bobby, who still had his eyes focused on me.

"Trying," she said. "I'm not so sure this was a good idea," she added in a lower voice, nodding toward Bobby. "As you say, the jury is still out."

Nevertheless, she pulled him back onto the dance floor, and I retreated again to get another soda. Twice I was offered something hard to drink. I avoided that and the offer of Ecstasy.

"Don't need it," I shouted. "I'm high already."

Some of them weren't too sure that I wasn't. I could see that I had become the big subject of discussion.

Then, finally, as I had expected, Shayne Allan made his grand entrance with three of the other boys who were on the league-winning baseball team with him. As always, it was as if the king had arrived. I was probably the only one who deliberately headed in the opposite direction, deciding that it was a good time to get something more substantial to eat.

I filled a plate with some Chinese food and found a chaise longue as far away from it all as possible. I watched the others laughing, getting more and more into some hard liquor, passing around some X, and beginning to pair off and find privacy somewhere nearby. Charlotte had made a number of announcements forbidding anyone to go into any other place in her house but the bathrooms. There was the large cabana, however.

I looked for Ellie, but she had dragged Bobby off somewhere, too. Neither was in sight. I feared that I was going to have to find another way to get home, but I wasn't thinking about it just yet. I certainly had tried to participate in everything I could. I was as friendly as I could be. No one could say I was antisocial tonight.

"Bored?" I heard, and looked up to see Shayne standing there, his arms folded across his chest. I couldn't help it. I laughed. "What?" he said.

"You remind me of the statue of the Indian outside of McKinley's hardware store."

He unfolded his arms quickly, but to my surprise, he laughed, too. "To tell you the truth, I didn't expect to see you here," he said, pulling up another chaise.

"I didn't expect to see you, either."

"Is that right? Why not?"

"I thought you surely had something better to do."

"Like what?"

"Oh, I don't know. Brush your hair, try on clothes, whiten your teeth."

"Very funny. I like your hair up like that, and I like what you're wearing."

"Well, now that you approve, I might wear my hair this way again," I said.

He stared at me a moment. "You're different to-night," he said, narrowing his eyes suspiciously.

"Since I don't remember seeing you much at night, I don't know how you could make that conclusion."

"You want to dance?"

"I've been dancing all night while you were circling the wagons."

"What? What's that mean?"

"Deciding when to make your grand entrance."

"Why don't you like me?" he asked with an impish smile on his face. He was as good-looking as any movie star, I thought.

"I don't want to waste my time and effort."

"Why would that be?"

I knew he was just waiting to tell me that if I revealed that I liked him, he would tell me he liked me. "I figure that you like yourself so much you don't need anyone else to."

"Right. Prudence Perfect," he said, his eyes revealing that I had gotten to him, pierced his confidence and his armor of egotism. "Like you don't act as if you're God's perfect little female creation."

"You mean I have to act like it? I can't just be it?"

He started to turn away, but then looked back at me and laughed. "Okay, okay. Truce," he said, holding up his hands. He looked out at the others. Some of the boys were acting imbecilic already, having had too much liquor or too much Ecstasy.

"I feel the end is near," he said.

"There'll be some regurgitation."

He turned and stared a moment.

"What?" I said when I thought the silence had gone on long enough.

"You want to stay here to watch it?"

"Or?"

"Let's get out and just have some coffee or something at the diner."

"That's it?"

"Maybe a piece of apple pie."

"What about your devoted followers?"

"They'll find their way. I've trained them well." He waited.

Was this it, the inevitable rendezvous with destiny that Ellie said most of the girls expected for me?

Unlike what had been happening to me on the dance floor, I didn't imagine Brayden's face anymore. Shayne Allan was filling up my screen.

Go on, I told myself, *get them all clacking. Go off with him.*

"I like peach," I said.

"What?"

"Peach pie."

"Oh. You can have whatever you want," he said, laughing.

I hesitated and then rose. When I looked past him, past the lights, past the others toward the last round of fireworks going off, I thought I saw Brayden for a moment when the illumination washed away a pocket of darkness. I had been imagining him all night, but this time, he wasn't standing in anyone else's place. It really looked as if he was there. I think I gasped.

"You all right?" Shayne asked, reaching for my arm. Had I been swaying?

"What? Yes."

"You didn't take any garbage, did you?"

"No, nothing."

"Let's go," he said with a more commanding tone. Ordinarily, that might have turned me off, but right then, I welcomed someone else taking charge.

As we walked past everyone, I gazed back toward the place where I had seen Brayden. When it was illuminated again, he wasn't there.

Shayne took my hand, and we hurried out as if we knew that in a few minutes, the place would be raided. Most of the other kids had literally frozen in place to watch us leave.

"You make a grand entrance, and you make a grand exit," I said as we passed quickly through the courtyard.

"Only because of you," he said. He pulled me closer, and I didn't resist.

Poor Prudence Perfect.

I had left her behind, all alone.

6

Shayne

"So what brought you over to speak to me?" I asked Shayne as we drove off to the Echo Lake diner.

"An irresistible force."

"Yeah, right. What, did some of my friends whisper in your ear? Did they tell you I was dying for you to come to me or something?"

I now felt more certain that this was the major reason both Charlotte and Ellie were intent on my attending the party. They had decided to play Cupid, but in this version of the myth, I was going to get a mortal lover. If anything did happen between Shayne and me, they, especially Charlotte, would claim credit for engineering the whole thing. Why was it that girls who had trouble finding romance for themselves tried so hard to create romances for other girls? Was it their intention to live through them, have vicarious love affairs?

"What's more complicated than the mind of a teenage girl?" Dad would often ask. He had become an experienced diamond cutter and compared trying to understand teenage girls to the geometric precision cutting of a precious diamond. Do it well, and you'd catch more brilliance. "Understand a teenage girl, and you'll save your sanity."

Mom and I would laugh, but I wasn't going to disagree with him. I knew what he was talking about. I was having trouble understanding myself.

"No. I don't need anyone to tell me what to do," Shayne said. "I'm not kidding. When I first saw you tonight, I was very attracted to you. At first, I didn't know who you were. You looked that different, and I don't mean just the way you're wearing your hair and the way you're dressed. I saw something different in your face. There was like a glow around you."

"A glow?"

"Well, something," he said, struggling to explain. "Something made you stand out in the crowd. How's that old song go?" he asked, and then started to sing, "Some enchanted evening . . . ."

Laughing, I said, "Yes, well, all right, I guess we are like strangers. We can both probably count on our fingers how many words we have actually spoken to each other."

"It's not my fault," he said quickly. I gave him a look that said, *Please, spare me.* "Well, maybe it is somewhat," he quickly corrected. "But you scare me, Amber."

"What?" I started to laugh. "I scare you?"

"No, I'm serious."

"Okay, I'll bite. How can I scare a big, strong boy like you?"

He looked forward.

"Well, how?" I followed up more firmly when he didn't appear to want to answer.

"Give me a chance. I'm trying to figure out how to say this so I don't sound too egotistical."

"What a challenge for you."

"There!" he said, pointing at me. "That's exactly it."

"What?"

"You're the only girl in this school, the only girl I've met, who isn't afraid of putting me down, of getting me to dislike her. That makes me feel a little insecure. I'm like a prizefighter whose manager has set him up with weak opponents, and finally, he has to fight someone who can fight back. Know what I mean?"

I remembered thinking I was like a prizefighter when it came to Brayden, a prizefighter who couldn't land a blow.

"I don't watch prizefights," I said.

"You get the point. I know you do. You're just making it harder for me."

I smiled to myself. I was, and I was enjoying it, too. I was riding a wave of greater self-confidence that seemed to have begun when I decided to put my Prudence Perfect image in a drawer and lock it. It happened after I had been with Brayden in the woods. Everything right now seemed to stem from that. Strangely, even though we hadn't gone all the way, as they say, I no longer felt so innocent. I never thought of myself as shy, but perhaps I was. At least, I was until tonight. Shayne wasn't wrong. I was different and I liked the way I felt. I liked the sense of danger. Ellie would laugh, but right now, I liked being with a guy who wasn't safe.

"I don't enjoy putting you down," I said. "You just make it impossible not to most of the time. If you went to Hollywood, you wouldn't need a publicist or even a manager. No one could sell you better than you sell yourself, Shayne."

"So? Is that so terrible? My dad's always telling me not to be ashamed of my abilities and accomplishments. I admit that my mom's always telling me to be more humble, but they both brag me sick when I'm out with them. It's not always my fault."

"Poor, poor Shayne Allan," I said. "The object of so many compliments he can't get the real him out."

He shook his head. "There's no winning with you."

He sounded as if he was already willing to give up, and I wasn't sure that I would be happy about it. "I'll tell you what to do."

"What?"

"Try talking for a while without saying *I, me, my,* or *mine.*"

"How would I do that?"

"Talk about yourself in the third person."

"Huh?"

"You know what the third-person point of view is, Shayne. Just try it. You'll see. Remember your Shake-speare, o future valedictorian. 'The eye sees not itself, but by reflection, by some other things.'"

He smirked. Then he thought about it for a few moments and said, "Okay. I'll try it. I'll try anything to please you."

"That's your last *I* until I say otherwise. Otherwise it won't work."

"Okay, okay. Shayne hears you."

We pulled into the diner parking lot, parked, and got

out. It was late. There weren't many people there, but the manager, Mr. Freid, knew us both well, and out of the corner of my eye, I saw him give Shayne a thumbs-up. I smiled to myself. We took a booth near the front, where we could look out at the parking lot and the highway. I just ordered coffee and a piece of peach pie, but Shayne ordered a cheeseburger, sweet potato fries, and coffee.

"I thought we were just having coffee and pie."

"I didn't have anything to eat at Charlotte's."

"Shayne didn't," I corrected.

"Right. Shayne didn't. He was too busy trying to figure out who you were."

"Yes, and his problem was how to do that while being surrounded by the members of his mutual admiration society."

"Who says the admiration is mutual?"

"Spoken like the Shayne Allan I know."

"How'd he get in here?" he asked, and pretended to look around for himself. I smiled. "So, how's your summer been so far?" he asked.

"Okay."

"Just okay?"

"These days, being just okay is terrific."

"That's not so good." He paused and thought a moment. "Many times I . . ."

"Shayne," I corrected again.

"Shayne often wondered what it would be like to be with you, to talk to you alone like this without an audience."

"But Shayne was afraid, you said."

"He told you. He isn't used to being rejected."

"No one can get used to that. So, tell me the truth now. What changed Shayne's mind? And don't start singing 'Some Enchanted Evening.' They might ask us to leave the diner before I get my pie."

"Maybe not. Shayne's been told he has a pretty good voice. Mr. Jacobs has been trying to get him into the senior chorus ever since he was in ninth grade."

"But Shayne wouldn't do it. He might not stand out enough, is that it?"

He smiled and shook his head.

The waitress brought my pie and coffee and a coffee for him. "Burger will be up in a minute," she said.

"Shayne's not in a rush," he told her. She looked at him strangely, looked at me, shrugged, and returned to the counter. "Shayne doesn't know if he can keep this up."

"Shayne can," I insisted. "Don't you know? Shayne Allan can do anything."

He sighed.

"So? What's the truth about tonight?" I asked. "Why did you finally overcome your great fear of me? Tell the truth, for a change."

He thought a moment. "Maybe this third-person thing does make it easier." He straightened up. "Shayne kept an eye on you most of last year. He noticed you weren't interested in any other boy. No one seemed to get to first base, or if he had, he was tagged before he reached second."

"Is everything Shayne thinks of analogous to a sport?"

He shrugged. "Shayne's an outstanding athlete."

"He's also an outstanding scholar. He should reach higher sometimes."

"Okay, okay. You sound like Shayne's mother."

The waitress brought his burger and fries. "Shayne says thanks," he told her.

"That's nice. I hope Shayne pays," she said, and we all laughed.

I let him start to eat, sipped my coffee, and ate some pie. "So?" I said.

"So, Shayne didn't feel pressured. He was taking his own precious time, waiting for the right moment, hoping for some sign from Amber that would encourage him, but Amber was too stuck on herself."

"She was not!"

"Shayne thought so. Then he heard tonight that she had met a new boy, a good-looking new boy."

"Aha!" I cried. "You were pushed in my direction. I'll kill that Ellie and Charlotte."

"They meant well. For Shayne, that is."

"So, Shayne admits that he was pushed in my direction."

"Not pushed, encouraged. Then he thought about it and decided that just maybe he was being stupid and would lose his chance, so he decided to swallow his pride and . . ."

"He admits that his pride was always in the way?"

He paused and nodded. "Maybe. No. Yes."

He ate more of his burger. We stared at each other for a few moments, like two chess players waiting for each other to make a bad move. I ate more pie, drank more coffee, and sat back.

"I think Shayne's making a little progress," I said.

"Is there really a new boy in town?" he asked. "Shayne hasn't heard."

"What is this? Is Shayne a gunslinger worried that someone faster on the draw has come to Echo Lake? You sound like you're in the movie *Shane*."

He laughed, and then he looked serious. "Yes, when it comes to Amber Taylor, Shayne is worried about someone being faster on the draw," he said. "Maybe we should talk about what Amber likes and doesn't like. Is the new boy someone she could like?"

"Why don't we just talk about Shayne for now?" I said. "We have to work on his rehabilitation and see if he's a lost cause or not."

"Thanks a lot."

"Besides, doesn't Shayne know anything about romancing a girl? The same is true for a girl romancing a boy. What she doesn't talk about or want to hear about is another girl, and a boy should feel the same way hearing about another boy."

He nodded. "Shayne understands. Okay. I think he might like his rehabilitation. As long as it doesn't take that long, that is."

"How long it takes is up to Shayne," I said.

He smiled softly, lovingly, at me. Now that I was sitting right across from him and really looking at him, he didn't seem at all intimidating. In fact, he looked like a little boy, excited and happy.

"How come Shayne's never gone with one girl for very long?" I asked.

"Different reasons. No one reason fits everyone."

"Maybe Shayne can't make a commitment. Maybe he's always worried that there's someone better looming on the horizon."

"Maybe. Maybe you're the one looming."

I smiled and ate some more pie to keep myself from blushing. During the last twenty-four hours, I had been with two very good-looking boys. One had stirred me as I had never been stirred, but the one I was with now held out the promise of a full relationship, no baggage to worry about, no formidable emotional and psychological problems to overcome. Suddenly, my quiet, uneventful life was filled with very dramatic and exciting choices.

I finished my pie, and he finished his burger. Then he slapped his chest.

"Me Shayne. You Amber," he said, imitating Tarzan. I laughed. Someone put on the jukebox, and Tony Bennett singing "I Left My Heart in San Francisco" came on.

"Shane's parents love this song."

"I think mine do, too."

"Whatever happened to romance?" Shayne asked, obviously now imitating his father.

"Why do these kids wear rings in their noses and dye their hair orange and purple?" I followed.

"When they're older like us, what will be their musical memories? You can't understand half of what they listen to, and they can't, either. It's just noise."

"They're all in their own movie."

"Right," he said. "Exactly. Why don't you and Shayne go somewhere where you can really talk about this and come up with a solution?"

"Talk?"

"Whatever's necessary."

"Right. That's what I thought. It's getting late."

"Shayne has no curfew."

"Amber does, and Shayne shouldn't be thinking only of what's good for Shayne," I said sternly.

"Got it," he said, saluting, and signaling for the check.

After he paid and we rose to leave, I glanced out the diner window and froze for a moment. I thought I saw Brayden standing just on the outer edge of the parking lot. He looked very unhappy. Could he really have followed us from Charlotte's party?

"Something wrong?" Shayne asked.

"What? No," I said, looking out again and this time not seeing him. I hurried to catch up, and when we stepped out, I looked around again, but I didn't see him. I concluded that I was just tired and my imagination was running rampant.

"Supposed to be nice tomorrow," Shayne said. "Shayne can get his dad's motorboat if Amber would like to picnic on the lake."

"Who else is coming?"

"No one else. Why, do you need a chaperone or something?"

"No. I just thought Shayne would have one or two of his shadows."

"Not this time. So?" he asked. "What do you think? Take a chance with Shayne?"

I thought about Brayden. I was still upset about the way he had deserted me in the woods, and from the way he was acting and what he had said, I didn't see us doing much more than taking a walk. He resisted my invitation to show him around or even meet my parents. He hadn't invited me into his house to meet his mother. Right now, I had to admit that I was a little afraid of meeting her. Maybe if he saw that I was starting to see Shayne, he would be more willing to do more things, meet other kids, go to a movie, something. Perhaps I was being mean, or maybe this was just what he needed.

Anyway, it felt good to have two very good-looking boys vying for my attention.

"Okay," I said. "What time?"

"Shayne will come by about eleven."

"What do I need to bring?"

"Just yourself. Shayne will pick up some subs and stuff before he comes for you."

On our way to my house, we talked about what we hoped for our senior year and what we thought we might do afterward. Shayne had already won a number of scholarships, two of which were athletic. I wasn't sure what I wanted to study, so I was content for now to plan for a liberal arts education, at least for the first two years.

"Sounds like the Taylor family jewelry store might come to an end, then."

"Maybe. Maybe I'll marry someone who wants to be in business, and we'll come back here to live."

"Here? Don't you dream of getting away?"

"No. I mean, I want to travel and see things, but I have a suspicion that I might not be happier somewhere else."

Shayne shook his head. "Shayne knows he'll be happier somewhere else."

"Shayne should read his Thoreau again, and more of him," I said. As soon as I said it, I felt as if Brayden was sitting right behind me. I even turned around to look, which was ridiculous. Shayne didn't notice.

"Right. 'Time is but the stream I go a-fishing in.' Sounds great until you want to buy new shoes."

"Shayne misses the point," I said.

"Shayne wants to miss that point," he replied.

It was really the only discordant note between us so far. He laughed, and I let it pass.

After we pulled into my driveway, he reached for my hand.

"May Shayne kiss Amber good night?" He smiled. "Ordinarily, Shayne would just do it without asking."

"Well, then, there's hope for Shayne yet," I said, and kissed him before he could kiss me.

The surprise on his face made me laugh. "Can Shayne leave the third person behind tomorrow? It's getting a little crowded."

I pretended to debate with myself about it a moment and then nodded. "But it might be necessary to resurrect him again, so keep him handy."

"Right. Good night."

"Night," I said, and got out of the car. He watched me walk to my front door and then backed out slowly, pausing to look back at me. I waved, and he drove off.

Just as I reached for the front door, I heard, "And so the beautiful butterfly was born."

I turned sharply to my right and saw him standing there in the corner of the front porch. How could I not have seen him when I first started for the house? What did he do, float over the railing? Or was he just waiting for me in the shadows, waiting most of the night?

"Once again, you succeeded in frightening me."

"Sorry. Where were you?"

"I told you about the party. I asked you to go. Afterward, I went to the Echo Lake diner with Shayne Allan. He's on course to be valedictorian, and he's one of our top athletes."

He dropped into the wooden rocker. "So, it looks like it was better for you that I didn't go. Was it fun?"

For a moment, I felt terrible rubbing Shayne in his face. Probably, if Brayden was at one school long enough, he might be a candidate for valedictorian, not that it was the criterion I set down for a boyfriend. It was just that I thought, even from the limited time I had spent with him, that he was capable of doing great things, too. It wasn't fair to him to move him around like furniture.

Then I remembered why I was upset with him.

"Forget the party. Where were you? What happened to you? How could you just leave me sleeping out there in the woods?"

"I had to go, and I didn't want to wake you. It wasn't like I left you in a lair of poisonous snakes. You were pretty safe."

"Well, why did you just leave?"

"I had to get back for my mother," he said.

"Did something happen?"

"Yes, something happened. It's still happening," he said in that cryptic tone of voice I was getting used to.

"What?"

"I told you. She's not well."

"But why? I mean, she must have been well once, right?" I asked, stepping up to him.

"It's complicated," he said. "Tell me about your party. You look very nice, by the way."

"Thanks. It's probably still going on, and I'm sure Charlotte's parents will be pretty upset about it when they find out. There were fireworks. I thought that was reckless. It's pretty dry out there. Lots of booze and stuff like X. You know what that is, I'm sure."

"Yes, I know. So, it was getting out of hand?"

"I wasn't eager to hang around to find out." I leaned against the railing and looked at him. "I thought I saw you there."

"Saw me?" He smiled. "And how could that be?"

"I'm sure you could have found her house. You seem to be able to find anything around here."

He laughed. "So, this Shayne Allan was your knight in shining armor who came to your rescue?" he asked, nodding toward the driveway.

"Yes. His parents have a place on the lake. I agreed to go for a picnic tomorrow. He has a boat. Or, rather, his father has a boat."

He nodded. Then he stood up and looked at his house. I turned and could see that the attic light was still on.

"Isn't your father coming home soon? You shouldn't have all of the burden on your shoulders."

"Soon," he said, walking slowly to the steps. "Have a good time on the lake. Maybe you can show him the place I showed you."

I nodded. He didn't sound upset. I was hoping to hear at least a note of jealousy. I guess if I had to char-acterize how he sounded, I would say resigned, like someone who knew that he couldn't compete. I attributed that to his responsibilities at home.

I felt a great sadness come over me. I wanted to reach out to him, to tell him that I might change my mind and not go with Shayne if he wanted me to spend the day with him, maybe help him with his mother in some way, but he just smiled and walked away.

"I'll see you tomorrow afterward, maybe," I called.

"Oh, sure," he said. "You'll see me. Don't worry about that."

He walked into the shadows and toward his house. I watched for a moment and then entered mine. I was filled with so many different feelings and emotions that I couldn't see myself falling asleep for hours. Both of my parents were upstairs, but Mom called to me from her bedroom. I knew that just like any other time I was out, she would keep one ear listening for my footsteps on the stairway.

I walked up to their open bedroom door.

"Have a good time?" she whispered. Dad looked asleep, but I suspected that he wasn't.

"Yes, but I didn't stay until the end. I went to the diner with Shayne Allan for some peach pie and coffee."

My father couldn't pretend any longer. "You didn't have enough to eat at the party?" he asked, turning around to face the door.

"I wasn't going for the pie as much as for other reasons, Dad."

He turned to Mom. "Translate, please," he said.

"She was exploring the possibility of a relationship," Mom said.

"A relationship? I remember that."

She poked him, and he turned over to fall asleep again.

"Night, honey," Mom said.

"Night. Oh. I'm going to picnic on the lake with Shayne. He has his father's boat."

Mom just smiled. Dad waved without lifting his head.

I entered my bedroom slowly, reluctantly, like one who knew she was about to do battle with her own thoughts and wished there was a way to avoid being alone.

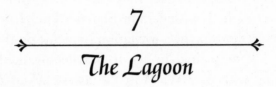

7

The Lagoon

I slept later in the morning than I usually did because I went to bed later than I usually did, and I did have trouble falling asleep again. While I was preparing to go to bed, I had thought about how much of a good time I'd had at the party and with Shayne afterward, but then I began to feel sorry for Brayden, especially when I remembered how he was when he walked away from me on the porch. It was so unfair that he had to be chained to his house because his mother was so ill and his father was not there to help. What kind of a man was he? I wondered. What kind of a father and husband? I couldn't even begin to imagine my dad being like him under similar circumstances.

These thoughts lay so heavily on my mind that after I had gotten into bed the night before and tried to envision Shayne and relive the events of the evening, I had seen Brayden's face instead, just the way I was seeing him in every boy's face at the party. It was as if I had spent time at the party and the diner with Brayden and not Shayne. I heard Brayden's voice in my mind when I should have been hearing Shayne's, and when I recalled kissing

Shayne good night, it was Brayden's lips I pressed mine to and not Shayne's.

In fact, when I awoke, I lay there for a while thinking more about Brayden than Shayne. Had I been too quick to accept Shayne's invitation to picnic on the lake? Should I have waited to see if Brayden wanted to do something with me? Was I just as awestruck as most of the other girls with our school's most popular boy now that he was paying attention to me? Would I have the same fate as the other girls Shayne hit on? How would I face that, especially if I had driven Brayden away?

While I was thinking, the phone rang. At first, I thought it might be Shayne, but as if she couldn't start her day without first finding out what had happened between Shayne and me last night, it was Ellie who called. She sounded very tired, almost as if she were talking in her sleep, her voice straining and cracking.

"Where did you two go?" was the first thing she said after I said hello.

"Just to the diner for coffee and pie," I replied. "You sound like you just got in."

She laughed. "You're not far from wrong. Just coffee and pie? Why?"

"It's all I felt like eating," I replied. I knew what she was really after, but I thought I would tease her.

"No, I mean, didn't you do anything afterward, go anywhere else, do anything else exciting?"

"He took me home, and I went to sleep."

"Oh, Amber." She groaned with disappointment. "I hope you weren't a bore. Everyone was surprised and delighted with you last night. You're not going back to being Prudence Perfect, are you? You didn't disappoint him and make him feel like a fool for wanting to be with you? I warned Charlotte that you could do that. I told—"

"So, this whole thing was your and Charlotte's plan from the start? That's why you were so intent on my going to Charlotte's party?"

She was silent. It was as good as admitting to it. I sat up quickly.

"Did you two approach him and tell him about the new boy in town and that I was interested in him, and then, when I told you that Brayden wasn't coming, you called Shayne? Is that what went down here, Ellie?" I demanded to know.

"We were just trying to help you," she whined. "What are friends for?"

"That's a good question. What are they for?"

"Well, all I can say is, you blew off a great opportunity. Shayne is really—"

"Shayne's picking me up later this morning," I said, quickly interrupting what I knew would be a long lecture about my missed opportunity for a great romance. "We're going boating and picnicking on the lake."

"Really?"

"Unless he doesn't show up, yes, really."

"Just the two of you?"

"Just the two of us. He's getting his father's boat."

She was silent a moment, and then, ironically, the heavy syrup of jealousy was layered over her next words. "That's great. I'm happy for you. I told you that you two should be a thing."

"Thing?"

"A couple. You know what I mean. Will you call me when you get home and give me real details this time?" Before I could say no, that I didn't kiss and tell, she added, "I wish Bobby's family had a place on the lake and a boat. We went to that silly little clubhouse behind his house that he and his father built. And we didn't have any coffee and pie."

"Sorry to hear it," I said.

"I meant, we didn't need that. We had a better dessert." She laughed. "I'm sure you will, too, eventually."

"I wouldn't jump to any conclusions about anything yet, Ellie. The truth is, I'm really just getting to know Shayne. He might as well have just entered the school as far as I'm concerned. And I think the same is true for him when it comes to me."

"So, what about your new very good-looking neighbor? Is he already yesterday's news?"

"The jury's still out."

"Huh? What does that mean?" She was really waking up now. "You mean you would still see him, go out with him, too? You can't play both of them," she said with a moan. I could almost feel through the phone how much the idea intrigued her. "Can you?"

"Now, Ellie, would Prudence Perfect even think of such a thing?"

I could almost see the dam holding back her imagination break open and rush out in all directions.

"Well, I guess you could have a great ménage à trois," she said. "Male bookends."

"Control yourself, girl," I said, even though in my

own imagination, that had already taken shape, but in a way she could never envision.

"Will you call me later? Will you?"

"Yes," I said. "I can't talk anymore. I have to get up before my parents leave for work."

"Don't forget to call me," she cried into the phone quickly. I hung up and got out of bed. I knew it was already too late to greet my parents before they left for the store, but I didn't want to talk to her anymore. I put on my robe and slippers and ran a brush through my hair. When I went down to the kitchen, I found a note that Mom had left on the kitchenette table:

"Call me if you need anything. Otherwise, have a great day. I know I don't have to tell you to be careful, but be careful, and don't worry about anything. I left you a beach towel in the laundry with your beach bag."

I folded it up and smiled. Who else had a mother like mine? Most of the time, she really was more like an older sister. I wondered if there was more pressure on a mother to be more of a friend than a parent when there was only one child, one daughter in the family. If anyone would feel guilty for not having another child to be with me in this life, it was my mother.

I made myself some breakfast and went out on the porch to get myself more woken up. Luckily, it was going to be a great day to go boating on the lake. The sky was only spotted here and there with small, puffy clouds, and there was barely a breeze. What's more, it felt as if it was going to be one of the warmest days of the summer, if not the warmest. I sat in my robe and slippers and looked at the front of Brayden's house, wondering what his plans were for the day. Would he spend all of it at home? Were his little walks around the area really all he could do?

I saw a grocery delivery truck approaching and watched it pull into Brayden's driveway. From where I was sitting, I couldn't see the front door, so I rose, walked down our driveway, and watched the delivery boy get out with a box of groceries. He went to the front door and knocked. When it was opened, I was hoping to see Brayden, but I was surprised instead to see his mother. She wore an ankle-length baggy black dress. Her face and hair were wrapped in a black scarf, making her look like someone with the mumps or a swollen jaw. I could barely make out her eyes and mouth. She paid the delivery boy quickly and took the box. I could see that he wanted to carry it in for her, but she was not letting him set foot in the house. Before she closed the door, she saw me standing there. I started to wave at her, but she looked at me with what I thought were cold gray eyes and closed the door so fast and hard that it left me with a chill.

I hurried back into the house. I was actually trembling. The unpleasant look on her face when she saw me was startling. Did she know that Brayden had made friends with me? Did he tell her? Did she resent it, thinking that I might take up more of his time, time he would otherwise spend with her? Or was her reaction to me simply part of her illness, in that she would have reacted to anyone the same way? She looked as if she was terrified of setting one foot out that door and into any sunshine. What I managed to see of her face looked so pale, chalky white.

Where was Brayden? Was he still sleeping? Surely he would have been there to carry in the box of groceries. Was she really so bad that she couldn't even shop for herself? Why hadn't her husband hired a full-time nurse to care for her if she was so ill? Once again, I wondered why his father would depend on his teenage son to look after her.

I shook off my questions and went up to take a shower and dress for the picnic with Shayne. I didn't want him to see the darkness in my face and start asking questions. I put my bathing suit on first. I really had only two suits, a one-piece and a two-piece, both in a rhinestone pink. When I tried them on, I realized that I hadn't bought a new suit for nearly a year. They both felt a little tight, with the top of my two-piece almost like the top of an abbreviated bikini because of how much larger my breasts had become.

If I wore it, I thought, I'd bury Prudence Perfect forever. I turned every which way, gazing at myself in the full-length mirror. I pictured Shayne's face after I stripped down to my suit. The look I imagined coming into his eyes brought a blush to my cheeks and neck, but rather than any shame or embarrassment, it brought a sense of power with it. How easily I could make him tremble with desire, I thought. I held a pose, lifting my breasts and turning my waist. Was this a terrible thing to feel? How do you know when you've moved from pride into arrogance, an arrogance that causes you to flaunt yourself and perhaps diminish the respect any man would have for you?

Afraid of just that, I quickly took off the two-piece.

For a moment, when I stood there naked, I had the feeling that Brayden was watching me. I had closed the curtains fully, but although I knew he couldn't see me, I stood there frozen, just the way I might be if he had somehow walked in on me. It was a little creepy but also titillating. Why was my imagination so active, my body so electric? I closed my eyes and saw him close to me as he was in the woods. I felt his lips on mine just as they were in my dream, his hands caressing me. I was shocked and surprised by my own moan and snapped my eyes open. Then I reached for the one-piece and hurriedly put it on. As I did so, I pictured Brayden standing behind me, a wide, impish smile on his face.

It made me move faster, choosing shorts, a blouse, and a pair of sandals. I worked on my hair, pinning it back, put on a little lipstick, and grabbed my book and went down to wait for Shayne on the front porch. I knew I was fooling myself, thinking that I would actually get some serious reading accomplished. I wasn't only watching and waiting for him; I was also watching for Brayden. I saw some of our other neighbors on the street. Some were outside, working on their flowers and lawns. Some were talking, but there was no sign of Brayden.

The moment I saw Shayne's car turn onto our street, I put my book on the small table and grabbed my beach bag, in which I had the beach towel Mom had put out for me, some money, my hairbrush and lipstick, and my cell phone, and I walked to the driveway.

He pulled in and got out quickly to open the car door for me.

"Morning," he said. "You look terrific."

"You sound surprised," I said, getting into his car. He laughed and hurried around.

He was wearing a pair of light blue shorts and a darker blue T-shirt. He had on a hat with a wide brim. I thought to myself that he could easily become a male model. Everything he wore looked good on him—or, rather, he made everything he wore look good.

"Everything about you surprises me, Amber." He shifted into reverse. "That's what makes you so interesting, or should I say exciting?"

He backed out. I saw him pause to look at Brayden's house, but he said nothing, nor did he ask anything. I was glad of that. We drove away slowly. All of the neighbors standing outside their homes paused to look at us. I saw expressions of satisfaction on their faces, as if they had a vested interest in my finding a boyfriend. Maybe they did. Most of them had lived on this street as long as we had and had watched me grow up.

"Did you hear about Howie Knapp?" Shayne asked.

"No, what?"

"He lost control of his father's Lexus, drove off the road last night leaving Charlotte's party, and knocked over the Templetons' brand-new white picket fence. His rear wheels got stuck in the ditch, so he couldn't just drive away. They called the cops. He and Mitchell Frank were in quite a daze and spent the night in jail. They're actually going to have to appear in court. Too much X or booze or both. I guess Charlotte's going to be put in a dungeon when her parents get the full story."

"Ellie didn't say anything when she called me this morning."

"It's just getting around. Maybe she wasn't there for the wild end."

"No. She went off with someone." I didn't say whom, and he didn't ask. I smiled to myself, thinking just how uninterested Shayne was in her, with her lauding him every time she had the opportunity. Maybe he was more oblivious to his admirers than I thought. I wasn't sure if that was good or bad. It could mean that he was so arrogant that he wouldn't even acknowledge the girls who drooled over him.

"Yeah. Anyway, afterward, the police raided Charlotte's house, found more drugs, I heard, and lots of beer and open booze bottles. She didn't have much time to clean up the mess. They also found the illegal fireworks and Audrey David passed out on a chaise longue at the pool. She had to be taken to the emergency room to have her stomach pumped. I heard they took down the names of anyone else still there. We got out just in time."

"We did. My parents didn't call me from the store this morning. Maybe they haven't heard yet."

"My parents haven't heard yet, either, but they will. I still had a big to-do at my house this morning," he said. "Not because of Charlotte's party. My brat sister wanted to come along in the boat with two of her friends. My parents were going to give in until I whispered in Wendi's ear, reminding her that I knew where her stash of pot was hidden in her bedroom. I was about to announce it, too, when she piped up and said she had changed her mind. Nothing as effective as blackmail when it comes to my bratty little sister."

"Everyone I know thinks your sister's picture should be next to the word *spoiled* in the dictionary."

He nodded. "No, it should be next to *spoiled rotten*."

"Don't your parents realize it, what she is and what she's becoming?"

He tilted his head and looked at me with his eyebrows raised. "My parents? Remember the famous Toby Glocklin story, the girl who plagiarized a short story and had it published in the high school literary magazine?"

"I heard about it, but that was what, nearly ten years ago, right?"

"Right. Her parents were brought in, and the dean, Dr. Littlefield, placed the story she plagiarized next to hers in the magazine and showed them how it was taken word for word with only very small changes."

"So? How does that relate?"

"It's what her mother said when she was confronted with the solid evidence in his office. She said, 'In an infinite universe, anything's possible.' In other words, it was just a coincidence that Toby wrote the story practically word for word. How's that for being blind to your kid's failings? I'm afraid that's true for my parents and my sister."

"I can't see my mother or my father saying something like that. They would never make such ridiculous excuses for me."

"You never gave them the opportunity, Prudence Perfect."

"And I don't intend to, either," I shot back. I think my eyes were as big as Mom's when she was annoyed or infuriated by something or someone.

He pretended to cower. "Okay, okay. Don't vaporize me."

"Just watch where you're driving. I don't want to end up in a ditch, too."

"Yes, boss," he said, flashing a smile. I held back as long as I could and then laughed.

A little while later, we turned down the road that led to the homes on the west side of the lake. I had never been to his home and had seen it only from a boat recently when we had been invited to the Mallens' house for the day. Shayne's family's house was a large two-story with an enormous back deck that looked out over the water. The dock was right behind the house. It had a good half acre of lawn and some wooded area on both sides. Most of the lake homes were beautiful large structures, but I thought his family's was one of the nicest with its blue and white decor.

I had never seen it from the front, and when I did, I thought it was even more impressive.

"I didn't realize how large your house is," I said.

"It's eight thousand square feet and has six bedrooms. Wendi thinks there are two for her. Half the time, she has someone sleeping over."

"It's beautiful. I love the stone and the wood and those large windows."

"They wanted as much natural lighting as they could get. It took nearly three years to finish when you consider all the detailed work inside."

It was very quiet, with just the sound of motorboats on the lake.

"Is your family here?"

"My parents are visiting friends," he said, "and Wendi decided to visit one of hers when she couldn't get to go boating, so for most of the day, it's just us."

"And whoever else is on the lake," I said.

We walked up to the porch. There was a wooden swing wide enough to hold four people.

"This looks so relaxing."

"Try it."

I sat on it and looked out at the landscaped front and surrounding trees. Anyone turning into Shayne's driveway would surely feel as if he or she had left all the commotion and noise of everyday life behind. Between the rear of the house with its view of the lake and this, I wouldn't care to leave home, I thought. I laughed to myself, thinking of Thoreau. This would be a little over the top for him.

Shayne sat beside me, lowering himself tentatively, with a smile on his face.

"It's not the hot seat," I said.

He laughed. "I don't actually sit here much," he said. "Actually, I never sit here, but watching you and the way you appreciate everything makes it look more inviting than ever."

"It's so peaceful. You're lucky, Shayne."

"I know. How else would I have gotten you out with me today?"

"I think that took a little more than luck."

He smiled. "I hope so. I should have told you to wear a hat. Do you have any sunscreen in your bag?"

"Oh, no. I didn't think . . ."

"No problem. I've got some in the house. It gets

pretty hot out there, but the breeze can fool you. I learned the hard way when I was younger. I got so sunburned that I nearly ended up in the hospital. I'll give you one of my baseball caps. I picked up our subs this morning and have it all in the kitchen. C'mon," he said, standing up and reaching for my hand.

He led me to the front door and unlocked it. The house was as impressive inside as the outside had promised. It had a vaulted ceiling in the entryway and beautiful tiled flooring that flowed gracefully into the large family room. Everywhere possible, there were windows so that the house was as bright inside as could be. What a contrast, I thought, to the dark, cold home Brayden was trapped in.

I could see the patio doors that led out back and the walkway to the dock. Shayne went to the kitchen to get the subs and drinks and returned with a baseball cap as well as the sunscreen, as I looked around. The fireplace must have taken a long time to build, I thought. It went as high as the ceiling, and these ceilings were at least eighteen feet high. He put the cap on my head.

"Perfect," he said. "It looks way better on you than it does on me, too."

"Are you absolutely sure?"

"I'm, shall we say, overly confident, but I'm not stupid. I know beauty when I see it."

I glanced at him. He looked sincere, but there was still that twinkle in his eyes that kept me from trusting him.

"Speaking of beauty, this is such a beautiful room. It's large, but it looks comfortable and warm."

"I'll show you around when we return," he said. "We have a great entertainment center."

"Okay."

We headed out the back and down the slate steps to the dock. I paused to look around the property, the wide patio, the barbecue area, chaises, and an outside fire pit. Then I turned to look up at the house.

"Now that I'm here and see it close up, I think this is probably the most beautiful home in Echo Lake," I said. "It's much nicer that Charlotte's, even though they have more land."

"My mother would have it no other way," he replied. "If someone built one larger, we'd have an addition put on the following day." He gazed out at the lake, standing with his hands on his hips and smiling.

"Do you like your mother?"

"Like her? Sure. Why?"

"You blame her for a lot."

"It just sounds like it. Whose shoes would I rather be in?" He nodded at the lake. "Maybe I take this all for granted too much. Glad you're here. It's like having my eyes opened. What a day, huh?"

"Yes," I said, taking in the lake. There were already a half-dozen boats on it and two small sailboats. We could hear the laughter and the screams of people enjoying the water. Someone went by on water skis.

"You ever do that?"

"No. It looks hard."

"Oh, it's so easy. I'll get you up on skis, if not this time, next time."

I knelt down to feel the water.

"I know it feels cold, but once you're in it, you'll love it," he said.

"I haven't gone swimming yet this summer."

"Well, let's not waste time."

Shayne explained that his father's boat was an eight-and-a-half-foot Azure with a 450-horsepower engine. It was white with a thick brown stripe. I thought it looked brand new and said so.

"It is brand new," he said. "Actually, it's only a month old. This is probably the tenth time it's been out. It has an extended swim platform, so we'll ride around and then anchor and take a dip, okay?"

He helped me into the boat. The white cushion seats were very comfortable.

"Have you been in a boat much?" he asked as I moved nervously to keep my balance. He undid the mooring.

"No, not at all."

"We'll go slow," he said. "Or not," he added with a smile.

I sat up front, and he handed me the sunscreen. I began to dab it on my face. When I was finished, I handed it back to him. "Thanks."

He reached out to spread some around my lips and around my nose. "Can't take any chances with this face," he said. Then he put some on, too.

"Whose face did you mean?" I asked, and he laughed.

"You know what's going to happen if I keep seeing you?"

"I have a few ideas."

"No, happen to me, I mean. I'll develop an inferiority complex."

"If I could accomplish that, they'd probably send me to the CIA's psychological ops department."

He widened his smile. "Where have you been all my life?"

"Two feet back, covered in the long shadow you cast."

"Okay, okay," he said, holding up his hands. "I surrender. I won't even celebrate my birthday . . . more than once a year."

It was my turn to smile. Could he be charming, after all? Maybe it really was just a case of everything coming too easily to him. I sat back and closed my eyes a moment to feel the breeze and the warm sunshine. The lake had a freshwater aroma that came from the plants around it and the fish that swam in it. It was as if every green leaf radiated the scent of life itself, flourishing, rich, and healthy. Suddenly, I felt his lips touch mine. It was surprising but soft and warm. I opened my eyes as he pulled back.

"Couldn't help it," he said. "You are too beautiful to resist."

"Why do I think you've used that line before?"

"You're just naturally skeptical. That's all right. I'll wait."

"For what?"

"Your faith in me, in my honesty."

"Let's hope it happens before either of us reaches social security age."

He roared and then got behind the steering wheel and started the engine. He backed up, slowly turned, and headed out toward the middle of the lake. Try as hard as I could, I wasn't able to hide my excitement. I squealed with delight as the boat bounced when he sped up and the water spray sprinkled my cheeks. After we made one large circle, he slowed down.

"You want to try it?"

"What, steer?"

"All of it. It's easy. C'mon," he said, stopping to change seats with me.

I eased into the driver's seat, and he showed me how to accelerate. I started very slowly.

"Watch where you're going," he advised as I kept dropping my eyes to my hands. We were heading for one of the sailboats. He reached around to help me turn the wheel. Our cheeks were touching. "Go on, you can go faster now," he said. "That's it."

I was really having a great time. He sat back and watched me with a wide smile on his face.

"What?"

"I just love the way the excitement radiates in your face."

As we crossed the lake, I thought of something. "I want to show you a place on the lake," I said, and turned the boat so that we headed toward the small lagoon Brayden had taken me to.

"Don't get too close here," Shayne advised. "There are stumps and large rocks. We never come down this way." He reached over to turn the wheel a bit. "So? What's the big deal?"

"It doesn't look the same at night," I said, not hiding my disappointment. I didn't see as many birds, either.

"You were here at night? With whom?"

"It doesn't matter. I don't see it the same way. Sorry."

He studied the shore suspiciously. "Let's get back out to the middle," he said. "We'll take a nice dip and then have some lunch."

I slipped out of the driver's seat, and he took over. As we accelerated and turned away from the lagoon, I looked back and was positive that I saw Brayden standing very close to where we had been and looking out at us. He was so well hidden by the leaves of the bushes that I was sure that Shayne couldn't have seen him. Even before we turned too far to see him, he was gone.

The sight of him quickened my heartbeat but also seemed to bring me back to earth. Shayne looked at me and saw the difference in my face.

"You all right? You're not getting seasick or something, are you?"

"No, I'm fine." I forced a bigger smile.

He glanced back toward the lagoon. "You know who owns that lot? Your wild friend Charlotte's family."

"She's really not much of a friend."

"I didn't think so."

"Why is the lot undeveloped?"

"Her father thinks it will double in value or something. That's what my father says. He tried to buy it once from her father. Did Charlotte take you there?"

"No."

"So, if Charlotte didn't take you there, who did?"

"Nobody," I said. "I just took a long walk one day."

He nodded, but I could see that he didn't believe me. I wondered myself why I hadn't told the truth. It was almost as if I wasn't sure if I really had been there or I had dreamed it.

Or maybe I was feeling guilty again for enjoying myself with a boy who could do what he wanted and had no dark and dreary life pulling him back into the shadows, where only loneliness and sorrow dwelled.

Suddenly, I had become a keeper of secrets, and for some reason, that made me feel even closer to Brayden.

8

Birdsong

The water was cold, but Shayne was right. After swimming for a while, it didn't feel bad at all. He had some tubes and even a raft. He helped me up onto it, and then, holding onto the raft and kicking, he pushed me in a circle around the boat as I lay there soaking up the sun and feeling like a queen. He returned to the boat and plucked a soda out of the box onboard. He poured it into a plastic cup and brought it to me on the raft.

"Your Majesty might be thirsty," he said.

"Thank you, Prince Charming. I am."

I took a long sip and looked out at the lake, the beautiful houses, the other wealthy people enjoying their boats. It wasn't hard to see yourself as special when you had all of this at your beck and call, I thought. It had a way of seducing you. I wasn't sure I wouldn't be as arrogant as he was if I lived this way.

"You look too pleased with yourself," he suddenly declared, and turned over the raft.

I screamed and used the emptied cup to heave water on him. We frolicked about until he pulled me to him and kissed me while I held on to the edge of the boat. He pressed his body against mine and told me to hold on or we'd both drown. He was fooling, of course.

"You're taking unfair advantage," I said.

He shrugged. "I don't know what else to take," he said, kissing me again.

I broke free and kicked back.

"I'm drowning!" he shouted, pretending to be pulled down under the water. When he came up, he spurted at me like a whale.

I screamed and splashed at him. He went under again and then came up beside me, but he didn't touch or kiss me again.

"Let's eat. I'm starving," he said, and climbed up onto the extended platform, reaching for my hand and helping me on. He threw me my towel, and we settled down, unwrapping the sandwiches and opening our drinks.

"How many other girls have you taken out on the lake?" I asked.

"You're the first."

I tilted my head with a skeptical expression.

"It's the truth."

"How come?"

"I don't know. Yes, I do. I knew you would appreciate it more. Most of the other girls I know would rather hang out at the mall or . . ."

"Or?"

"Do other things," he said with a sly smirk.

"What makes you think I don't?"

His eyes widened a bit, and then he laughed.

"No, I'm serious. I'd like to know why you said that."

"I don't know. When I look at you, I think, *That girl has class.*"

"Which means what?"

"Why this third-degree questioning?" he asked. I saw that he was looking a bit uncomfortable.

I looked out over the water toward the lagoon. Really, why was I asking these questions? Even I could feel the antagonism in my voice. It was almost as if I wanted this to fail, this budding relationship. It was too good. We looked too perfect. Whatever the reason, something was gnawing at me.

"You want to try waterskiing?"

"Not today," I said, which assumed that there would be a tomorrow.

He nodded. "How about I take you to this restaurant in Greenwood tonight?" He smiled. "My dad's an investor. We eat for free."

Greenwood was a large town about twenty miles southeast of Echo Lake. I had been there only because it had a well-developed mall with some large department stores.

"Okay," I said. "What time?"

He looked at his watch. "My parents and my sister could come back anytime soon. Let's get back to the house so I can show it to you without being interrupted, and then you'll tell me how much time you need to get ready to go to dinner. I am your loyal servant," he added with a mock bow.

"Okay."

The truth was, I hated leaving the lake. I thought I could stay out there until nightfall and maybe even after that.

"We can do this again next weekend and stay much later on the water if you want. Maybe by then you'll get your courage up for a waterskiing lesson."

"Maybe," I said.

He cleaned up a bit and then raised the anchor and started the engine. I sat back as we started off toward his dock.

All of this had come as a real surprise. A little more than twenty-four hours ago, I would have laughed at the idea of Shayne Allan and me becoming what Ellie called "a thing." In the meantime, I had met Brayden and, especially after our short time in the woods, imagined that we might become "a thing."

Did this all happen as suddenly and as surprisingly to other girls as it was happening to me? I wondered. For most of my teenage life, most boys were little more than an interesting distraction. I had begun to worry that something might be seriously wrong with me because of my reluctance to get too involved with any one boy and my failure to get very excited about anyone. I knew I seemed "different" to so many of them, and I was seemingly either above or simply outside of everyone else's experiences and needs. It was how I had earned their nickname for me, Prudence Perfect, but along came Brayden, and I could feel a change coming over me. Was it simply a case of belated maturity? Or was something magical finally happening to me?

A part of me was afraid to think too hard about it, for fear that it would all go poof in a sudden cloud of smoke. Maybe certain things in life, certain things that you do and feel, shouldn't be analyzed at all but just enjoyed for what they are. Besides, I thought, thinking a little more about Brayden, everyone is entitled to his or her own little secrets, whether they are secret feelings or secret fears. Perhaps I had been too severe a judge. So far, this afternoon with Shayne certainly made me feel guilty for looking down on him and ridiculing him. Just the little I knew already about his family made me think that he was under different kinds of pressures from the pressures other boys at our school endured. Rich or poor, everyone had his own particular burdens.

I helped him tie up the boat at the dock, and then we headed back to the house.

"You can use one of the spare bedrooms to change out of your wet suit," he said. "Or you could use mine."

"I'll use the spare one," I said.

"I was afraid you'd say that."

"Then why did you offer?"

"To see if I was wrong. I can hope, can't I? You shouldn't be afraid," he added. "It's as easy as waterskiing."

"But the landing isn't as soft when you fall," I said, and he laughed.

"Okay, go on and be a challenge. I can take it."

Can you? I wondered, *or will you find a convenient excuse to abandon the effort?*

He took me upstairs and showed me the guest bedroom. It looked as large as my parents' master bedroom. He explained that his father had designed the house so that all of the bedrooms had a view of the lake.

"Sure you don't need any help?"

"I think I can manage alone."

He surprised me by kissing me quickly and then backing away.

"Don't know what you're missing," he said. "Take a shower if you want. Maybe it will save some time. Come on downstairs when you're ready. I'll show you our entertainment center." He walked off to his own bedroom to change.

I went into the bathroom with my bag and began to change and brush my hair. Even though the bathroom was equipped with all sorts of shampoos and conditioners, I didn't want to take a shower there. I could see that even with only a few hours on the lake, I had picked up some color. I was glad now that I had used the sunscreen. My complexion was such that it didn't take much to get me red and peeling, especially the skin on my nose and above my eyebrows.

I did use the dryer to brush out my hair, and then, after I put on some lipstick, I headed out and down the stairs.

"I hope you remade the bed," I heard, and turned at the top of the stairs to see Wendi and one of her girlfriends standing just down the hallway.

"Excuse me?"

She looked at her friend and then, smiling widely, came down the hallway toward me. Anyone who knew Shayne and then looked at Wendi would wonder if they had the same father, even the same mother. She had black eyes and hair. Most brothers and sisters shared some feature, but neither her chin nor her redone nose nor her ears and eyes resembled Shayne's. She was barely five feet two, if that, and had a stocky build. Both of Shayne's parents were tall. His mother had a fashion model's figure, and his father was an athletic-looking man. I had seen them both often at basketball and baseball games. As she drew closer, I thought Wendi would single-handedly make some plastic surgeon wealthy. I foresaw liposuction, breast enhancement, and endless Botox in her future.

"The maid is off today."

"What's that supposed to mean?"

"I figured you'd be one of those who played dumb," she replied, obviously egged on by the wide smile on her companion's face. "How long have you two been up here?" she asked. "We just got here."

"As long as it took for me to change out of my bathing suit and brush my hair, if you must know."

Wendi looked at her friend and smiled. She kept looking at her when she spoke to me. "It doesn't take my brother long to get any girl out of her bathing suit." She laughed, and her friend, who was a little more timid, just continued smiling.

"Well, I hate to disappoint you, but this is one girl who didn't need his help," I said, and turned away.

"I hope you weren't a virgin when you came here," she called after me, laughing. "Our maid will ask about the bloodstains. Looks like he won another bet," she shouted after me. "He told his friends he could nail you."

I kept descending, but the anger in my body rose like mercury in a thermometer. I thought it might blow off the top of my head. Shayne, who was waiting in the family room below, turned, took one look at me, and came hurrying over.

"What's the matter?"

"I had the pleasure of running into your sister."

"I didn't know she was back," he said, looking toward the stairway. "What did she do?"

"It's not what she did. It's what she said, but forget it. I don't want to give her the satisfaction of knowing she bothered me."

He took a step toward the stairway.

"Don't start anything, please, Shayne," I said. "I can see she's just hoping for that."

"Okay, but maybe now I will tell my parents about her stash," he said.

"From what you're saying, it won't do much good." I looked at my watch. "If you want to go to dinner, I'd better get home."

"Sure. I'll show you the rest of the house next time."

I was already heading toward the front door. He caught up quickly and hurried ahead to open the car door for me, just as his parents pulled into the driveway. Shayne's father stopped. They were driving a light yellow Bentley convertible. His father was in a bright yellow sports jacket with a black tie, and his mother wore a light blue shawl over her strapless dark blue dress. She had a different hairdo from the one I remembered. This was a short pixie hairstyle. I thought she had the face for it. She reminded me of the actress Keira Knightley.

"How was the lake?" Shayne's father asked.

"Great, Dad."

"Boat performed well?"

"Everything was great."

"Hi, Amber. How are your parents?" he asked me.

"Very good, thank you, Mr. Allan."

"I'm coming in to see your father soon," Shayne's mother said, leaning over to talk to me. "I saw a necklace he made for Morgan Brice. Gorgeous. We're lucky to have so talented a jeweler in this town."

"Thank you, Mrs. Allan."

"Is your sister back yet?" she asked Shayne.

"I think she's been back for a while. Check the safe," he said.

Her smile faded, but his father almost smiled. "Where are you two headed?"

"I'm taking Amber home to change. We're going to Salmon Bend in Greenwood for dinner."

"Make sure you pay this time, Shayne. Don't let them tear up your bill," his father said firmly.

"Okay, Dad."

"Nice to see you, Amber," his father said, and continued on to their garage.

"Your mother always looks like she has just stepped off a magazine cover," I said. "I don't know how she does it."

"She has an army, the beautician army. I have a suspicion there's a hairdresser hanging in her closet," he told me. I knew he meant it to be funny, but he sounded almost resentful, sarcastic. I was tempted to ask him again if he liked his mother. "C'mon, tell me. What did my sister say to you?"

"She asked me if we remade the bed in the guest room and if I was a virgin. She said you won another bet you had made with your buddies about what you could do to me."

"That bitch," he said. "I'll handle her later."

"Something tells me you're better off ignoring her," I said.

He looked surprised at my reaction. "Most of the girls she's confronted at our house would like to feed the fire if she was burned at the stake."

I said nothing, but I wondered how many other girls he meant. How many were at his house? Did he tell me the truth when he said he hadn't taken any other girl out on the lake? I knew from the chatter in our cafeteria that he saw girls from other schools, girls he had met during away basketball and baseball games. Maybe there was some truth to what his sister claimed. What was I to believe?

As we turned onto my street, my eyes were drawn to Brayden's house. There was a late-model Mercedes sedan in the driveway. It wasn't the car I had seen that first day when his family had arrived and were being moved into the house. It had an Oregon license plate. Did they know some people here? Were friends or family finally visiting?

It occurred to me that Shayne had rarely, maybe never, been down my street. It wasn't a through street, so anyone turning down it would be doing so to visit someone, and there wasn't any other student from our school living here. I felt confident that his parents weren't friends with any of our neighbors, either. Maybe he really didn't know which house was the house of a new resident unless that information was something Ellie or Charlotte had given him. Just as when we had driven out earlier, he barely glanced at it as we turned into my driveway. He looked at his watch.

"How's an hour and a half sound?"

"Fine. How fancy is the restaurant?"

"Oh, it's not fancy. It's what my mother calls casual fancy."

"I don't know what that means."

"You'll choose the right thing to wear, I'm sure."

"Thanks. I love the pressure."

He laughed. "I'm wearing a black shirt and white pants. No jacket. Take it from there."

"Okay."

I started to get out, and he reached for my arm to make me pause.

"Amber, I hope you had a good day so far despite the evil dwarf."

"I did," I said, but even I detected some unhappiness in my voice. Some things you just can't disguise. "Does she know you refer to her like that?"

"I think she's gotten the hint, yes."

"My mom's always saying you get more with honey than you do with vinegar."

"She hasn't met my sister yet. Give her a chance," he muttered, and leaned over to give me a quick kiss. I said nothing, just got out. He backed up quickly, this time not looking back to wave. I had the feeling he was burning with rage inside and wanted to get home to go at his sister.

Even the richest, most successful families ruptured with jealousies and meanness, I thought. What was the secret of true happiness? In fact, why were my parents, who were far less well-off financially, far happier people?

When I got into the house, I called the jewelry store to tell my parents that I was going to dinner with Shayne. My mother demanded a detailed description of the afternoon on the boat. I knew she was listening keenly to my voice as I spoke, searching to discover whether I had really enjoyed myself. I told her what Shayne's mother had said about Mrs. Brice's necklace.

"Good," she replied. "When the wealthier women come in because of something another has bought, they always want to outdo it."

I laughed and then hurried up to shower and change for dinner. When I glanced out my window at the front of Brayden's house, I saw that the car that had been there was gone. I looked across at his bedroom window, and as usual, I could see nothing because of the glare.

As I showered and dressed, I asked myself how serious I wanted things to get with Shayne Allan. One time, when my mother and I had talked about first romances, she had said, "Sometimes you get like a car that has lost its brakes. You have to steer more carefully and wait until the road flattens out and you can roll to a stop."

How easily that could happen with Shayne, I thought. I had really enjoyed being with him the night before and certainly today. I felt myself forming an entirely different opinion of him, and yet I also sensed the hesitation, that foot on the brake that Mom mentioned. I didn't want to be simply another one of his conquests, and his sister had planted the thought well in my mind. Although Wendi had always disgusted me and struck me as being someone who would enjoy someone else's unhappiness, I couldn't help thinking that maybe she wasn't exaggerating all that much. It wasn't difficult to imagine Shayne sweeping away any other girl and taking advantage of opportunities in that house, especially when his parents weren't there. I knew there were girls in my school who wouldn't care, girls who might even see it as some sort of accomplishment. Ellie struck me as one of them, but that was not me and would never be.

When had what you thought of yourself become so unimportant? I often heard girls brag about how they had taken advantage of a boy they were with, but I always felt they were trying to convince themselves as much as they were convincing others, despite all the hoopla about liberated women. Maybe I was simply born too late. Maybe I belonged in a previous century. Maybe what Brayden said his mother believed about reincarnation wasn't something to be so easily set aside.

Despite the fun Mom and I made of Dad's love of old movies, I truly enjoyed watching them, especially the costume dramas about lords and ladies. Most of the other girls I knew found them boring and silly. Was that what I was, boring and silly? I was trying not to be. Was I trying too hard?

Because of what Shayne had said he was wearing, I chose a solid black light V-neck sweater and a pair of black jeans. Naturally, I put on one of the necklaces my father had created for me. It was a chakra he had designed. According to ancient Indian medicine, our bodies were composed of six chakras, or energy wheels. The chakras were associated with certain colors, body parts, and functions, and by wearing the six, you were supposedly helping your body to maintain balance. The necklace had three strands with sterling silver and semi-precious stones.

With my hair up and the color I had gotten from being in the boat on the lake that day, I thought I looked very attractive. As usual, I then felt guilty for having those feelings. Why couldn't I be more like some of the girls in my school who believed that if you had it, you should flaunt it—otherwise, why have it?

While I was gazing at myself in the full-length mirror, I thought I saw someone move past my opened bedroom door. I turned quickly, my heart thumping. For a few moments, I just stared, holding my breath and trying to remember if I had closed the front door completely behind me when I had entered the house. I was thinking too hard about Shayne, the afternoon, and his bratty sister.

Crime, as other people knew it in other communities, was practically nonexistent in Echo Lake. Despite having all of the seasonal homes that were empty most of the year, we had very few instances of break-ins. Someone would probably have to go back as far as the nineteenth or early twentieth century to read about an armed robbery or a murder here. Nevertheless, the usual paranoia about crime existed here. People still locked their cars and their homes and used alarms and security cameras.

I approached the doorway slowly and peered out. I saw no one, but I went down the hallway to look in at my parents' room. I even checked their closets and bathroom before returning to my own room. I gazed again at myself in the mirror, but I couldn't help but glance at my doorway, too, every other moment. Finally, I just had to go downstairs to be sure I had closed the front door. I even examined the rear door. They were both closed and locked. *Whatever it was,* I thought, *it was in my imagination.*

I returned to my room to get a jacket. I chose my light pink leather one. Before I could go downstairs, my phone rang.

"Why didn't you call me?" Ellie asked. "I've been sitting by my phone."

"How did you know I was home?" I countered.

She laughed. "A little bird told another bird who told me. So?"

"What does that mean? It didn't have anything to do with Shayne's sister, did it?"

"No. Why do you ask? Tell me," she pleaded.

"There's nothing to tell except that she's as ugly on the inside as she is on the outside."

Ellie laughed. "So? What about the time you spent with Shayne? Don't tell me it ended like last night?"

"I had a great time, and it hasn't ended yet. We're going out to dinner. He'll be here any moment, so I gotta go."

"Oh. Well, I guess you won't call me tonight, but call me tomorrow."

I realized something. "Why didn't you tell me about all that happened after Charlotte's party?" I asked before I hung up.

"Oh, that stuff. Forget it. It won't matter. They'll all get away with warnings, maybe some probation."

"It would matter if someone had been seriously hurt," I said.

"Right, Prudence," she said, then laughed and hung up.

I went downstairs again and out onto the front porch, fuming from talking to her. The descending sun blocked by the trees layered the usual shadows over Brayden's house and grounds. I stood staring at the dark house, wondering when I would see Brayden again. When I stared at his house, it seemed to me that the shadows actually moved in a circle.

"I'm right here," I heard, and spun around. "I told you you would see me again."

"I didn't think I wouldn't see you again," I said. "But why do you have to sneak up on me like this all the time?"

"Sorry," he said, dropping into the rocker. "You look a little upset. Wasn't it a good day on the lake?"

"You were there. You should know," I said, folding my arms across my breasts and stepping up to him. "I saw you, so don't deny it."

He smiled. "I'm not denying it. I guess you were showing him the lagoon."

I felt myself calming. "Yes, but you were right. It didn't look the same in the daytime."

"Did you tell him who had brought you there?"

"No."

"Why not?"

"That's none of his business," I said, and he smiled.

"I thought you would feel that way. I'm not sure he would have appreciated it, anyway."

I pulled my head back. "How do you know what he would appreciate and what he wouldn't?"

"I listen to the birds," he said, gazing at the street.

"What?"

"Birds gossip. Didn't you know that?"

"Yes, I just heard about that." I saw no point in telling him about Ellie, since he hadn't ever set eyes on her.

"So why are you upset?"

"How do you know I am?"

"Do you know that we all have auras around us, a sort of luminous radiation?"

"You mean chakras," I said, fingering my necklace.

"Yes, something like that. Well, I can see your aura's kind of dark right now."

"Oh, you can see it? What else can you do? You read thoughts, read auras, find things here that others take a long time to find, have super hearing . . ."

He started laughing. I stopped and suddenly felt the anger receding in me.

"I'm just annoyed with a so-called good friend."

"Why?"

"She's just a busybody sticking her nose into other people's affairs."

"Yours?"

"Forget it. Is your father back?"

"No."

"I saw a car there when I returned before."

"It was the landlord," he said. "Checking up," he added, pursing his lips and looking annoyed.

"Oh. Was there something wrong?"

He looked at me as if I had asked the dumbest question of all.

"I mean, with the house or anything?"

"No."

"Who is the landlord? I mean, is he someone who lives here?"

"No. He lives in Portland." He stood up. "Your date is almost here," he said. "Watch yourself." He stared away, this time walking off the porch and toward the front of his house.

"What's that supposed to mean?"

He paused and shrugged. "It means don't do anything he would do."

"What?"

He pointed to a pair of robins dropping from a tree limb to the lawn to hunt for worms. "The birds, remember? They gossip."

He kept walking.

"You don't make any sense, Brayden," I called after him. "You're infuriating!" I cried. He lifted his hand but kept walking.

A moment later, I saw Shayne's car approaching. When I looked back, Brayden was gone. It was as if he fled or disappeared before Shayne could see him. But I had to add another thing to my list. He seemed to be able to sense the future. I wondered if he could sense his own.

I wondered if that was what really made him so sad and bitter.

9

An Unpleasant Evening

"You're looking better and better every time I see you," Shayne said after he got out of his car to open the passenger door for me.

"Thanks," I said.

"Think I have anything to do with it?"

I paused, pretending to give it great consideration. Then I shook my head. "No."

He laughed and gave me a quick kiss on the cheek, but I was still distracted by Brayden's appearance and disappearance. I hesitated before getting into Shayne's car and looked toward Brayden's house.

"Anything wrong?" Shayne asked. He looked at Brayden's house, too.

"No."

I got in, but Shayne continued to look at the house and then headed around the front of the car to get in.

"Anyone live in that house?" he asked, nodding at it.

"A family recently moved in, yes."

"Doesn't look like it. It's actually an eyesore on the street. Is that where this new boy lives?"

"Brayden Matthews, yes," I said.

"Well, I heard he doesn't like going to parties. Ellie and Charlotte told me about him. Why is he so antisocial? Shy? Does he have an ugly scar? Maybe his family is hiding out. You know, like in the witness protection program or something."

"Don't be stupid."

"So? What's the answer?"

"He has a very ill mother to care for. His father is away a lot."

"Well, I'll feel sorry for him as long as he stays away from you," Shayne said, and then laughed. "Oh. My sister has been confined to her room, and her friend was sent home. She can't have any friends over for a month," he said as he backed out of my driveway.

"What did you do?"

"I told them how unpleasant she was to you and then sort of directed my father to what she had hidden in her room."

"I'm sure she'll blame me."

"If she does anything else to bother you . . . hey, I like that necklace. Your father made it?"

"Of course," I said. "Do you want me to describe what it is?"

"Sure."

I did, thinking of what Brayden had told me, but I wasn't sure that Shayne was paying very much attention. Almost as soon as I finished, he said, "Mel Quinn's parents went to visit his uncle. They're not back until late tomorrow. He's having a sort of house party tonight."

"I thought we were going to dinner."

"Sure. I mean, maybe we can stop by afterward."

"Is it going to turn out to be another Charlotte Watts party?"

"Only three couples invited, and that includes us. There'll be no fireworks except for the fireworks we make together. You know Mel? He plays third base."

I laughed.

"What?"

"You had better become a professional ballplayer of some sort, otherwise you won't be able to identify your friends."

"Very funny," he said. "Well, anyway, Mel's a good guy. You know him."

"Not very well," I said. Actually, I did know something about him, having heard him discussed by other girls. They said he had a sign on his bedroom door: "Check your virginity before entering." Why would his parents permit it? I thought. But I had also heard rumors about his father having extramarital affairs. "If you don't mind, I'd rather skip the party."

"Really? Why?"

"I don't have a good feeling about it."

He looked at me as if I had gone crazy and shook his head. "Feeling? How can you have any feeling about it? You've never been to a party at Mel's, have you?"

"No, but that doesn't matter."

"That doesn't matter? Oh, I get it. You're back to being Prudence Perfect, and so soon, too," he muttered.

"I am who I am, Shayne. If that discourages you, feel free to turn around," I said.

The look he gave me this time had no amusement in it, but no apology, either. For a while, neither of us spoke. Then he smiled. "Maybe you'll change your mind after you have a great dinner."

I didn't reply. It was a quick ride to Greenwood. As if he thought it might influence me to go to the house party, he talked about Mel Quinn's athletic ability.

"I don't recall you being at many of the baseball games last year," he said. He smiled. "I always look at the cheering section."

"I was at a few."

"What's a few?"

"Three."

"Now, what sort of school spirit is that? You don't belong to any clubs or teams, either, do you?"

"I help out at the store after school. It gives my mother time to do her errands. We're not that busy yet that time of the year, so we don't hire any part-time help."

"Such a serious family," he said, wagging his head and smiling.

"Isn't yours serious about many things?"

"My father, I suppose." He thought a moment. "I don't think I ever hear my mother talk about doing any real work. She never had a job. She met my father while she was attending college, and they got married about a month after she graduated. My maternal grandparents are probably richer than we are. My uncle and my aunt have summer homes in Europe and live in Montecito, California. Ritzy neighborhood. You ever been there?"

"No."

"What about your uncles and aunts?"

"I have only one aunt. She's on the East Coast. We don't see her and her family that much."

"I hardly see my uncle and aunt, but they have come up occasionally to see me play ball. From the sound of it, they might have been there more than you."

"Maybe."

He looked as if he had gone into a sulk for a while, and then he perked up again. "I haven't decided on a college yet, have you?"

"No."

"I have a full scholarship to USC. Did you know that?"

"I heard you had offers, yes."

"That I do," he said proudly, too proudly for me. "Here I am, one of those who don't need any financial aid being courted by colleges. Oh, well, when you have it, so many want it."

"I think you need more lessons on that inferiority complex," I said.

He laughed. "As long as you're the teacher, I'll learn."

"Maybe I'm not as good a teacher as you think."

He didn't answer. We pulled into the parking lot of the Salmon Bend restaurant. It was just outside of Greenwood and was, as Shayne would explain, actually built from what had been a large residence.

"So that's why there are all these separate dining rooms," he continued as we approached the entrance. "I made sure we were in the smallest, most romantic one. I have my own table reserved, as you can imagine."

"Yes, that's not hard to imagine," I said, and he laughed.

"How am I going to impress you if you take it all for granted?"

"That is another challenge you might not meet," I said. He held his smile, but there wasn't any joy behind it, not even any glee.

He opened the door, and the hostess immediately greeted us. It was clear that she knew who he was. I could see that he enjoyed the way she fawned over us, over him, calling him "Mr. Allan" and leaving another couple waiting as she escorted us to our table in the dining room at the right. It had about six tables, and ours was near the window that looked out on a very large pond.

"It's a salmon farm," he said as he pulled out my chair. "You'll see there are a half-dozen different dishes made with salmon."

"Oh," I said, unable to hide my disappointment.

"What?"

"I . . . my mother and I prefer wild salmon. It's healthier."

"Ah, that's just a bunch of garbage. Don't believe it," he said.

The waitress, a woman who didn't look much older than a high school student, hurried over to our table. She had short dark brown hair that looked as if someone just learning how to cut hair had done the hairdo for her. The ends were obviously uneven. I could see by the way her eyes brightened that she knew Shayne well and probably had a crush on him. She handed me a menu, nearly poking me with it because her eyes were so fixed on him, waiting for him, like some prince or young king, to bestow one of his handsome smiles on her. He looked up, flashed a smile, and took the menu.

"What's good tonight, Joyce?" he asked.

"Oh, Chef has made your favorite, the wrapped salmon," she said. It was as if I wasn't even sitting there.

"Well, he knew I was coming," he said. She nodded, smiling so brightly that I had no trouble imagining that she had heard he was coming, too. "It is good," Shayne told me. "He seasons it with just enough salt and pepper and coats it with Dijon mustard before wrapping it in phyllo dough and baking it. Healthy, healthy. Don't worry about the wild and the farm thing," he advised— more like ordered.

"I'll have the vegetarian platter," I said. "No salad needed."

Shayne shook his head. "Give her what she wants, and give me the wrapped salmon. Serve them together. I won't have any salad tonight, either. And Joyce," he added, leaning toward her, "a bottle of my mother's Chardonnay served the way you know how."

He reached up to touch her hand. I thought that if her eyes had been bulbs, they'd have exploded. She hurried off.

"They'll serve you alcohol?"

"Joyce'll get it for me. No one will notice. You'll see why. Anyway, even if they do, they won't say anything. You like white wine?"

"Yes, we have it often at home, but . . ."

"Stop worrying. My father has fifty-five percent of this place. Even if Maurice sees it being poured into a different bottle, he won't say anything."

"Who's Maurice?"

"The manager. He's seen it done before, actually, but when it's the son of the majority interest holder . . ."

I leaned back and looked at him. "How does it feel to be able to get away with so much more than other people just because your father's rich? I mean, look at Charlotte Watts and how much trouble she's been able to escape because of her father."

"That's America," he said. "Get used to it."

"Not the America I live in."

"Sure it is. I'm sure that if you got yourself into something, your dad would call on some influential people and get you out of it, too. He might even call my father or Charlotte's."

I thought about it. He was probably right, if I did get into something serious somehow, but the realization didn't make me feel any better. He could tell. The expression on my face was too revealing.

"You're not some kind of idealist, are you?"

"No. I just have these funny ideas about fairness and equality."

He laughed.

Joyce brought us the wine. She explained that she had someone in the kitchen named Brody uncork it and pour it into what looked like a large bottled water. Shayne gave her a five-dollar bill.

"For Brody," he said. She nodded and pocketed it quickly. "Excuse the glasses," Shayne said when she poured the wine into the water glasses. "Taste it."

I did.

"Well?"

"Very good," I said. I looked at Joyce. "Russian River Reserve?"

Joyce looked at Shayne, who was smiling.

"I didn't tell her," he said.

"Yes, that's it," Joyce said unhappily. She put the basket of bread down.

"Could we have some olive oil?" I asked.

"Good idea," Shayne said. Joyce sauntered off.

"What is she, your private waitress here?"

"She likes taking care of me and my guests. I tip her well."

"I have the feeling she's hoping for more."

"They can hope," he said.

"I feel sorry for her. She should have other goals in life."

He laughed, but she returned quickly with the olive oil. As soon as she left again, he reached across the table to take my hand. "Didn't you have a good time on the lake today?"

"Yes, of course."

"I thought you and I were really getting along."

"Who says we're not?"

"You just seem suddenly different, more like you were before we went to the diner last night," he said. "Matter of fact, I felt that as soon as I picked you up."

"I don't know why," I said, but I couldn't help wondering myself, because I knew it was true. Maybe it had something to do with Brayden. I hardly knew him. He was a tight ball of complications, for sure, but every time I had any contact with him, it had an effect on me. The truth was, he was still in my head from the short conversation we'd had just before Shayne arrived.

"You don't relax enough," Shayne said, nodding to himself as if he had landed on the right answer. "You think and worry too much. Get over it. Let's just have a good time. You've got to let your hair down, let go sometimes and howl at the moon."

"Why is that something a boy always says?" I asked.

"Oh, there are girls who tell other girls the same thing. I'm sure you've heard it many times."

"What does that mean? 'I've heard it many times?'" I asked, taking my hand back just as Joyce brought my vegetarian dish and his wrapped salmon.

"Is there anything else you need?" she asked.

"Not at the moment," Shayne told her. "Stay close just in case there's some sort of an emergency."

She widened her smile, glanced at me like someone who wished she could make me evaporate, and walked away.

I started to eat and sipped some wine.

"This is so good. You should have ordered it," he said, savoring his salmon and perhaps overdoing it to make his point. I ignored it.

"So," I continued, "what did you mean about my hearing that many times?"

"C'mon, you know how most of the other girls think of you, Amber. I'm not telling you something you don't know. Anyway, who cares what they think of you? Surprise them. Make them eat their hearts out," he said, chomping away at his salmon dish and drinking his wine. "Have a wild time."

The vegetarian platter wasn't very good. Some of the grilled peppers and the eggplant were overdone. I was sure the chef gave it the least amount of his attention. He probably resented someone choosing something so blah and simple over his specials. Shayne poured me more wine. I was filling up on that and bread.

"I could order you something else," he said, seeing how I was playing with my food.

"No, that's all right. I'm not that hungry."

"Wrong way to be in a place like this," he said, going after every morsel of his main dish. He drank all of the wine in his glass and poured himself some more. Then he sat back. "Mel's ordering in some pizzas, if you get hungry later."

"I told you that I'd rather we not go there," I said, pushing my plate away.

"Well, what do you want to do, just go home?" he countered with annoyance on his face. He looked at his watch. "It's early."

"Let's just go for a walk."

"A walk? Where?"

I shrugged. "You could take me home and we'll take a walk."

"You'd rather do that than go to Mel's and party?"

"We enjoyed nature today. Why not stay with it?"

He stared at me a moment and then shook his head.

Joyce came hurrying over. "Finished?"

"Yeah, tell Chef he outdid himself, but he needs to work harder on the vegetarian dish," he said.

She smirked and took my plate. "Dessert?"

"No. We're going for a walk," he said with the tone of someone who was being led to the gallows. He took out a twenty and a ten and put them on the table. "There's your tip. You know how to handle the rest," he added.

She smiled.

He stood up, and I did, too. After she took her money and walked off, I asked, "What about what your father told you?"

"What?"

"About paying the bill."

"Oh, he just says that when someone else is around. Forget it." He reached for my hand.

The hostess rushed over to be sure we had enjoyed everything. "Have a good night," she told him.

"We're trying," he said, rolling his eyes.

She gave him a knowing smile that told me he had brought other girls there, girls who were probably far more compliant.

"You don't really want to just go for a walk, do you?" he asked when we got into his car.

"Not unless you want to," I said.

"Good. Then we're off to Mel's."

"No. We're off to my house. You're off to Mel's."

I could see him fall into a sulk very quickly. It was obvious that Shayne Allan was someone who almost always got just what he wanted, especially from any date.

"I tell you what," he said after a while, "why don't we go to Mel's, and if you don't like it, we leave. How's that? You might just have a good time!" he added, the frustration palpable.

Brayden's half-joking admonition resonated: "Don't do anything he would do."

Why was I remembering that and giving what he said any credence?

"You don't believe whatever my sister told you, do

you? She hates anyone else having a good time, because she's so miserable most of the time."

I didn't say anything.

"You've got to fight back this urge to be Prudence Perfect. I thought you did a good job of it today on the lake."

"I must be tired," I said. "I'm not used to being in the sun all day. Just take me home."

"But you wanted to go for a walk, I thought."

"Maybe next time."

"Right, next time," he muttered. "You didn't like your dinner at my father's restaurant, and you don't want to veg out at Mel's with some of my friends. Two strikes."

"Do you get a home run every time you're at bat?"

"No, but I get a hit most of the time," he countered. "C'mon. We'll listen to music, talk . . . he's got some good wine. I know now that you like wine and know what's good. It's really early. I don't want to end our night like this."

"We can sit on my porch for a while," I said.

He looked at me, shook his head, and accelerated. He didn't say another word until we turned into my driveway. He didn't get out to open my door. He sat there staring at the steering wheel.

"You were sure different on the lake," he said. "I really believed that this Prudence Perfect crap was just that, crap spread by jealous bitches."

"I'm sorry you feel that way. I happen to believe that relationships are built slowly and carefully."

"Relationships? I'm not looking to get married, Amber. I thought we'd just have a good time. Look around, will you? That's what's going on. Kids our age are having a good time. They're not establishing lifelong relationships. Jesus, what are you, all of seventeen? This isn't the Middle East or something."

"I'm not looking to get married, but that doesn't mean I can't put some value and meaning into being with someone. Maybe everything you do is just another ball game to you, Shayne, but I like to think I'm playing in the World Series with whomever I meet. I think that analogy will help you understand." I opened the door and got out.

"You have to win a lot to get into the World Series," he called as he began to back out. I watched him drive off, speeding away and having to hit his brakes at the end of the street to make the turn. I stood there for a while, thinking. Was I being too prudish? Did I fit the name Prudence Perfect? Was I afraid that I would lose control, speed down that hill without brakes like Mom had said, and he would take advantage of me? Would that be so terrible?

The hens will be clucking now, I thought.

"You made the right decisions," I heard, and spun around to see Brayden sitting on my front porch.

"What are you doing here?"

"I had a feeling you'd be home early. I just wanted to make sure you were all right."

"Why did you have the feeling I would be home early?"

"You told me I had extrasensory powers, didn't you? Why the surprise?" He stood as I walked up the steps. I looked at the lighted window. I didn't hear the television but assumed Mom and Dad were both in the living room reading.

"Did you meet my parents?"

"No."

"They didn't hear you out here?"

"I wasn't exactly noisy. You want to go for a short walk? You look like you're wrapped pretty tight."

I smiled and shook my head.

"What?"

"That's what I first asked Shayne to do after dinner, go for a walk."

Brayden smiled. "Well, let's not disappoint your feet," he said, taking my hand.

10

Eyes Behind the Eyes

"You know, Brayden, I think it would be nice if you told me a little more about yourself. After all, this is our second walk in the dark in a matter of days," I said. "And I don't mean general stuff."

"What do you want to know about me? For a long time, my mother home-schooled me. We were on the go too much when I was younger, but no matter where we lived, what school I attended when I was in junior and senior high, I had top grades." He laughed. "One school had something called Super Honor Roll, and I was one of two in my class. Most of the time, I was ahead of the other students because I read a great deal on my own. I never formed a serious relationship with television or Facebook," he added, which made me smile.

"I haven't, either, although my father tries to get me to watch old movies with him all the time, and often, I do it on my own."

"I was told I was three grades ahead in my reading when I was first enrolled in a public school."

"So, that's why you're so confident about being ahead

or at least up-to-date with everyone here if and when your family decides to stay?"

"Yes. You're reading *Brave New World* this summer. I saw it on the porch," he added quickly. "I read that novel when I was twelve. Remember what Thoreau said about books?"

"No. What?"

"'Read the best books first, or you may not have a chance to read them at all.'"

"So, you can thank Thoreau for making you the student you are."

"Actually, I have to thank my father for most of this. He was always pushing books at me, bringing one home from a trip for me, telling me this one was essential or that one was more important than what my teacher was having me read. Whenever he was home for a long period of time, which might mean a week, he would talk about the book I had read or go over my math assignments with me. He actually taught me calculus before I was introduced to it in school."

"Really?"

"Yes. My father was what you would call a child prodigy. He graduated from high school at the age of thirteen and acquired a bachelor's degree at sixteen. He went on to do graduate work in economics at Harvard. There were many articles written about him. He worked in a government program by the time he was twenty. If you care to check it out, go on the Internet and look up Sanford Arlen Matthews. He has published ten books on various economic theories and concepts and one study of the great American depression."

"You sound very proud of him," I said as we turned the corner. I hadn't realized how far we had walked because I was listening so keenly to every word.

"I'm proud of him as an economic genius, but if I were in a department store that had a section on fathers, he wouldn't be my choice."

"Oh." *How sad,* I almost said.

"I think I've suggested that he's not very good at expressing his emotions. I'm sure he believes that emotions are a detriment, a weakness. They cloud good judgment. If he had the ears, I'd call him Spock from *Star Trek.* Occasionally, his humanity broke through."

"Your mother must have seen more in him to marry him," I said.

He paused and looked out at the busier street of Echo Lake. Then he turned toward another street that wasn't a through street. He walked a little faster, as if he had seen something on the busy street that he wanted to avoid. I looked back, saw nothing unusual, and then caught up.

"Sometimes I think she pitied him more than she loved him," he continued. "He became a kind of project for her, a small pile of clay she thought she could mold. It figures, she's an artist. Despite the way he is, he loves her as much as he could love anyone and has tried to be more . . . human. He's in awe of her art, and he is her biggest advocate. He'd do his best never to miss any of her art openings or award ceremonies. She designed the covers of five of his books, by the way. The publishers weren't happy about it because they were a little esoteric, but he wouldn't agree to a contract without her on it."

"Well, that's romantic . . . in a way," I added, and he laughed.

"Yes, in a way." He paused and looked at one of the houses on the cul-de-sac. "Your mayor lives here."

"I know."

"His wife takes her first lady of Echo Lake status quite seriously."

"How do you know that?"

"You don't follow the social columns in the *Echo Lake Times*?"

I laughed. "How do you do that? I haven't seen the paper delivered to your house. I did see some groceries delivered there," I added quickly. "Your mother came to the door."

"Oh?"

"She looked like she was standing guard or something. She wouldn't let the delivery boy bring the box in. She took it even though I could see that it was heavy, and she saw me."

"Did she?"

"Yes. I waved, but she slammed the door closed."

He nodded as if it was not a surprise.

"Did you tell her about me?" I asked.

"Not in so many words, but she knows about you."

"What does that mean?"

"She senses you. Be careful," he said, smiling. "Or you'll end up in one of her paintings."

"You make it sound terrible. I've seen her paintings on the Internet. I like them."

"She's changed her style lately," he said.

"Oh? Like what?"

"Like nothing you've seen. I hope she'll return to her more successful work."

We continued walking silently for a while. I felt as if I was peeling an orange or unwrapping a package. Little by little, I was getting better at forming a picture of who he was, what his family was like. I thought about his mother again.

"What did you mean when you said your mother senses me? You make her sound like a hound dog or something."

"If we go through here," he said, ignoring me and indicating the space between the mayor's house and the one on his right, "we'll cut around and come out just behind your house."

"Is this all you do all day with your spare time, explore the grounds around everyone's home?"

"No. I'm also working on a book of poetry entitled *The Eyes Behind the Eyes*."

"What's that about?"

He nodded at the path. "Shall we?"

"Okay, okay, I'll go. I'm sure you know your way around safely."

He laughed and reached for my hand.

"Well?" I asked. "What's your book of poems about?"

"I think we all have a second set of eyes that we don't realize exists. Not even doctors know. Some psychiatrists might, but I haven't seen anything written about them."

"I still don't understand."

"Well, with the eyes we know we have, we see what everyone sees generally. The same colors, shapes, events. But with the eyes behind the eyes, we see beyond, we see deeper, we see what's really there. That's why sometimes, when someone smiles at you, you don't trust the smile. You don't realize it, but your eyes behind your eyes see through the smile and know it's not true. Some people have those eyes wide open, and some haven't opened them at all yet. Mine are wide open."

"That's pretty deep," I said. "What makes you so deep?"

He paused to show me that I had asked a good question. For a long moment, he just stood there thinking.

"I'm not sure if it's a gift or a curse," he began, "but you might say it was forced on me almost the way anything you inherit is forced on you. People always say they can't choose their relatives. It's supposed to be a joke, but it's true. They can't. They're born into that clan or whatever. You're born with so much you can't change. Oh, there's plastic surgery for the superficial stuff, but you are who you are. That's what I believe. If you try to change that, you run into some serious trouble."

"I don't know anyone my age or even a little older, even a lot older, who talks like you do," I said.

He shrugged. "As I said, a curse or a blessing. Not sure."

We continued walking.

"I think it's a blessing," I said. He shrugged.

"So, why did you come home so early from your hot date?" he asked. When I didn't answer, he paused again and looked at me.

"Let's just say there was an attempt to change who I am and leave it at that."

He laughed. We continued walking and reached a point where we were on the path we had taken from my house to the stream. I looked back toward it.

"Still can't forgive me for leaving you?"

How could he see what my thoughts were, my expression, in this darkness?

"I was quite surprised and, to be honest, a little shocked and disappointed. Maybe a lot disappointed."

"Sorry," he said. "It couldn't be helped." He sounded very sincere and very sad.

"It's all right. I got over it, but . . ."

"But?"

"I didn't get over my dream."

"Which was?"

"That you kissed me. You didn't sneak a kiss when I was asleep, did you?"

"No, but I had the same dream," he said. "Probably at the same time." He stepped closer.

Over my shoulder, the moon slipped between two soft gray-blue clouds and washed his face in a silvery light that made his eyes dazzling. He hesitated just as he had that first day when he had reached for my hand. I could see the desire but also the fear. It wasn't like the fear of a boy who was unsure if the girl he was about to kiss would reject him and embarrass him. It was a different sort of fear, the fear of someone who thought he might fail and, as silly as it sounds, miss my lips with his. To help him overcome the hesitation, I moved forward, too, and we did kiss.

It was the kiss in my dream, the same kiss that felt as if his lips had settled on mine and formed themselves

perfectly to fit my mouth. I could feel that same excitement flow into me, softening me but causing me to want
more from his kiss. My hands went to his shoulders,
my arms tightening so that he wouldn't step away. And
when he did, I pulled him back.

"Amber," he whispered. "Wait."

Wait? I thought. *That's what Prudence Perfect would
do, would want, and might even say, but not me, not now.*
I stepped toward him and drew his lips back to mine,
eager to feel him slip his kiss from my lips and to my
neck. I moaned and turned my body even more into his.
He embraced me and held me close. I wanted him to feel
the thump of my heart, the warmth of my breath on his
neck. He stroked my hair, and then he suddenly stopped,
shook his head, and turned.

Without another word, he started away.

"Brayden, what's wrong?" I called.

"I've got to go," he said, not looking back. He looked
down like someone who was ashamed. "You'd better go
home."

Before I could reply, he disappeared into the shadows.

I stood there, confused and disappointed. Before I
could take another step, I had to calm myself and feel
the passion in me reluctantly retreat to that corner of my
heart where it had been resting and waiting to be nudged
into action, demanding that every part of me come alive
as it had never come alive. The woman who waited to be
born inside me moaned in despair and frustration.

I followed him into the darkness, walking softly,
listening for his footsteps, hoping that he had decided to
turn back and come to me in the shadows, but he didn't.

I stepped into my backyard and gazed up at the lighted attic in his house. I didn't see him or his mother, but for a few long moments, I stood there, anticipating him looking out and down at me. Instead, the lights suddenly went off, and the entire house fell into darkness, silhouetted by the moonlight like something his mother might have painted with only black and gray swallowed in the silvery glow. A lone crow settled on the roof and sat as if it were on a great nest waiting for something as dark and eerie as itself to be born.

I walked around to the front of my house. The television wasn't on, but my parents were surely waiting up to see how my date with Shayne had gone. They would both be reading and waiting. I was so confused about the night's events that I was afraid to enter the house. What would I tell them? That I'd had a disappointing date but met our new neighbor and gone for a romantic walk? The stunned looks on their faces would only add to my own bewilderment.

I sucked in my breath and walked into the house.

"I thought I heard a car pull in a while ago," Dad said when I stepped into the living room. Mom turned to anticipate my answer, too. "We thought we heard it leave earlier. Where have you been?"

There was no lying about it, I thought. "I did arrive earlier, but I went for a walk with Brayden," I said.

"Who?" Dad asked.

"The boy next door," Mom said, smirking at him.

"Oh, right. But . . . I'm confused. Didn't you go out with Shayne Allan?"

"I did. We went to dinner."

"In Greenwood," Mom said, nodding. "So, what about that?"

"It was all right. Nothing special. He wanted to take me to a house party afterward, but I didn't want to go. I'm afraid he doesn't take rejection well."

They stared at me almost expressionless.

"You must have heard about Charlotte's party."

"Yes, we heard late in the day," Dad said. "You didn't say anything, but we weren't worried about you being involved in any of that."

"I could have been," I said. "You can get blamed sometimes by just being there."

"She's right, Gregory," Mom said, narrowing her eyes suspiciously. "Why did you go on a walk with the new neighbor when Shayne brought you home?"

"Brayden was out there, and I thought a walk would do me some good."

"Nature boy," Dad said. "When am I going to meet this descendant of Thoreau?"

"I'll try to get him to come to the store tomorrow, maybe."

Mom shook her head. "But you sounded like you had a very good time on the lake with Shayne today when I spoke to you earlier," she said. "Didn't you?"

"I did."

"So?"

"It's complicated," I said.

Dad turned to Mom. "It's complicated? Please translate again."

"I think she needs to digest it all herself because it's all happening fast. Girls are . . ."

"Complicated," Dad said, nodding.

Mom winked at me to let me know it was all right not to keep explaining, but I knew she was planning to talk to me a lot more about it all.

"Were you busy?" I asked, hoping they would say very and ask me to come in tomorrow, even though we had Mrs. Williams.

"We were fine," Mom said. "Don't worry. Enjoy your weekend."

"Okay. I'm going up."

"I guess you're tired," Dad said. "Two young men in one night."

"Gregory Morton Taylor . . ." Mom said, accompanying it with her big eyes.

"Just joking," Dad said, and shrank in his chair to return to his book.

I hurried up the stairs. Dad was joking. He meant no harm, but it wasn't funny to me. I felt as if I had fallen into a whirlpool of conflicting emotions, twisting and turning me every which way. A part of me was asking what I had done. Why had I suddenly been so unpleasant, so tough on Shayne? After all, what should a boy, any boy, whether he had Shayne Allan's good looks and intelligence, athletic abilities, and wealth or not, want to do with a girl he found attractive and interesting? What's wrong with him wanting to make love, have fun, enjoy the relationship? Why was my Prudence Perfect so stern and negative when it came to him but suddenly ready to surrender and take a chance with a boy who had the emotional and psychological baggage of Brayden Matthews? Was I looking to be unhappy, to wallow in sadness and misery?

Or was it that constant, plaguing question? Was I simply too frightened to be with a boy like Shayne Allan, too afraid of where it would lead? Did I feel more comfortable with Brayden because I believed it would lead nowhere? Look at how he had fled from me when our passion had just become emboldened.

Was what I wanted out of a boy, any boy, unreasonable at this age, this strong, extra feeling as close to everlasting love as could be? Why should I expect Shayne Allan to be as serious as I was? It was almost as if I was holding his good looks and accomplishments against him. After all, I did enjoy being with him during the day. I was excited about the boat, the house, all that he was able to offer. It was fun. What was wrong with just having fun? Besides, I knew that if I became his steady girlfriend, every girl in the school would be envious, and I would suddenly be the most popular girl in the school. Why wasn't that enough? Why wasn't that important enough to me? What made me so different?

Brayden seemed to be as serious as I was, maybe even more serious and more concerned. But did being around someone like him do me more harm than good?

What if I had never met Brayden, never heard his words resonating in my head, not seen his face almost everywhere I looked and felt him near me? Would I have been as cold to Shayne's advances? Would I have been able to have more fun, to relax and let go of Prudence Perfect? I almost resented Brayden moving in next door now. Maybe I should have ignored him that day when he was peering through the hedges. Who his age does something like that anyway, and besides, where was this

going? Yes, his kiss thrilled me, and yes, I enjoyed walking and talking with him, but where else would we go?
Wouldn't everyone, even my own parents, think I was a
fool to choose someone like Brayden over someone like
Shayne, especially if after the summer Brayden and his
parents were gone? What then?

I could confide in my mother. We were close, yes,
like sisters, but we weren't sisters, and no matter what
her experiences were when she was my age, they were
her experiences, and they had occurred at a different
time, a time when girls my age were living in a world
without the same sort of pressures and values, or lack of
them, as girls were facing today. No matter how sympathetic my mother was, how understanding, and no
matter what similar examples she described, they weren't
going to be exactly like mine, nor would they resemble
the experiences other girls my age were having now. I
couldn't imagine her having met a boy like Brayden, for
example.

What I wished I had now was a truly close friend, a
real best friend, someone who didn't drink out of the cup
of envy, someone who cared about me enough to think
only of me and not herself in my shoes. Or wouldn't it be
great to have a slightly older sister, I thought, someone
who shared a room, who went to sleep in the next bed,
and who would talk all night, listen and talk, until we
were both too tired to breathe another syllable? How
lucky the girls in my class were to have someone like
that.

All of these thoughts, these questions, wracked my
brain. I sat, staring at myself in the vanity mirror and

growing so dizzy that I had to close my eyes and take deep breaths. For a few moments, I sat with my arms folded under my breasts and rocking myself. Suddenly, I heard a gentle knock on my bedroom door and looked up to see Mom.

"You all right?" she asked softly, closing the door behind her.

I nodded and then shook my head.

"Oh, Amber, darling, what is it?" she asked, moving quickly to my side to embrace me.

I rested my head against her shoulder just as I always did when I was a little girl. "I'm just very confused."

"Boys can do that," she said, wiping strands of my hair off my forehead. "What really happened with Shayne Allan?"

I sat up and took a deep breath. "We did have a good time at the lake. He was very nice and I thought that I had been wrong to be so critical of him. I thought that his family made him act arrogantly, and I really believed that he was trying not to be, at least with me."

"So? That sounds very promising."

"But he was different tonight. He was more like the Shayne Allan I knew from afar, and I guess I didn't want to be just another . . ."

"Another conquest?" she said.

"Yes."

"I'm proud of you," she said, and kissed me. "Don't agonize over it. You have wonderful instincts." She rose.

"Maybe I don't, Mom. How do you know I do?"

"I know," she said. Was she talking herself into it? I didn't have her confidence.

She paused at the doorway and tilted her head. "What I don't understand is this boy next door. You've met him a few times and seem to like him but haven't brought him around. I know I should go over there to welcome his mother and father to the neighborhood . . ."

"She's a recluse. She has things delivered to the house. I saw her in the doorway accepting groceries, but she wouldn't even acknowledge me when I waved."

"Well, you have to feel sorry for her, then. She surely has no friends here yet. First chance I get tomorrow, I'll knock on their door anyway and make an effort. I've mentioned them to a few people, but no one seems to know anything at all about them. The real estate agent, Beverly Bell, told me all she knows is that the house is owned by someone named Marcus Norton from Portland. He owns considerable real estate in Oregon and never put the house up for sale. There's no indication that this family is buying it, either."

"No, just renting to see if they like it here. I told you."

"Yes, but . . . well, maybe when I get to meet Brayden or his parents, I'll have a better feeling about them. You haven't met his father, either, then?"

"No. Brayden says his father's still away."

"Okay. Bring him around the store tomorrow, and don't give what happened tonight with Shayne a second thought."

I knew she was right, but I also knew that I wasn't going to stop myself from having a second and third thought. I prepared quickly for bed and crawled under my blanket, wrapping it around me tightly and pressing my face against the pillow, hoping to rush myself into sleep.

I did fall asleep sooner than I had expected, but my eyes snapped open a little after four in the morning. For a moment, I lay there a little dazed, and then I turned and saw the glow of light spilling from Brayden's bedroom window. I rose slowly and peered between my closed curtains. It was the first time I had seen his bedroom so bright, even though the shade on the window was drawn down completely. I stood for a while wondering what had gotten him up so late. Was something wrong with his mother? Everything else about the house was quiet and dark.

I waited and watched for as long as I could, but, growing tired again, I retreated to my bed. I didn't fall asleep until the light spilling from his bedroom had been shut off. It was the first thing I thought of when I awoke in the morning. I had overslept again and knew that my parents were already gone. I dressed and hurried downstairs. I thought I would have a little breakfast, and then I was determined to go to Brayden's house and knock on the front door.

But when I opened mine to step out, he was standing there as if he knew I was coming.

11

Portrait

"Brayden, what's wrong?" I asked immediately after he raised his head. The expression on his face told me that something wasn't right. "I was just coming over to see you and . . ."

"It's my mother," he said. "She had a bit of a nervous breakdown last night. My father had made arrangements for her to check herself into a clinic not far from here, and she has done so. I'll be gone for a little while."

"Oh, I'm so sorry. Is there anything I can do?"

"No, but thanks for asking. I'll be around as soon as I can."

"Has this happened before? I mean . . ."

"Yes, but it usually works out all right. She'll be fine. A few days, maybe a week," he said. "The doctors reconsider her medications, stuff like that."

"Your mother can just check herself in like that? I mean, she wanted to do that?"

"Yes. She knows when she's in greater trouble."

"Is your father coming home?"

"He's already at the clinic, but I think he'll return to

his work from there. He's working in Los Angeles, so he could get to her easily today."

"Shouldn't he stay with her until she's cured?"

"Amber, I'm afraid my mother will never be cured. She'll get a little better, well enough to cope, but . . ."

"Why not?" I asked, stepping out and closing the door behind me. "I don't understand. Does she have a fatal disease?"

"We all have a fatal disease," he said.

"But her condition is mental, right?"

"Yes, but mental problems affect you physically, too."

"Well, where is this clinic? I don't know of anything like that in Echo Lake."

"No," he said, smiling. "It's not in Echo Lake. It's closer to Portland. Okay. I've got a few things to do in the house, get some things for my mother, and then I'm off."

"What do you do there? You can't stay with her, can you?"

"I can stay close to her. That's what's important now."

He turned to leave. I had the feeling that I would never see him again. Impulsively, I followed him and reached for him. He turned slowly, and I thought his eyes had changed color, looking suddenly more gray in the sunlight.

"Are you really coming back?" I asked.

He smiled. "I'll be back. I promise," he said. He leaned forward to kiss me softly on the cheek and then turned and walked very quickly toward his house. I watched him go all the way this time. He sensed it and waved from his porch before entering the house. For a few moments, I stood there staring at the closed door. Then I turned and went back inside.

I wasn't sure what I was going to do with myself. I thought about going to the store and working, even though they had enough help, but I knew that would disappoint my mother. I had been hoping to spend most of the day with Brayden, getting to know him more and maybe getting him to do some fun things with me. I actually had a day designed. I thought we'd go for a drive so I could show him some of the more beautiful places in our immediate area. I anticipated us having lunch somewhere, and afterward, I'd invite him to my house, ostensibly to do more talking but maybe to do more than just talk. In my mind, a day like this could go far to solidify a relationship between us. If that happened, I had all sorts of suggestions for other things we might do and had even thought that I might be of some assistance to him in helping his mother come out of her shell.

Once these first steps were taken successfully, I expected that I would find a way to introduce my parents to him and his mother, and that might even go further to help her. If we had some success, I thought it would ensure his family's staying in Echo Lake. I imagined what it was going to be like to introduce him to our school, to the students I thought he might like. I foresaw the envy in my girlfriends' eyes, and in my mind, I luxuriated and basked in the jealousy and rage I would see in Shayne's. My senior year of high school would turn out to be the best school year of my life. Brayden and I would become that "thing" Ellie had predicted Shayne and I would be.

We would spend every weekend night together and study together, either at his house in his room or in mine. We'd be invited to all of the parties, because whoever had one would want us to be there. Everyone would see how special we were. Almost every other student in our class would want to be friends with us, hang with us at lunch, and be interested in what our plans were for the weekend. I pictured many of them listening keenly to anything Brayden said because he was so special and intelligent. Naturally, every girl in my class would flirt with him, but they would clearly see how futile it was because he was too devoted to me.

I hesitated to think of love. Despite how attracted I was to him and how much I hoped he was attracted to me, for me, love still seemed to be something beyond our teenage years, an emotion that needed maturity. Yes, we could have sex. We could express just how much we were attracted to each other. We could even cling to each other with far more passion than older couples evinced, but that final leap, that final step that in essence declared that we wanted to spend all our lives together, remained something reserved for that time in our lives when we would be truly independent, when every decision we made would be made ourselves for ourselves, and we would either enjoy or suffer the consequences without having the safety net that our parents provided.

Was all of this simply a daydream, a fantasy? Maybe none of this was in Brayden's thinking. Perhaps to him, I was just a pleasant way of passing some time. Maybe even if he did end up staying, none of what I imagined would take place anyway. He could be attracted to a different girl. After all, there were other attractive girls in school. Just because I was the first to meet him and we had kissed didn't guarantee any of it.

And besides, I thought, didn't he just tell me that his mother would never be cured? What sort of a high school life could he have? Look at the way he had to live now. Parties, dates, trips, all of that seemed impossible for him. How could I have designed such a happy scenario? There I was again, living in my own movie. From the first time I had set eyes on him, I had pictured us on some big screen, acting out our developing relationship. I was still doing it.

Get real, Amber, I told myself, and sulked about it for a while.

Suddenly, I wondered why I hadn't volunteered to go with him to the clinic, at least for the day. I could even have taken him in my car, and he could have called me when he wanted to return. I had the whole day off. Why didn't I show him that I wasn't selfish and immature? Surely he would have appreciated the company, even if I'd spent the whole time waiting for him in some lounge. I could have met his father, too. I hadn't even thought of it. Maybe that was why he had come over in the first place. He had hoped I would suggest it. He certainly couldn't invite me to join him on such a sad trip.

Sure. That was it. *How stupid of me,* I thought, and quickly got up and hurried out the front door, down the driveway, and around to his house. I knocked on the door and waited. I heard nothing, so I knocked again. Had he left right away? Didn't he say he had things to do in the house? I hadn't seen any car in his driveway when I first stepped out and watched him go back to his house after we had spoken. He must have called a taxi, or maybe he was still waiting for it to arrive. But why wouldn't he answer my knocking on the front door? I knocked a third time and then tried the door handle. To my surprise, the door opened. It hadn't been locked. He was surely still inside, then, I thought, and called for him. I waited and listened but heard nothing. I called again. Still, silence was all that answered.

I started to turn around to leave, but stopped. Although it was morning and there was a partly sunny sky, the house was so dark inside. When I stepped to my left and gazed into the living room, I saw that the curtains were drawn closed. To my right, the same was true for the dining room. Its window curtains were shut. There wasn't a light on anywhere. Because some light seeped in around the curtains and shades, it was a hazy sort of darkness, almost like a fog.

I looked at the straight stairway. It seemed to lead up to a wall of even thicker darkness. Why didn't they want the sunshine in their home? Was this part of his mother's illness, this clinging to shadows and avoiding bright days? She must be in some deep depression. Maybe the life they led had finally had an effect on her.

Even though Brayden and his mother had been living there for a while, the house felt empty and still uninhabited. There wasn't an unpleasant odor, but it smelled to me like a house that still harbored a damp, dank scent. It was as if no one had cooked or baked anything in it for years. There were no aromas associated with polish or any cleaning fluid, either. I detected only the smell of the wood and the old carpet, an odor you would smell in a very old, deserted house.

When I looked at the furniture more closely, I thought that everything appeared to have been there for years. Nothing new had been bought for the house. What they had brought looked insufficient, too. The dining-room table was too small for the room, and the same was true for the sofa and chairs in the living room. It looked more like furniture from a small apartment. I wondered if it really was their furniture or furniture that they had rented for the time being.

Everywhere I looked, I saw boxes not yet unpacked. Many had books in them. Nothing had been put on the shelves in the armoire in the dining room, and nothing was on the shelves in the living room. There were no pictures on the walls in either room and no newspapers or magazines in the living room. When did they plan on doing the rest of the unpacking? What had Brayden and his mother been doing in there these past days?

I wandered into the kitchen and saw dishes and pots and pans still in boxes. There were only a few plates and glasses on the counter, along with a single dish towel. There were a few pieces of silverware in the sink and a single coffee cup. I opened the refrigerator and saw that there wasn't very much in there. Now that I thought back, the box of groceries I had seen delivered wasn't that large when you considered that there were two people to be fed. The cabinets were the same, barely stocked.

More curious than ever, I decided that I had to go upstairs. First, I called for Brayden again, just in case he had been in the bathroom or in his room and hadn't heard me knock or enter. There was still only silence. I began to ascend very slowly, listening keenly for any sound. I did feel terribly guilty about entering the Mat-thewses' house when no one was there and snooping like this, but my curiosity was just too strong. It was like a magnet drawing me up those creaking stairs.

I paused at the top and turned to what I knew had to be Brayden's bedroom. Without any lights, the shade drawn closed on the only hallway window, and all of the doors closed, it was as dark as night. Nevertheless, I went forward and paused at Brayden's bedroom door. I knocked.

"Brayden? Are you in there? I've been calling."

I waited but heard nothing except the sound of what I thought to be a stronger breeze crossing the roof of the house and sliding along the windows and rain gutters. It sounded like some giant blowing out his birthday candles. After a moment more, I opened the door of Brayden's bedroom. His shade was drawn down, but there was enough light leaking in around it to give me a view of the room. I stepped in and slid my hand up the right side of the wall, looking for a light switch. There was none there, nor was there one on the left side. I realized that there was no ceiling fixture in the room. Any illumination would have to come from the two lamps on the night tables beside the double bed, which was neatly made, the pillows looking untouched. I stared at it for a moment, then reached under the lampshade of the closest lamp and turned it on.

I saw that he had a matching dresser and a computer desk. Unlike the furniture downstairs, his furniture looked too large for the size of his room, but what impressed me the most about his room was how neat and organized it was. Over on a computer desk was a closed laptop. Next to it was a pad with a pen beside it. I could see that there was nothing written on the pad. On the wall above it were some achievement awards, each from a different school. To the right of the table were three wall shelves all filled with books. I went around the bed, saw a pair of slippers on the floor, and turned on the lamp on that side, too. Now that the room was better lit, I could see that unlike the rooms downstairs, it looked cleaned and polished. Nothing had been left packed. I stepped up to the bookshelves and perused the titles.

There were books on philosophy, economics, and history, and many classic novels and plays. He wasn't exaggerating about his reading habits and accomplishments, I thought. My eyes went to the dresser. Finally, there was a picture in this house. I looked at it closely. It was a picture of Brayden when he was much younger, maybe ten or eleven. He was standing with two people I assumed were his parents. His mother was a very attractive woman and not anywhere as thin as she was now. She had a beautiful figure, shoulder-length dark hair, and a soft smile that radiated her beauty and intelligence. His father looked much like the man I had glimpsed that first day. He wasn't even smiling. I saw that Brayden held only his mother's hand. His father looked impatient, probably wishing that the photographer would speed up.

I recognized the background. They were in Rome at the foot of what was known as the Spanish Steps. I put the picture frame down and looked at the windows that had their shades down. I wanted to peek out and see what the view of my bedroom window was like from his. I had left my curtains open, and despite the difference in the height between our two houses, there was a good view of most of my room. I tried to imagine Brayden watching me at night. Then I turned and looked at the rest of his room. The closet door was slightly open, so I peered in at his clothes. They were all hung neatly and organized. I remembered what he had told me about that military-style shirt he always wore, how he had many of the same one, but I didn't see any hanging in his closet.

It was terribly snoopy of me, I know, but I looked into his dresser drawers, too. Everything was folded neatly in them, but again, I didn't see another military-style shirt.

I looked into his closet again and saw a box on the floor next to where his shoes were. All of his shoes looked polished, his sneakers clean. I knelt down and lifted the top of the box and saw all sorts of mementos from places he and his family had gone. There were postcards, brochures, and some maps. I found an album in which there were many pictures of their trips. Turning the pages was like reviewing his aging from an infant to a teenager. It was that well organized. Most of the backgrounds were recognizably famous world sites, such as the Eiffel Tower in Paris, Trafalgar Square in London, and the Vatican in Rome. I put it all back the way I had found it, turned off the lamps, and left his bedroom. I was going to leave the house but decided instead to look in on what was surely his parents' bedroom, the bigger one.

The furniture there looked more as if it belonged. Nothing was too small or too large for the space. There was a king-size dark maple bed with matching night tables and two dressers. I imagined that one was for his father, one for his mother. If it was anything like the dressers for my parents, his mother's was the larger one.

Dad was always complaining about how little space he had in his own house.

What struck me immediately about his parents' room, however, was the lack of any pictures of them. There was no wedding picture, no picture of them at any party or even on any trip. Instead, there were at least a dozen pictures of Brayden. They were everywhere possible, two on the walls, four on the top of each dresser, and two on the night tables. I knew that most parents who had only one child doted on that child, but this looked over the top to me. I couldn't imagine him not being embarrassed if anyone looked in and saw how he was almost idolized.

I thought that I would leave quickly now, but when I stepped out of the master bedroom, I looked at the short stairway that must lead up to the attic, his mother's art studio. Did I dare? He had said that the clinic she had gone to was closer to Portland. He couldn't go there and be back this soon. He was probably not even there yet. I could safely sneak a look at her work, I thought, and headed for the attic stairway.

This was the darkest part of the house. There weren't many steps to the stairway, but I could barely see them. When I reached the door, I took a deep breath and opened it. The window shades had been drawn closed up there, too, but again, there was enough light leaking in around them to help me navigate into the attic. Here there was a ceiling light fixture. I found the switch and turned it on. The illumination seemed to cascade down over the easel upon which was the most shocking painting I had ever seen, shocking because it was clearly a portrait of Brayden, but everything about him was distorted. It was as if she meant to depict his face on a raindrop. The shape of it was elongated in places and widened in others. His eyes looked as if they were spilling out of their sockets and running down his cheeks. His cheeks were porous, the skin looking magnified so that each and every pore was clearly seen. His nose was shaped strangely so that it seemed to be riding on a wave, and his mouth, wide open, was cavernous and dark like the inside of a pipe. She had done the head, but the neck was still in a drawing stage, and it, too, looked like liquid, spilling out from under his chin and jawbone.

I actually gasped and stepped back.

Why would his mother create such a distorted, horrible picture of him?

Was this evidence of her mental problems? Was this what he meant when he'd said she'd changed her style lately?

It looked nothing like the artwork credited to her on the Internet. How could Brayden watch her paint such a version of him and not complain? Was he afraid that it would make her worse if he did? Could he possibly tell her it looked good? This picture belonged in someone's nightmare and not in any frame on any wall in any house, much less theirs.

I glanced at the paintings covered with a gray sheet on the floor. Did I want to lift that sheet and see any more of her grotesque work, the babbling of a disturbed mind? *No, thank you,* I thought. The portrait of Brayden was enough to guarantee a nice nightmare that night. I practically fled the attic. I was halfway down the stairs when I realized that I hadn't turned off the light. Reluctantly, I turned around and hurried back up. I reached for the light switch but stopped.

Was my mind playing tricks on me?

The bizarre portrait of Brayden looked different. The right eye looked as if it had poured farther down the right cheek. I stood there staring at it and then, as quickly as I could, switched off the light and left the attic, this time making sure to close the door. I left the house as if I were being pursued and ran back to mine. Once I was inside, I felt silly. There was no one chasing me. Why was I running?

I went to the kitchen to get a glass of water and then returned to the living room and looked out toward Brayden's house. I would not tell him what I had done. He might get very upset. I wouldn't tell my parents, either. First, they would be angry that I had entered and explored someone else's home like that, and second, once they heard what I had discovered in the attic, they would surely want me to stay away from Brayden and the Matthewses.

I sat thinking. What had come over me? I would not like it very much if someone had done what I had done and gone through my things the way I had gone through Brayden's. I never did anything like this. I tried rationalizing away my guilt by telling myself that I never would have done it if he wasn't so damn secretive. And anyway, I'd had good intentions. I had gone over there to volunteer to go with him. *Stop beating on yourself,* I told myself. The best thing to do was to try to forget it. I decided that I would go into town and stop at the store after all. The truth was, after what I had seen, I wanted to be around my family.

I started on my walk, looking back twice because I felt as if I were being followed. When my gaze went to Brayden's house, I saw that a window shade in his parents' bedroom was up. I hadn't done that, and I was almost positive that all of the shades had been drawn, the curtains closed. I stared at it for a moment and then continued walking, only much faster. I was halfway to the store when Charlotte and Ellie pulled up to the curb. I was almost glad to see them, as silly as I knew they could be.

"Well, her walk hasn't changed," Charlotte told Ellie.

"I don't know. Don't you think she leans back a little more than usual?"

The two laughed.

"All right, Laurel and Hardy, what's this about now?"

"Laurel and Hardy?" Ellie said.

"They were a big comedy team in the movies once."

"When? I've watched television since I was old enough to sit by myself," Charlotte said. "And I never heard of them."

"Right after the Treaty of Ghent."

"What?"

"Forget Laurel and Hardy. What's the joke?" I looked at Ellie. She had that self-satisfied grin embedded in her face, the one that I knew usually accompanied juicy gossip.

"Cell phones are buzzing thanks to Wendi Allan."

"About what?"

"About walking in on you and Shayne in the guest

room in their house at the lake yesterday. Did you know he makes notches in his jockstrap?" Charlotte laughed. "You're a notch in a jockstrap."

I felt the flush come into my face. "She's lying," I said. "That didn't happen. I just used the guest room to change and . . ."

"I heard he's already confirmed it," Charlotte added. She looked at Ellie. "Tell her."

"Tell me what?"

"He told Bobby, who told me this morning."

"He's lying, too. He's just angry because I wouldn't go to a house party with him last night."

"You'll need a letter from a gynecologist," Charlotte said. "You can carry it in your purse and flash it whenever anyone says you're no longer a virgin."

"Frankly, my dear, I don't give a damn," I said.

"Huh?"

"She's just quoting some old movie," Ellie said.

"*Gone With the Wind. Gone With the Wind.* That's not just some old movie," I said, and imagined my father standing beside me and smiling. "I don't care what Shayne and his evil brat sister tell people. They're both lying."

"You know what he'll do next, don't you? He'll claim you were a disaster in bed, and that was why he left you. He did that to Donna Parks, remember?" Charlotte asked Ellie, who nodded. "You'd better come up with some good stories about him."

"No one would believe her," Ellie said quickly. "Not about Shayne. So, what really happened? Were you a perfect Prudence Perfect or what?"

"Well, let's see," I said, putting my hand on my hip and pretending to recall. "I tried to talk to him, but he could only hear his own voice. I tried to kiss him, but he had his lips pressed to a mirror. I reached for his hand, but he was holding his own, and when he realized I had been with him for more than an hour, I had to remind him who I was. Otherwise, it was a Prudence Perfect date."

"Sour grapes," Charlotte quipped, but Ellie just stared at me.

"C'mon. What really happened, Amber?" she asked. "Why did you mess up your date with Shayne? You decided you'd rather be with your new neighbor? Is that it?" She turned to Charlotte. "She was planning on seeing them both."

"Both? I want to see this new neighbor. He compares with Shayne? Maybe I should have another party."

"After all that happened, your parents would let you?" I asked, astounded.

She laughed. "They'll go away again."

"Right. Easy come, easy go. Which reminds me. I have to go to the store. Please do your best to defend my honor," I told them. "I'd do it for you two, especially you, Charlotte, although I think you'd want it the opposite way, right? You'd want to be that notch in a jockstrap. Almost any one," I added, and walked away. I could feel the shock on their faces splashing against my back.

I swear, I felt as if Brayden were walking right beside me and smiling.

12

Shadows

My mother was surprised to see me, but if she was upset about it, she didn't show it, not that she would have when we were in the store.

"Guess who came in for a new bracelet this morning?" she told me. "Shayne's mother."

"Right," Dad called to me from behind his worktable in the rear. "I figure if you go out with ten different boys this year, I'll sell ten different bracelets."

"Stop it, Gregory. Where are you going, honey?" she asked. I realized that her smile indicated that she was anticipating that I had something planned to do with friends.

"Nowhere special," I said. "I just decided to take a walk to town and stop by."

Mrs. Williams was with a customer on the other end of the store in front of the ring display, but I could see that she was listening to our conversation, too. Maybe she was afraid I would return to work on the weekends and she would lose her part-time position. Mom's eyes darkened. There was no sense even trying to hide my unhappiness from her. I glanced at Mrs. Williams again, and then I turned and walked a little farther away. Mom followed.

"What's wrong?" she asked.

"Brayden's mother took ill."

"Ill? Is she in the hospital?"

"No. It's more of a nervous breakdown, I think. She checked herself into a clinic. Brayden's father apparently had set something up in the event of something like this happening."

"Clinic? What clinic?"

"I don't know the name of it. Just some place closer to Portland. He looked so sad and overwhelmed when he came over this morning to tell me. I felt so sorry for him, just having moved here and all. I'm sure I'm the only one he knows, especially with his mother being the way she is."

"Well, maybe now you can invite him to our house to dinner. He can eat with us every night if he wants until his mother can come home."

"No, he came over to tell me he would be gone for a while."

"Oh. You mean he'll be with his father?"

"He just said he had to stay close to his mother. Maybe there's a place for relatives at the clinic or something nearby, or maybe his father set something up in a motel for him. He didn't say, exactly. He just said he had to be with her, near her."

She nodded. "Well, he sounds like a very devoted and mature young man. I look forward to meeting him as soon as he and his mother do return. I am sorry we have ignored them until now. Not very neighborly of us and not like us."

Seeing how sympathetic my mother was, I was tempted to tell her what I had done, how I had gone into Brayden's house and gone through it and up to the attic, and what I had seen. I wanted her to understand how seriously ill Brayden's mother really was. I was thinking now that she would be even more sympathetic, and, contrary to what I had feared, she would not be upset about my seeing him.

"We'll talk about it later," she said as two more customers entered the store before I could say anything about what I had done. I started to go to help her, but she waved me off. "You've still got the rest of your weekend to enjoy, Amber. Go on," she said firmly. "We're doing fine."

I looked at Mrs. Williams, who had finished with her customer and, with a much more comfortable expression on her face, was moving to help Mom. I nodded at her and left the store. Our village was busy. The traffic was much heavier than usual, and the bells on the shop doors were ringing so much it sounded as if Christmas had come in July. I suppose with the added business, other store owners, like us, felt it was like Christmas.

For a few moments, I stood on the sidewalk looking in both directions. Now that my short, bittersweet romance with Shayne Allan was over almost before it had begun, and Brayden was gone for I didn't know how long, and I wasn't working with my parents, it occurred to me how much of a loner I had become. My choices looked so limited. I could repress my intelligence and wallow through the day with Ellie and Charlotte and other girls like them, doing inane things and swimming in the gossip that would most assuredly center on my aborted relationship with Shayne, or I could take a ride myself, maybe go to the mall and look at some new things for myself. But shopping alone was never satisfying for me. I thought about calling someone, but then I thought that it was just the wrong time to seek out classmates to do anything. I was confident that there would be quite a few girls who would go somewhere with me, but it would be primarily to pick up some erotic, smutty little detail they could exploit.

Feeling defeated, I started for home.

When I reached Mrs. Carden's house, however, I smiled to myself, recalling how Brayden had characterized her as interesting because of the way she spoke to her clothing, her "errant children." Many of the things he had said to me rolled through my mind. Right now, I wondered if maybe he wasn't better off than I was when he was made to travel and hop from one school to another. If he didn't make any satisfactory relationships in one place, he probably just shrugged and looked forward to another. Maybe it never bothered him to feel like a loner, and that was why he wasn't so enthusiastic now about getting to know more people our age in Echo Lake. Was that sort of independence good or bad? Surely there was a point where you needed close friends. You had to feel you belonged to something, somewhere.

When I reached his house, I paused and looked up at the bedroom window that had had a shade raised when I left for town. I stared up at it, surprised. It wasn't raised now. Had I seen that because I was closer when I was looking up at it? When I had seen it before, had it been only an illusion caused by reflecting sunlight? Had the sun been that high by then? I couldn't remember, but how could it have been up then and be down now? Had his mother come right back for some reason? Had her breakdown been less severe than it seemed? After seeing the portrait she was painting of Brayden, I couldn't imagine it being less severe. What should I do? Go up and knock on the door again? Open it and call for him if no one responded? I certainly didn't want to go exploring for myself again, not in there.

In fact, every time I looked at Brayden's house, something about it seemed different, whether it was the way the shadows played on the windows and the walls or the way birds, except for an occasional black crow, seemed to stay away from it, even away from the trees and the yard. Looking at it now, I could understand why Brayden wasn't happy about staying there by himself. Even with the condition his mother was in, she was company, and of course, she was family. I couldn't imagine what it would be like to go through many days without either of my parents right now. Why was his father's work so important to him, so important that it took precedence over his own family in what might be their greatest time of need?

Sometimes, even with the silly little things I witnessed between my classmates and their parents, I felt that I lived on an island. There was so much that separated me from other girls my age, and boys, too. For some, my devotion to my parents wasn't only not cool, it was bizarre. If anything, they accused me of being the immature one. I should be more self-centered, less responsible, and more daring. Who went through all these years without ever having seriously annoyed or disappointed his or her parents? It was as if because of that, I couldn't be trusted. There were many times, like now, when I seriously wondered if I was too much of a goody-goody, if I enjoyed being Prudence Perfect after all.

I paused in front of Brayden's house and continued to debate what I should do. I did feel silly being frightened of a house. *At least go up and knock on the door, Amber,* I told myself. Otherwise, I would seem indifferent. I approached the house slowly, hoping that if they were really back, Brayden would see me and just come out, but the door didn't open. I stepped up to it and knocked. I waited and then knocked harder. There was no sound within. I looked at the handle. *Don't do it again,* I told myself. No one was home. He would surely have come to the door. Convinced that he wasn't there, I turned and walked off his front porch and hurried up to my house, as if the horrid vision of that portrait in the attic was pursuing me.

After I had been home for a while, I began to receive some phone calls from other girls at school who were friendlier to me than most, some of whom I had thought I might call. In every case, however, they were fishing for details about my dates with Shayne, hoping to learn more about the stories Wendi had been spreading. Only Marilyn Myers came right out and asked me if I'd had sex with him.

"Is it true?" She quickly followed with, "I really wondered if you ever would with anyone."

"When I do," I snapped back at her, "it won't be just anyone, and it certainly wouldn't be someone who puts making love to me on the same level as scoring a basket in a basketball game."

She giggled. "You sound like you did," she said, "and now regret it. Right?"

"Think what you want, Marilyn, but you're right about one thing. If I did have sex with him, I would regret it."

"No one's going to believe that."

"I don't care. Look, I'm busy doing things that have some meaning. Thanks for calling with your concern," I told her, and hung up before she could even think of a way to protest her innocence.

I wasn't really on any island, I told myself. That was another illusion I had created for myself. If I were on an island, I would be beyond the reach of all of this. Never before did I regret living in a small community as much as I did at that moment. The best thing about living in a city was that you could be anyone you wanted and anything you wanted, because you were constantly surrounded by strangers who didn't know whether you were lying or telling the truth about yourself. You could find new friends just by crossing the street.

I tried to calm myself by doing some reading, but that didn't work. I couldn't concentrate on anything I read. I was much too fidgety. I had to find something satisfying to do. Finally, I decided that I would prepare dinner for my parents and myself. I called my mother and told her I was going to the supermarket. "What would you two like?"

"Oh, Amber, this isn't why I wanted you to have free time. I don't want you to be concerned about us or the house. I want you to have fun."

"I know, but right now, this would be fun for me," I said as strongly as I could.

She was silent, and then she asked my father what he would like for dinner. I could hear him in the background.

"Amber Light is preparing it? Tell her to make what she made for my birthday."

"Did you hear that?" Mom asked.

"Yes."

"If you continue to spoil him, what am I going to do when you leave for college and after you get married?" she asked.

She was joking, of course, but maybe it was part of my problem that I couldn't see myself leaving home to go to college. Like every other junior last year, I was told I should be considering schools. Some were looking for the colleges that were farthest away. Once going to college was mentioned, it was almost expected that you would say, "I can't wait to get out of this place." I never said it. Actually, I never thought of college as a form of escape.

The only colleges I took seriously anyway were colleges in Oregon, especially Portland.

"I'll send home care packages," I told her, "instead of you sending them to me."

She laughed. "Knowing you, you probably will. Okay. You know what to do," she said.

I set out immediately for the supermarket. I would be preparing blackened salmon with chipotle squash puree and mango rice. I thought I would make some brownies, too. Dad loved them. Having this to do kept my mind busy, and for a while, I really was happy. Unfortunately, when I turned the corner of an aisle in the supermarket, I ran into Megan Thomas, who had made the word *ostentatious* hip the year before. I could wait forever for her new word, but the moment she saw me, her eyes widened, and I would soon learn it. She looked so pleased at the sight of me. It was as if she had won the lottery. She stepped away from her mother quickly and literally turned my grocery cart around so that our backs would be to her.

"Oh, I'm glad I met you. I, for one, never dreamed you would be so promiscuous," she began. "In fact, I would have bet my college fund against it. I would have said *promiscuity* wasn't anywhere near your vocabulary."

Before I could respond, she attacked me with machine-gun speed.

"Tell me. What did he do to get you between the sheets? Were you always hoping he would be the one? I bet you were. Is it true he had to get the sheets washed before the maid saw it and told his mother? Oh, was it painful making love for the first time? It was a little painful for me the first time," she added, looking back at her mother.

"I imagine it would be painful for you all the time," I said when she turned back to me.

"Huh?"

"I hate to disappoint you, but you've been abused."

"Abused? What do you mean?"

"Your ears have been filled with lies, and they've infected your brain and now your mouth. See your doctor or your dentist to have the word *promiscuity* extracted." I spun my cart around sharply to walk away from her.

I saw her glaring at me a few times before I left the store. I'd never had any great affection for her, nor she for me, but there was no doubt that she would rush right to her phone when she arrived home and elaborate on anything she had been told, claiming that she had heard something from me or that her questions had pushed a button, forcing me to reveal things I never would have otherwise. I realized now that this was one of those stories that never went away. They just got fatter and fatter until they exploded. *Prepare yourself for more questions and stupid remarks like hers,* I thought.

I couldn't wait to get home again and throw myself into the dinner preparations as soon as I unpacked the groceries. Mercifully, my phone didn't ring again before my parents returned from the store. I had the table in the dining room set with our best china and glasses, a vase of wildflowers I had picked in the yard, and a bottle of Dad's prize white Burgundy from France. When they arrived and saw it all, they were both delightfully surprised. Dad was already salivating over the aromas flowing from the kitchen.

"Is that brownies I see?" he asked, nodding at where I had them cooling on the kitchen counter.

"It is," I said.

"Oh, honey, this is wonderful," Mom said. She started to help out, and I stopped her.

"No, tonight you two sit, and I'll do all the serving."

"But . . ."

"You've been on your feet all day. Please," I said.

"I'll just change, then," she said. "Gregory? Are you going to follow your marching orders?"

"Absolutely. I might even put on a tie," he said jokingly, but he did come down to the dining room wearing one. Mom wore one of her prettier dresses, too.

The dinner went perfectly. Dad was in a great mood because they'd had one of their best days yet at the store, and the orders for some of his unique jewelry pieces were continuing to build. He even thought aloud about the possibility of expanding the store. The video rental store next door was struggling and could go out of business any day, he said. "We could have the wall torn down between us, and we'd have double the space."

Mom was more cautious, but I could see the excitement in both their faces. Their energy, their joy, and our wonderful dinner did a great deal to drive the blues out of me. All of the gossip and cattiness going on around me suddenly seemed insignificant, but I was also wise enough to realize that when we'd be clearing the table, washing up the dishes, and settling into the remainder of the evening, all of it would come back at me for sure.

And it did, with a phone call from one of the girls, Evelyn Laskin, who sat next to me in two of my classes but rarely spoke to me. I made the conversation short, cutting her off immediately with "I'm on another call." Lying to her didn't seem wrong or weak of me. It seemed the perfectly right and normal thing to do.

I looked in on my parents in the living room.

"I'm taking a walk," I told them.

"Oh? I thought your nature walker was gone for a while," Dad said.

"But not nature," I told him, and he laughed.

They returned to their reading, and I left the house.

Tonight we were having partly cloudy skies with a slightly stronger breeze. The darker shadows cast by the clouds seemed to slip and slide as if they were undecided about where to rest for the night. It was funny. For years, I had looked at Brayden's house unoccupied, but it had never looked as dark and empty as it did tonight. *I guess it's all my imagination,* I thought, and walked on, imagining him alongside me. When I reached the place where he had taken me off the road, between the Knotts and Littlefield homes, I paused. *Do I dare?* I thought, and surprisingly, with little fear or hesitation, I began to follow the path he had led me on that first night.

It was quite a bit darker, but somehow I didn't step into any puddles or mud. I went through the woods easily and arrived at the small lagoon. Just as on that night, I saw all sorts of birds. The clouds shifted, and more stars began to appear. The twinkling light danced on the surface of the lake. *Why can't it always be like this,* I thought, *quiet, beautiful, and inspiring?* When you thought about it, most of the grating and unpleasant noise in this world was made by human beings. Even the persistent caw of a crow had a place in the symphony of night. From way across the lake came the murmur of voices and some laughter. Either some people were in a boat that I couldn't quite see or they were out in their yards facing the water. It was difficult to make out words, the sounds undulating and perhaps driven this way and that by the breeze. Strangely, all of this beauty suddenly made me feel even sadder.

And then I heard what sounded like branches cracking off to my right, deeper in the forest that surrounded the lake. It could be almost any animal, I thought, but

my heart tripled its beat. The cracking stopped and then
started again and then stopped. Any other girl, even
most of the boys I knew, would surely turn and hurry
away, but I didn't. I couldn't explain it, but not only was
I not afraid to remain, but I took some steps toward the
sounds, listened, and moved ever so slowly between the
saplings and older trees and bushes, listening keenly and
studying the dark shapes ahead of me.

When I was a good ten or fifteen yards in, I saw a
shadow slip between two trees. It was not a deer and certainly not a fox or a raccoon. I didn't think it could be a
bear. Could someone have seen me enter the woods and
walk to the lagoon? Had I been too deep in thought to
hear him following me? Of course, there were criminal
events here and there in some of the other communities
between Portland and Echo Lake, and a girl had been attacked on the highway when she had car trouble the year
before. Was I a fool to be so oblivious to the possibilities
that hovered around me in this world? Had the relative
safety of life in Echo Lake made me careless, innocent,
and naive after all?

As these thoughts occurred, my skin tingled with the
cold chill that rushed up and down my spine. I saw the
shadow move again. This time, I was positive. There
was someone there. Who would be walking alone in the
woods at this time of the night? I hesitated, took a deep
breath, and thought about turning and running as fast
as I could, but I didn't. I would never be able to explain
why I had come here at night alone to anyone, but even
more difficult to explain, especially to my parents, would
be why or how I drove back my fear and, instead of

fleeing, walked slowly toward the place where I saw the shadowy figure. From what well had I drawn this surge of courage? Why did I have such confidence? Or was it simply arrogance and stupidity? I took another deep breath. Finally, I paused and called out, "Who's there?"

For a long moment, there was nothing but silence. Even the breeze stopped playing with the leaves, and I could no longer hear the sounds of music and voices floating over the lake. It was as if I had crossed into another, darker world, fallen through some black hole, but unlike Alice, I hadn't dropped into a Wonderland but into a nightmare. I was too frightened now to cry out again. My legs seemed frozen. I could barely breathe.

"Who's there? Is someone there?" I called. I waited for about ten seconds, and then I decided to turn and go home.

But it was too late.

"What are you doing here?" I heard on my immediate right, and spun around to see Brayden Matthews.

13

Thoreau

Starlight was captured in his eyes. The rest of him seemed to be cloaked in a shadow that began to lift away with a shifting cloud. For a moment, he looked larger, his shoulders broader, but I soon realized that was all part of the shock of seeing him appear seemingly out of nowhere. I stood staring at him, speechless.

"I thought it was you, Amber," he continued, his voice soft, soothing, chasing the trembling out of my body. "When I heard someone walking around at the lagoon, I told myself it could only be you this time of night. Who else cares or knows how beautiful it is? Who else would come out here now? But why did you come tonight? Tell me, what brought you?" he asked like someone full of wonder, hoping to hear that it had something to do with him, something magical.

I wondered myself and stood there caught up in his question, but then I realized that this wasn't a dream. He was really standing there beside me.

"The bigger question is what are you doing here tonight, Brayden? And why are you walking in the woods like this in the darkness?"

"I wasn't walking through the woods. I heard you come looking for me. I'm going to stay here for a few days," he said casually, as if it was nothing surprising.

"What? What do you mean, stay here? Why? What about your mother? Isn't she still at the clinic? And your father? Is he still there? I don't understand what's going on. When you left, you implied that you would be gone for a while."

"Things changed."

"But . . . where are you going to stay for a few days? I don't understand what you mean by staying here."

"I fixed up that cabin I told you I found," he said, nodding to his right. "Come on. We'll talk there."

He started away. When I didn't move, he paused and looked back.

"It's all right," he said. "Come on." He held out his hand.

I started after him and took it. He tightened his grip as if he never wanted to let go.

"When did you return?" I asked him as we walked.

"About two hours ago, I think. I can't be sure." He smiled at me. "'Time is but the stream I go a-fishing in.'"

"Never mind all that," I said with a schoolteacher's firmness. "Don't try to distract me. Why are you here and not at home? And what do you mean, you fixed up the cabin? Why? When did you do that?"

"Questions, questions," he said. "You'll have no trouble being a mother."

"I won't keep asking questions if I can get some answers," I replied, and he laughed but said nothing more.

We walked on until we came to a small clearing, and

there, as he had described, was a small log cabin. Trees and bushes had grown around the sides of it thickly enough to keep it well hidden from anyone coming from any other direction. It didn't look much larger than someone's toolshed, but I imagined that when it was built, it was considered at least average.

"I suspect this is quite old," he told me. "I'm surprised some local historical society hasn't laid claim to it. Whoever owns this land surely must be aware of its existence."

"The family who owns this land isn't very interested in preserving history. They're interested in preserving wealth," I said, and he laughed and turned to me.

"I'm really glad you came."

"And I will be, too, when I know what's going on."

"Patience, patience," he said.

He opened the cabin door and stepped in. The top of the doorway was low, so he had to bend a little. I did the same. He immediately turned on what looked like a battery-powered lantern. It wasn't very strong but threw enough light for me to see his sleeping bag spread over the old wood-slat floor, a box full of other camping utensils, and what looked to be some canned food. The cabin did look cleaned up, but there wasn't much to it. It was only one big room. The two windows were boarded up.

"What are you doing here?" I asked. "Why are you camping out here?"

He sat beside his sleeping bag and folded his legs before he looked up at me.

"Sorry there's no furniture."

"Brayden," I whined.

"Okay, okay. It's like this. My mother is going to be there for a while, and it's better that I don't visit her every day. I decided not to stay at some Bates Motel near the clinic."

"Bates Motel?"

"*Psycho*. Remember the movie? You must have seen it."

"Yes, my father insisted when he thought I was old enough to be scared half out of my mind, and my mother is still bawling him out for it."

He laughed.

"What about your father? Didn't he want you to go with him in the meantime?"

I lowered myself to the floor to sit across from him, hoping that I wasn't sitting on or near any bugs that could come up through the slats.

"And do what? Hang out at a better hotel or motel? He works all day, with working dinners and sometimes working even into the night. Time and normal activities get lost in some fog for him and his associates when they're into theoretical discussions. I accompanied him once and found myself more alone than ever. Half the time, I had to remind him that he had brought me along. No, going with my father was not an option."

"Well, I still don't understand," I said, looking around. "Why would you rather camp out here than be at your house? I'm sure you have a lot to do there yet while you wait for your mother to get better, and . . ."

"It's less lonely for me here," he said.

"Less lonely here? It's not exactly the place to meet people. Besides, I'd spend as much time as I could with you if you were home."

"You could do that here, too, if you want. When you're not working, that is."

"But . . ."

"I guess I take the Thoreau thing more seriously than most people do. I need to feel myself in nature now. It restores me, keeps me wanting to be here."

"I understand all that, but . . ."

"I'll do fine. Don't worry. In a few days, I'll be returning to the clinic, and my mother will be released, and things will return to the way they were."

"They weren't that good," I said. I was thinking now of my discoveries in his house.

"No, they weren't, but they were tolerable before this episode."

Something about the way he avoided looking at me when he said that told me that he was saying something he didn't believe himself.

"Did you return to your house first?" I asked, wondering if there had been some way for him to discover that I had been in his house. Perhaps I had left a light on or hadn't closed something.

"Actually, no," he said, which really surprised me.

"You came right here instead of going home?"

"I didn't see any reason to do otherwise," he said in a matter-of-fact tone, as if the reasons were perfectly clear. "I don't have anything cold to drink, but there's a bottle of some of that healthy water. You know, the water with electrolytes. My father always wanted my mother to drink it. He thought it would help somehow. Don't ask me how. Would you like some?"

"No. I'm fine. But I don't understand. If you didn't

go to your house first, how did you get the water and all of these other things here?"

"I stocked the cabin two days ago," he said.

"Two days ago, you knew you'd be here? But wasn't that before your mother got worse?"

"I anticipated it, and I also wanted to have an alternative to what my father would suggest I do afterward," he added.

"How could you anticipate it?"

"I've gotten so I can read my mother well enough to know when a time like this would come. That's one advantage of being around someone this ill for so long, not that I want the advantage." He looked at me with anticipation in his eyes, like someone who was waiting to see if the person he had spoken to believed him. I could accept what he was saying.

"You're so much closer to your mother than you are to your father."

He shrugged. "It's not all that unusual, and it works just the opposite for some, I'm sure. Mothers are deserting their children a lot more than they used to. But let's stop talking about my sad situation and talk about yours."

"What do you mean, mine?"

"I don't have to be a mind reader to feel that you're burdened with something. Does it have to do with your date the other night with the boy who you said tried to change you?"

"Yes. Remember? You shouldn't be surprised. You were the one who gave me a sort of warning about him."

"What happened? When we took that walk, you

didn't go into any real detail except to tell me you had asked him to go for a walk. I take it that wasn't very exciting for him, but this sounds like a lot more went on."

"I thought I could just forget it, but I see now that's not possible. It's like headline news around here now."

"I don't have a local newspaper, so just tell me."

I described the little to-do between Shayne's sister and me at Shayne's house after our boat ride, how Shayne had behaved at dinner, and how he had reacted to my not wanting to go to Mel Quinn's house party.

"I had no doubt what that would have led to if I had gone with him," I said. "He changed dramatically when he saw that I wasn't going to be talked into it."

"Impatient sort, isn't he?"

"Yes, but now that's not the worst of it," I said, and described the stories Shayne's sister was spreading and how other girls in my class were reacting. He nodded, looking very serious. I half-expected he would brush it all off as young-girl nonsense or something.

"And you're not sure how to handle it?"

"Well, it is a little new for me to be the center of everyone's excitement, especially under these circumstances. However, I think I'm handling it well enough for a novice. I made it very clear to everyone who called that nothing like Wendi described happened between me and Shayne and never will now."

He shook his head.

"What?"

"Remember, 'the lady doth protest too much, methinks'?"

"*Hamlet*. So?"

"Guilty people seem to protest more, because innocent people can't imagine anyone thinking they did it. Anyway, in this particular situation, I would advise you to go the opposite direction."

"Opposite direction? What do you mean?"

"Just hear me out," he said. "Tell them it's really all true, only you're the one who decided to break it up because he was a big disappointment in bed. I'm sure you can get a little descriptive and very convincing if you have to. The more detail you give about the sex or lack of it, the more they will believe you."

"What?" I asked, this time smiling. "Why would I do such a thing?"

"First, from what you're telling me now, I don't think this guy could handle it. He'd get his sister off you and run the other way as quickly as he could. Second, your clacking girlfriends would stop treating you as if you were the fool."

I started to shake my head.

"You can do it, Amber."

I sat back, my arms behind me, my hands flat on the floor, and thought. Then I laughed, imagining the reactions. "I think I could," I said.

"Sure you could. You'll be surprised how much respect you'll gain. Death to Prudence Perfect."

"Yes." I paused. "I don't remember telling you that some of my classmates call me that."

"You must have," he said, but he looked sorry he had said it. Had he been following me without my knowing and overheard Ellie and Charlotte Watts? "Regardless, if you do what I suggest, you'll be happier."

I thought for a moment and shook my head. "No. I think I'd rather my parents heard that I was still Prudence Perfect."

"Your parents don't have to live out there with these nasty creeps. Besides, something tells me your mother will realize what you're doing."

"How can you say that? You've never met her."

"Yes, I have."

"When? How?"

"Through you," he said. "You didn't turn out to be this great all on your own." I shook my head and smiled at him. Then I looked around the tiny cabin.

"You can't stay here, Brayden. You can't be serious. There's no running water, for one thing."

"I found a spring nearby, and I have a few bottles of that water."

"You don't have any real food."

"Thoreau had very little."

"It could get cold in the early morning."

"The sleeping bag is quite adequate. I've done it before and in much more challenging climates."

"It's a little claustrophobic," I said, looking around.

"It's big enough for me. I have a lot of thinking to do, anyway. Good place for it."

I looked at him suspiciously.

"What?"

"Where's your cell phone? I never see you carrying one. If you did stay here, wouldn't you need one in case your father called you?"

"You're right."

He reached into the box and produced a cell phone.

"I didn't see you had that before."

"You're right. I didn't. I didn't even want it now, but my father insisted I have it."

"I was wondering why you never gave me your cell-phone number. Or your house phone number, for that matter."

"We haven't had a phone installed yet. My mother has a cell phone."

"Oh. So?"

"So what?"

"What's your number?"

"Oh. I forgot. Wait a minute," he said, and searched the phone. Then he gave me the number. He flipped the phone closed.

"Don't you want to know mine?" I asked.

"Oh, right."

I rattled off both my cell and home numbers. He put them in his cell phone and put it in the box.

"Did you get to see your mother?"

"Yes. She was under some medication, so it wasn't much of a visit, and from what I understood, she'll be relatively out of it for a few days."

I sat forward. "What exactly happened that made her decide to check herself in?"

He stared at me a moment and then turned away. He was silent so long I thought he was unable to speak. I was sorry I had asked.

"Brayden? Are you all right?"

"Yes," he said. He looked at me a moment and then added, "I lied to you. I'm sorry."

"Lied? About what?"

"About my mother."

"That's okay. You're going through so much. How did you lie?"

"I'll tell you, but I don't want you telling anyone else, not even your parents. I know how close you are with them and how difficult it will be to hold back anything, but for now, I need you to do that." He fixed his soft, now warm eyes on me. "I think I can trust you more."

"Yes, of course you can. My mother and father would understand. They know how important it is to keep someone's confidence."

"Yes, I thought they would," he said, smiling. "The only thing . . ."

"What?"

"I hate bringing you into all of this any deeper than you already are. It's not fair to lay such a burden on you. You're struggling with your own personal and important issues right now. You don't need a new neighbor to un-load his troubles on your shoulders, too."

"Let me be the judge of what I can bear and what I can't," I said. "Don't you start treating me like someone fragile and weak, too."

He smiled again. "I thought you would say some-thing like that. You're right, of course."

"So?"

I felt myself tighten inside in anticipation. Maybe I was being a little overconfident. Maybe I had been too protected all these years, and now that I was swimming alone in the ocean of human conflicts, especially the more mature ones, I would turn and swim quickly in the opposite direction and rush home to my secure little world. The way his face turned even more serious, his eyes darkening, frightened me a little more than I cared to reveal.

"She didn't check herself in, exactly. My father brought her to the clinic."

"Your father was here?"

"Just in time."

"What do you mean?"

"My mother tried to commit suicide," he said. For me, it was like a clap of thunder in the log cabin.

"How?" I barely managed to get out.

"She deliberately took too many sleeping pills."

"I didn't see or hear any ambulance."

"There wasn't any. My father rushed her to the hospital himself. It happened late last night. After she was stabilized, he brought her to the clinic."

"And then you returned to get some of her things, and that was when you came over to see me?"

"Yes."

"Then this all happened last night after we took a walk?"

"As I said, late."

"Your father was home when we took the walk?"

He nodded. "I'm sorry I didn't tell you it all as it really happened when I came to see you. I didn't want to disturb you any more than you were, but I see now that you're the sort of person who deserves nothing less than the truth. I don't like being dishonest with you," he added, his beautiful eyes fixed on mine.

All of a sudden, I felt terrible about what I had done, sneaking into his house and snooping. If anyone was being dishonest here, it was little old Prudence Perfect. I couldn't hold his gaze. I looked away.

"What's wrong?" he asked. "Did I upset you with this news as I feared I would?"

I shook my head as the tears came into my eyes. "I did a terrible thing this morning soon after you came to see me."

"Oh?"

"I went over to tell you that I would be happy to go with you to the clinic, even drive you. I knocked and knocked on your front door. I didn't believe you had gone that quickly. Besides, I didn't see any car. I guessed you would call for a taxi, but I was hoping you were still home. I thought you might be upstairs, so I tried the front door, and it opened. I shouted for you, and then . . ."

"And then?"

"I went into your house."

"I see."

"I still thought you might be there, upstairs, and perhaps you hadn't heard me calling."

"So, you went upstairs?"

"Yes."

"And?"

"I went up to the attic, to your mother's art studio."

"And you saw her painting?"

"Yes."

"I wish you hadn't."

"So do I," I said. "It was nothing like her artwork on the Internet."

"No, it wouldn't be. I don't know if she'll ever paint like that again."

"What is it supposed to be? I don't understand."

"It's the way she sees everything now. Just imagine if your vision was covered by something that distorted anything you looked at. That's the way it is for her, as it might be for others in her situation, only she has a way of expressing it, her painting, her artistic ability. When therapists ask their clients to interpret something, they're using the art to get through, to look into their minds and understand the problems."

"Will they ask her to paint something where she is?"

"They might, but I don't know if she would. She'll paint something when that something is attacking her to get out. Do you understand?"

"I think so."

"I'm so sorry to bring you into this. It wasn't right. I should have just left you out there enjoying the scene."

"No, I'm glad you let me know you're here. Don't think that way."

He nodded, but I could see that he wasn't convinced. He lowered his eyes. I leaned forward and put my hand on his. When he raised his gaze so that his eyes met mine, I clearly saw all of the pain he was suffering. It wasn't hard to understand how much he longed for a normal life. Perhaps this was why he was so reluctant to meet others our age or become friends with those who might be his schoolmates. Their much calmer, settled world would constantly remind him of how difficult his own was and how much he would be unable to share.

"I hate to see you so sad, Brayden."

His fingers danced over my hand, and then he looked up and smiled. "I don't think I could remain depressed

around you too long, Amber. You wouldn't let it be. I bet
your mother is the same way."

"Yes, she is."

"You're very lucky."

"I'm lucky I met you," I said. His eyes seemed to find
their light again. He gazed at me, and for a moment, in
the dim light, his eyes appeared to be on fire.

Slowly, almost by an inch at a time, he brought his
lips to mine.

It was a soft but long kiss. I felt all sorts of doors un-
lock within me. He put his hand on my shoulder, and I
shifted so that I could fall into his waiting arms. He embraced me, and we lay back against his sleeping bag. He
glanced at it. My eyes followed his.

"It's kind of cozy in there," he said. "Even un-
dressed."

"I can't think of any other way," I told him.

14

A Real Wonderland

Would it make any sense to say we made love so softly, so gently and easily, that it didn't feel as if I had crossed any line or broken through any barrier? It was as if I was making love the way I had hoped and imagined it would be, the lovemaking of dreams, without any guilt or regret. I have heard other girls talk about their fears of becoming pregnant because of their loss of control or passion. There's that terrible time of waiting and praying for their next period, an anticipation almost like the anticipation of a patient waiting for results of a biopsy. Just witnessing that anxiety is enough for some girls to become chaste until they're married.

But then there are those girls who admit to making love out of fear that if they didn't, they'd lose their boyfriends, and for them, that was a major trauma. Some even think it makes them superior to their friends. They wear their loss of virginity like a badge. Most of the reasons I heard for their lovemaking sounded wrong to me. I felt above all that.

Ordinarily, I would have thought that in these great exploratory moments, I should be making more discoveries about the boy, but for me, it was as if I had just found my own body. Pleasurable sensations came to me from places I had least expected. No part of me was dull or insensitive. No matter where his lips met my skin, something electric, warm, and thrilling traveled to every other part of me. Even my fingers tingled.

I felt my whole body soften in his arms. It was a total surrender, a willing surrender. I was eager to see what other places on my body would tingle and awaken. The woman I often pictured curled up inside me like some mature fetus awoke and quickly unfolded throughout, slipping under my breasts, around my heart, and down through my thighs, even to my toes.

My breasts seemed to blossom under his touch, his lips. As small as our space was inside his sleeping bag, I never felt uncomfortable for a single moment. My whole body had turned into soft clay to be molded and shaped so it would fit neatly against his, but what surely made it more wonderful was the way we moved together as if we had truly become one body, every part of me anticipating every part of him.

Would it always be like this? How could any of my far more sexually active friends experience anything like I was experiencing? From what I heard them say, their sex seemed purely selfish, each of them caring only for what satisfaction he or she could draw out of the other. I thought of them as being crude and boisterous lovers who rushed in and out of pockets of pleasure, barely recalling where they had been or why. For them, sex was nothing more than a good piece of chocolate.

Making love the way Brayden and I were making love enlarged and expanded all of our senses. I knew that afterward, everything I thought was beautiful would be more beautiful. I would look forward to every morning more than I ever had, and I would even be more anxious to go to sleep, knowing that my thoughts and my dreams would be about Brayden, about us, about these moments. Everything, in fact, would have more importance to me. I would cherish time itself as I had never cherished it before, because every hour and every minute I could devote to our being together would suddenly be more valuable to me.

Of course, I thought that our lovemaking was soothing and comforting for Brayden, too, perhaps even more so than for me because of what he was experiencing and maybe because of what his life had been like until now, too. I felt his need, his hunger for something warm and bright in the midst of all this cold, depressing darkness that otherwise surrounded him. I had no way of really knowing for sure, of course, but something told me this was the first time it had been special for him.

Certainly, nothing happened that would telegraph any inexperience. He didn't fumble or grope like someone unsure of himself, but it was, as my father would say, like realizing that you have come upon an extraordinary, special jewel almost lost among very ordinary semiprecious stones. I felt cherished in his arms. He clung to me with a desperation that told me how much he needed me beside him. *How lonely and lost he must feel,* I thought, even as we lay quietly beside each other afterward, neither moving for fear that we would shatter the fragile bubble that, for the moment at least, gave us shelter from the ugliness and the sadness that visited too often.

Both he and I were so content that it was easy to fall asleep in each other's arms. The call of an owl, perhaps sitting on the roof of the cabin, which it probably had done many times before, woke me. The sound echoed in the small room. For a few moments, I didn't know where I was. The battery in the lantern was probably losing power, because the illumination it threw had dwindled to the point where I could just barely make out the door. My stirring woke Brayden.

"What time is it?" I whispered.

"I don't know," he said. Before he could utter it, I put my fingers on his lips.

"Don't say it. It's not a stream for me at the moment."

I slipped out of the sleeping bag and brought my wrist closer to the illumination to read my watch.

"Oh, no! I've been gone nearly two hours. My parents will be very worried. They're going to want to know why."

"It's better if you don't tell them about me," he said. "For now, okay?"

"You're definitely not returning to the house before you go back to the clinic?" I asked as I hurriedly dressed.

He got out of the sleeping bag and began to dress, too. "Yes, definitely not."

"I'm worried about you staying here that long."

"I'll be fine."

"How will you know when to go back?"

"I'll know," he said. "Remember, I have the cell phone."

"Oh, right."

"I'll walk you most of the way home."

"Thanks."

I slipped on my shoes and stood up. When he opened the door, the owl flew off the roof and swooped down in front of us before flying into the darkness. I thought it looked as large as a hawk and said so.

"No, it was an owl. They can get pretty big, especially when they spread their wings. I call them the guardians of the night. That's why he was on the cabin roof. He was watching over us."

He stepped back for me to go out of the cabin, and we headed across the small clearing back to the path we had followed to get there. It did seem darker than it had been. There was more cloud cover blocking out the starlight, but having less light didn't seem to bother him. He moved just as quickly, just as sure of himself. In no time, we were out of the woods and crossing the field that would take us back to the road I would follow home.

"I know you don't like lying to your parents," he said. "I'm sorry I asked you to."

"It's all right. I won't lie so much as be vague."

He laughed. "Yes, we were vague."

"You know what I mean."

"Of course." He paused. "It'll be fine from here," he said when we reached the road. He looked up it as if he never wanted to go back to his house, even get too close to it. Was it because that was where his mother almost died?

"Okay. I'll make some sandwiches for lunch tomorrow and bring something better to drink."

"Another picnic at the lake for you?"

"Yes, but this one will have a better outcome," I said.

"Will it?" he asked, suddenly sounding pessimistic and depressed again.

"It will if I have anything to do with it," I replied. "Besides, it already has." That brought back a smile to his face.

He leaned forward, and I did, too, so that our lips, like two messengers of hope, would seal their optimism with a kiss. I wanted it to last longer, but I was really afraid that my parents were freaking out.

"Good night," he said.

"Good night."

I started away and stopped.

"How will I know if you had to return to the clinic before I get to the cabin?"

"I'll call you. I have your number, remember?" he said.

"Oh, right."

"Stop worrying about everything, and get going. And be sure to be careful when you return to the lake tomorrow. It would be better if no one saw you."

"Right. I will."

I hurried up the street but paused once to look back. He was already gone. Moments later, I stepped up onto my front porch, took a deep breath, and opened the door. They didn't pounce, but they were both standing in the living-room doorway, looking very upset.

"Where were you, Amber?" Dad asked first. "Do you know how long you've been gone?"

"I'm sorry," I said. "I didn't realize the time."

"Where were you all this time?" Mom asked, a little more strongly.

"I went to that place on the lake I told you about. You know, with all the birds. The small lagoon."

"By yourself?" Dad asked.

"Yes." That wasn't a lie. I had gone there by myself.

"And you've been there all this time?" Mom asked.

"Yes. I went there to enjoy nature and think, and I fell asleep. I'm sorry."

"You fell asleep?" Dad asked, his voice awash in incredulity.

I nodded. That wasn't a lie, either.

"Didn't you realize how we would worry?"

"I'm sorry," I said. "As soon as I woke up and realized what time it was and how long I had been gone, I rushed back."

They just stared at me. I was wondering myself when was the last time I had done anything that gave them even half as much displeasure and disappointment. I had to go back years, to the time when I had let one of my classmates talk me into going for a ride with her brother who didn't have a driver's license, just a driver's permit. He wasn't old enough to have his own license yet, but he took sneak rides with their mother's car when she was away with friends or too busy with something else to realize. He got pulled over when he was speeding, and we were all reported. I really thought he was legal. I didn't understand, but that wasn't an excuse that would get me out of trouble. My parents made it clear that ignorance of the law was a person's own fault. I think I was more upset about getting them upset than they were. They never mentioned it again, but I had a feeling they were both thinking about it at the moment, just the way you might recall an old wound when a new one comes.

"I'm sorry," was all I could add again.

"Just go up to bed, Amber. I'll see about getting you a watch with an alarm on it," Dad said, half-kidding. Mom smirked at him, and he shrugged. "Can't hurt to have one."

"Night," I said, and hurried to the stairway, happy that I didn't have to explain too much more and actually distort and lie. When I stepped into my room, I let out a hot, heavy breath, and then I smiled with relief. I could go to bed thinking mostly about Brayden and our time together, and I could dream of what our day would be tomorrow and maybe even the day after tomorrow. Was I being selfish, thinking only about our pleasure together and not his mother? Was I guilty of hoping that she would stay in the hospital a little longer perhaps, with little reason for him to visit?

At first, when he told me he wanted to stay at the lake and sleep in that old cabin, I thought it was very strange and something he couldn't do for long, but now, after the time we had spent together, that old cabin, the woods, and the wonderful lake were something magical. I had feared that, unlike Alice, I wasn't falling into a Wonderland but into a nightmare. Now I felt as if I had indeed fallen into a real Wonderland, a Wonderland of our own making, filled with love and beauty, guardian owls, warm shadows, and brilliant stars.

I got into bed quickly. I heard my parents go to bed. Guilt did surge through me. After all, they had to get up to work. They didn't need to be put through tension and worry, which I knew they would both carry into their sleep. *I have to be more careful,* I told myself. *I will. This won't happen again. I'll find a way to make it up to them.* Comforted with the thought, I closed my eyes and almost instantly saw Brayden standing there, that promise and love making his eyes glitter like candles lit by the starlight.

I rose before my parents in the morning and rushed down to prepare breakfast for them. My mother gave me a look that told me she knew exactly what I was up to, some penance. Dad pretended to be surprised, but he knew, too. I apologized again for what I had done the night before, and they were soon back to their old selves, talking about the business and the plans Dad was pushing for expansion. I offered to go to work, but again, Mom insisted that I enjoy my time off.

"Find someone to do something with," she ordered. "For yourself," she added as they were preparing to leave.

I said I would. *If she only knew,* I thought, and followed them to the door.

My mother paused to look at Brayden's house. "Let me know when they're back. I really want to do something for that boy," she said.

"Okay."

She continued to hesitate, her gaze still on the house. "Have any of the other kids in town met him yet?"

"Not yet. Too much happened before he could get involved in anything."

She nodded. "Well, you can't solve everyone's problems, Amber. Think a little more about yourself."

"I will."

I watched them walk away. I could tell from the way they stayed close as they walked that they were talking about me. They had real worries about my future, about whether I was really enjoying my teenage years. I wasn't concerned anymore. *Soon,* I thought, *they'll meet Brayden, and they'll see that I'm quite normal and how special he really is.*

I went up to shower and dress and then have some breakfast myself. This time, when the phone rang later in the morning, I thought it could very well be Brayden. He had a cell phone, and I did give him my number. I was disappointed to hear a different familiar voice.

"Yes, Ellie, what's up?" I said.

"Nothing special for me, but I know exactly what you're up to," she began.

"What?"

"You're seeing your neighbor, aren't you?" she asked.

"Why do you say that?" I asked, afraid that we had been spotted last night. Perhaps Angie Littlefield had looked out her window and seen us passing between her house and the Knottses' house when he walked me back to the road. But that wasn't it.

"I was thinking about everything and what would make you turn off Shayne Allan after having made love with him in his house and came up with it. I couldn't imagine any other reason. So, when can I meet this new guy? I'll be honest about him. I promise. If he's better-looking than Shayne or in any way a better catch, I'll tell you. I know you think I'm so infatuated with Shayne that I put every other boy down, but—"

"That's not it," I said quickly. Suddenly, Brayden's

advice made more sense to me. "So you're convinced that I made love with Shayne?"

"C'mon, Amber. You're talking to me, not some of those empty heads we call our friends."

I paused and then sighed loudly enough to be heard over the phone. "Okay, I'll tell you, but try to keep it to yourself. It's not a nice topic for discussion."

"Sure. What?" she asked, now very excited.

"I did make love with him, but it was a disaster, and not because of me."

"What? Why? I mean, I don't understand what you're saying."

"Well, as you would expect, I was looking for a very special time."

"Yes, of course. So?"

"There's no nice way to put this. He underper-formed. You know what that means?"

She was silent a moment. Did she know? "Not ex-actly," she admitted.

"Haven't you heard of premature ejaculation?"

"What?" If she had been lying down, she surely had popped up, and if she had been sitting, she was standing now.

"We had hardly gotten started. Frankly, it makes a lot of sense when you think about him. He's so into him-self that he's interested only in his own pleasure. I was, however, quite surprised to see how unsophisticated he was when it came to sex. I mean, he's done quite a good public-relations job on all of us. You won't believe this, I know, but to me, it was as if he was doing it for the first time, not me."

"You're right. I can't believe this."

"Believe it. When I complained, I saw how his whole personality and attitude, especially toward me, changed. Yes, he isn't interested in seeing me anymore, but not for the reasons you thought. He's afraid I'll talk about him. I was going to let it go," I continued, now enjoying the roll I was on, "but when his bratty sister started to spread all those stories about me, I thought, okay, if this is how it's going to be, fine." I paused to let it all sink into her brain like a rock sinking in mud. "You know, now that I think more about it, I wouldn't be surprised to learn that he put her up to it so I would be too embarrassed to talk about what really happened. You know, like a shot across the bow of an enemy ship or the ship of a neutral nation to force them to stop and be inspected. My dad told me that happens often in wars. Well, Shayne and his sister have declared a love war against me. What do you think?"

"Maybe," she said, the possibilities creeping into her thoughts and raising doubts. "This is so incredible."

"You can just imagine how incredible it was for me, Ellie. A girl looks forward to her first time. I know you did. It didn't just happen by accident. You were ready for it, right?"

"Yes, of course. I told you about it, I think."

"You did, but your experience was ten times better than mine was. Believe me, I don't want to relive making love with Shayne Allan. You can't blame me, can you? Can you?" I asked when she didn't respond. She was still in shock a little. "What, you think I'm wrong to have told you the truth? I knew I should have kept my mouth shut."

"No, no. You did the right thing. It's good that you did."

"Now," I said in a softer voice, "Brayden is much different. He is a very polite and considerate person. No matter what we do, he's always concerned about my being satisfied, and I just told you how important that is."

"You made love to him already? What was it like?"

"You've heard people say it was night-and-day different to describe similar experiences, haven't you? Well, it was night-and-day different."

"Wow. I guess I can't let anyone call you Prudence Perfect anymore."

"Thanks."

"When can I meet him? Can I meet him today?"

"No. His mother is ill. I'll let you know. Maybe we'll double-date or something in the near future."

"Yes, yes. Who would have ever thought that Shayne Allan was . . ."

"Like a gun that misfires," I said, and she laughed. "Let's call him Mr. Misfire."

"That's good. Okay. Call me," she said. I could feel how anxious she was to get off the phone with me and start calling others, probably Charlotte Watts first. "Mr. Misfire" would spread like a wildfire.

"Ditto," I said, and hung up.

I felt so evil but so happy about it.

Thank you, Brayden, I told myself, and went off to plan our picnic lunch. I decided to cook up some chicken cutlets to make sandwiches and then thought I would surprise him with some fresh brownies, too. I turned on the radio and worked to music, feeling more alive and happy than I had all summer so far. As soon as I was finished preparing everything, I went up to choose what I would wear.

The weather was going to be perfect, hovering around eighty with just some scattered clouds and soft breezes. I decided on a pair of low-rider cargo shorts and a chicken-scratch tank top. A few years ago, my father had had some caps made advertising our jewelry store. Some had images of diamonds on the front, and some had rubies and emeralds. I had one of each, of course, and decided that today was an emerald day. I put on my emerald necklace, too. It was my birthstone. If Brayden asked me about it, I would tell him that my birthday was coming up, July 21. I hoped we would be doing something special together.

As I put on my lipstick, I studied my face. Did girls change when they become lovers? I wondered. Was there something, some look in their eyes, that revealed mature experience? Would my mother realize it? What would I say to her if she asked me? What would my father think? Would he say anything? Would I be a great disappointment to him? Would it change everything between us?

Someday, but not right now, I thought, my mother and I would surely talk about this.

Just before noon, I packed everything, including a light blanket that I was able to fold in a large, nondescript grocery bag, and headed for the lake. Before I stepped out, I called Brayden on his cell phone. I was afraid he would think it was his father or the clinic calling, but I wanted him to know I was coming. It rang and rang and didn't go to any voice mail. How odd, I thought, but then figured it was perfectly like him to leave the cabin without taking the phone. Whatever the reason for it, it didn't matter. I knew where to find him.

The moment I stepped out of the house, however, I froze. There was a car backing out of Brayden's driveway. It looked like his parents' car, the one I had seen that first day when they moved into the house. When it paused on the street, I had a closer look at the driver. It was definitely his father, the man I had seen, I thought. I called out to him and started down the steps, but he obviously didn't hear me. He accelerated and drove off. I stood there looking after him. Why was his father back? Was Brayden with him? Why wouldn't he call me to tell me? He had said he would. Was he in the house, then? I looked at it, then looked after his father's car, watching it turn off the street. I walked across the lawn and up to the front door.

I knocked and called and waited. There was only silence. I knocked again, and this time, when I turned the doorknob, I found that it was locked. Could his father have called him, and Brayden told him he would meet him somewhere, anywhere but the house? That was possible. He had seemed so put off by it when I had started for home and we had reached the street. But why wouldn't he answer when I called? Surely he would want to tell me what was happening. Confused, I stood there for a few moments, unsure of whether I should bother to go to the lake or just go home and call him again and again until he picked up.

I decided to go to the lake. It wasn't that long a walk. Concerned now, I walked faster than I usually did. At one point, when I turned off the road, I was practically running. I remembered his admonition not to be noticed, and I did avoid contact with anyone. The only one outside his or her house was Mrs. Carden, and she seemed oblivious to anything but weeding her small garden. In less than ten minutes, I was entering the woods and heading for the lakeside, where I would turn if I didn't see him and go on to the cabin.

I was practically running through the field and through the portion of woods before I reached the lakeshore. When I nearly stumbled, I slowed down. As I approached the water, I saw him sitting on a fallen log and gazing out at the lake. He appeared to be in such a trance that he didn't hear me.

"Hi," I called, and he turned and smiled.

"Hey."

"I tried calling you, but you didn't pick up," I said, coming up to him.

"Oh, I left the phone back in the cabin."

"You know your father came home, right?" I asked.

"You saw him?"

"Yes."

"Did you speak to him?"

"No, I didn't get a chance. He was backing out of the driveway. I called to him, but he didn't hear me, I guess, and drove off."

"Good," he said.

"Good? Why good? What's going on?"

"He came home to get more of her things. I'm sure he was in a bad mood. He saw how nothing much had been done in the house, and I wouldn't doubt that he saw the picture she was painting. He's not very pleasant when he's in a bad mood."

"Didn't he want to see you?"

"Yes, I'm sure he did," he said. "Let's try not to think about it, Amber. Let's just enjoy the time we have together."

"You make it sound as if it's not going to last."

"Remember Robert Frost. 'Nothing gold can stay.'" He smiled. "But why dwell on the sad things when we have these happy moments, right?"

I nodded. But deep down inside me, I heard the alarm bells ringing.

He kissed me, and I shut myself away from the discordant sound, something I would come to regret.

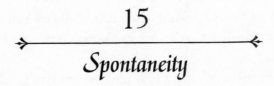

15

Spontaneity

I thought there were so many things very special about Brayden, but perhaps nothing as special as the way he could turn both of us away from the darkness and into the light. It was as if he had the power to draw the curtain closed on anything unpleasant whenever he wished to and then open the curtain on happiness.

"I want to show you something special," he said, taking my hand. "It's farther in the woods, past the cabin and just before the next property."

Intrigued, I walked with him, leaving our picnic lunch at the cabin. When we saw a doe and a fawn, I thought that was it. I had never come upon two of them so closely like this. It was remarkable how unafraid and unthreatened they both appeared to be. The doe looked up at us with almost as much curiosity as we had about them. The fawn came around its mother and glanced at us, too, and then the two of them started away casually.

"Was that it? Because it was certainly something special."

"Everything around here is special," he said. "That was just as much a surprise for me, however."

We walked on until I could hear water. He veered to the right and around some trees. Not far off, I could see the Russells' lake house. Mr. Russell was an important attorney who was being considered for state attorney general. He had twin girls, both now in the sixth grade. Their lake house was a modern A-frame about half the size of the Allans' home, but they had more decking. It ran around the sides of the house and also faced the lake. I saw the twins standing on the deck. They were light brunettes and tall for their age. I had babysat for them often when they were younger. I thought they were looking our way, but I didn't think they could see us through the trees.

"Here," Brayden said, kneeling.

It was a spring, the water sparklingly clear. It ran off toward the lake.

"Where's it come from?"

"The mountains, flowing underground for a good distance before emerging here. This water is delicious, far better than any town water. I poured out all that water I had and filled the bottles with this. Taste it," he said.

He cupped his hands to show me how. I knelt down beside him and let my palms fill. The water was cold but not icy. I sipped some and smiled.

"Yes, it's good."

"It's a very special spring. Let's bottle gallons of it and sell it as Amber Light."

I laughed. "That sounds like a beer."

"Yes, it does. It's just a fantasy, anyway." He sat. "But why not pretend this is truly a special spring? Drink from it and you'll always be young and happy."

"Ponce de León? His fountain of youth?"

"No, this is our fountain of youth, not his. If you're ever truly unhappy, make your way over here and drink from our fountain, and you'll wash away any sadness."

He sounded so convincing. I smiled and scooped up some more.

"Isn't it working?" he asked.

"Yes, but I wasn't unhappy."

"So? You'll be happier," he countered. He leaned over to kiss me. "See?"

I smiled. "Getting very self-confident, are you?" I teased.

"Because of the spring," he said, and then he took my hand and we stood. "I found another secluded place on the lake. It's not far from here. The land juts out far more on the left, so anyone in a boat would probably not be able to see us when we're in the water."

"In the water?"

"We'll go for a swim before lunch."

"But I didn't bring my bathing suit," I said.

"Neither did I," he said. "Either we're in nature or not, right? C'mon. I'll show you the place."

I followed him through the woods. We turned left and then down a small slope to the place he had discovered. He was right. It looked even more secluded than the small lagoon. We could hear boats on the lake, but they were far off, and I recalled Shayne being concerned about us getting too close to this area because of some stumps in the water. I imagined that most of the people who lived and boated on the lake probably knew about that.

Just before the water, there was a small clearing. The

ground was soft, with very tiny stones. It was like a private little beach.

"I would have brought the blanket I left back in the cabin and packed some towels if you had warned me about this," I said.

"Spontaneity. That's the secret to really having a good time. Planned things are . . . too planned. You need surprise."

"You might need surprise. I like to have some warning. Most girls do."

"Naw," he insisted. He began to undress. I looked around. Naturally, I was worried that someone could still come upon us. He paused, waiting to see what I would do. "We're pretty safe here," he said.

"I'm not so sure what you mean by safe," I said, grinning. He laughed, and I started to undress, surprised at myself for not hesitating.

He was in first, diving without hesitation.

"It's probably colder here than out in the center of the lake where I swam," I called out to him. "There's more shade. Right?"

"Not to me. It's like a warm bath."

"Yeah, right. A warm bath," I muttered to myself. "I must be crazy."

He turned to look out at the lake, and I slipped off my panties and stepped cautiously into the water. When I was only ankle-deep, he turned to splash me. I shrieked and then, half out of modesty and half to get it over with, dove in.

"Warm bath?" I cried after popping up. "You must have polar bear blood."

"Give it a few minutes. You'll get used to it and love it." He swam over to me.

It was colder than how it felt out in the middle of the lake, but it wasn't really bad. In fact, it felt more invigorating. I was able to stand, but the water was up to my neck. It was crystal-clear and easy to see to the bottom. Looking around us, I spotted some lake trout swimming amazingly close.

"Look," I said, and pointed to them when they came even closer.

"If you don't move, they'll swim right between your legs," Brayden said.

"No thank you."

"Then I will," he declared, and went under before I could say no. He lifted me up, and I screamed before I hit the water again. For a while, we were like two much younger children, teasing and taunting each other. When I was out of breath, he embraced me, and we stood quietly enjoying the moment.

On the portion of land that jutted out farther, I saw a raccoon. It paused to look out at us.

"We're being watched," I said.

"What?"

I nodded at it, and he turned to look.

"Oh."

"They have such humanlike faces, don't they?"

"Prettier than some human faces," he said, "especially the faces of the envious ones."

Above us, a flock of geese in their perfect V formation honked. It sounded more like a hink and a honk, but they were beautiful to watch.

"I guess I'm indoors too much. I never seem to notice all this."

"Pushing farther south," Brayden said, seeing what had caught my attention. "Seeing something beautiful like that must have reinforced Thoreau's beliefs."

"Were you always so into nature, Brayden?"

"No," he said. "Actually, I came to it quite recently."

"Why was that?"

"It became the only way for me to be in this world," he said.

I smiled. "You're an enigma wrapped in a puzzle," I told him. He nodded and fell back into the water.

"Don't be in a rush to find out what it all means. The fun is in the pursuit."

"Sounds like something someone who had something to hide would say."

"You talk too much," he told me, and came at me again. We kissed, and then he fell back into the water again, and the two of us began to swim. We didn't go far, but we were both above our heads. For a few moments, we treaded water and looked out at the activity across the lake. People were waterskiing, and there were also some small sailboats here and there, looking as if they were painted on the water. One of the motorboats crossing the lake seemed to be heading directly for us. We watched for a few moments. It wasn't turning.

"We'd better pull back," I said. He nodded, and we swam toward shore. The sound of the boat's motor grew louder. "Shayne told me not to get too close around here because there were stumps. Do you think this person doesn't know?"

"Maybe," Brayden said. We moved closer to the small part of the shore that jutted out to be sure we would be hidden from view. I watched the lake nervously. The boat appeared and then veered sharply to its left, turning away. I was holding my breath. It was Shayne's boat. He had another girl with him, and they were both laughing. I didn't recognize her and assumed that it was someone he had met at another school nearby.

"That's Shayne Allan. As you can see, he's heartbroken over our short romance," I said.

"Looks like he runs regular tours."

We waited until the boat was far enough away, and then we got out of the water.

"Here," he said, handing me his shirt. "Use this as a towel."

"But what will you wear?"

"Don't worry about it. I don't care if it's wet. It was used to dry your skin, so it's now very special to me. Here," he said, when I didn't take the shirt. "I'll do it."

He started to wipe my back and then worked over my shoulders.

"You're really very, very beautiful, Amber," he whispered, and kissed my neck. I laid my head back against his shoulder. We stood there for a moment, the slight chill over my body slowly evaporating with his body against mine. His hands moved down my sides and then up and over my breasts. I closed my eyes. My legs trembled.

"Let's get back to the cabin and get the food you brought," he whispered. "I'm sure you're hungry."

"I am. I didn't eat that much breakfast."

We both dressed quickly, silently. Neither of us spoke. I was still trembling, but not from the cool lake. He took my hand, and we walked back to the cabin, still not speaking. As we went through the woods, I saw rabbits and what I was sure was a small fox. It was as if all of the animals were following along with us. Even birds seemed to be flitting from tree to tree to keep up. The foliage was very heavy. In some places, the trees that had grown close to each other crossed branches, their leaves creating a green ceiling over the shaded, cooler places. We paused at one of those places, and he turned to me.

"You all right?" he asked.

"Yes, why?"

"You're so quiet."

"I'm just enjoying it all so much," I said. "Besides, you're not exactly a motormouth."

He laughed and kissed me softly. When he did, the sun moved as if it intended to send its rays between two trees and spotlight us in the woods. The rays fell around us. I was transfixed, caught up in a moment of pure ecstasy, but Brayden looked up at the sunlight and squinted. He looked very upset and unhappy for a moment, in fact. It was as if he thought the sun had disturbed us rather than highlighting us as something special. He turned quickly and, still holding my hand, walked faster through the woods, more like someone fleeing, again moving silently.

"Are you all right?" I asked when we closed in on the cabin.

"Yes, yes," he said with the rapidity of someone who

wanted to get the issue off the table. "Let's just get to our picnic."

We entered the cabin, and I picked up the bag with our sandwiches and the brownies I had made. He seemed suddenly distant to me and stood for a moment as if he had forgotten where he was and what was happening. I thought perhaps he was worrying about his mother.

"Maybe you should check your cell phone," I said. He looked at me, then nodded and did so.

"Nothing. C'mon," he said, grabbing the bottles of spring water. "We should sit close at the lake."

I could hear and even feel an urgency about him. He was acting like someone who expected to hear a whistle declaring an end to our enjoyment. Maybe he was anticipating a call from the clinic or his father, I thought.

We left the cabin, and he led me to another fairly clear area close to the water. I took out the light blanket and spread it, and we sat. He was still quieter than usual as I took out the sandwiches. I studied him. For all the time he had been outside, he hadn't picked up much of a tan. His skin was as clear as it was the first day I saw him, the same fair complexion, whereas I had begun to darken. Of course, I had spent hours on the lake in a boat, but Brayden never wore a hat, and he had told me that he was out every day.

"I made you some brownies," I said, and he looked at the food.

"Wow, that's great. Thanks."

"You said you were hungry."

"Yeah, sure," he said, and unwrapped his sandwich.

We sat there eating slowly and watching the activity on the lake. Whenever I turned my eyes to him, they met his. It was almost as if we were tuned to each other and our eyes moved in sync.

"So many boats out there today," I said.

"They ride those motorboats late into the night."

"Do they? What did you do this morning?" I asked.

"Nothing much. Waited for you."

"Well," I said, thinking that this might get him more animated, "you'll be happy to know that I followed your advice about Shayne."

He turned quickly. "How?"

"I told someone this morning that the story about me and Shayne was true, but I added the idea you suggested."

"Really?" He smiled. "And?"

"Well, I told it to this friend of mine, Ellie, who, although she pretends to be my best friend and is the girl I'm probably closest to, I'm sure has already spread the story, even though I deliberately asked her not to, knowing that she would. It's probably heating up cell phones as we speak."

He laughed. "I'm proud of you." He tapped his bottled water against mine in a toast. "Great sandwich by the way," he said. "Thanks."

"I'm actually a pretty good cook. I've been working with my mother in the kitchen ever since I could hold a dish. You'll have to let me make you a real dinner soon. My mother keeps asking to meet you."

"Does she? You're a complete woman, Amber. You're bright and beautiful and compassionate and capable.

Someday some lucky guy is practically going to rupture his tongue rushing to say 'I do.'"

"Why can't that be you?"

He smiled but lost the smile quickly and turned away.

"What?" I asked.

"I wouldn't bet too much on my future."

"Why not?"

"Let's just take it an hour at a time. I won't even say day," he told me.

It was as if a dark cloud had moved over the sun. I felt the chill shoot through my body. All of his trouble and sadness came rushing in around us as though we had left an opening in the wall of happiness we had built around ourselves. It was always waiting, lurking just outside, hoping to have an opportunity. Right behind it came reality, angry that it had been put aside and not given the respect it deserved. Here we were, pretending to be in our own safe, magical place, while not that far away, his mother floated in some pool of great depression. From the way he had described his father and from the little I knew, Brayden was more like an orphan, someone who did not know his own past and did not even dare to dream of his own future.

I reached out to touch him. His arm felt strangely cold. For a moment, it was as though he had lost all feeling and didn't realize my hand was on his forearm. Finally, he turned and smiled.

"Let's not get ahead of ourselves, Amber. These hours are too special to lose or damage by worrying about what's to come and what isn't."

"Okay," I said in a tiny voice, the voice of someone much younger, the voice of a little girl who was afraid of losing her childhood faith and imaginary friends. Somehow, at one time or another, when we reach a certain point, we know we'll soon cross a line and leave that precious place where all hard and true realities are uninvited, where we can curl up comfortably around our dreams and feel invulnerable and protected.

Brayden's right. Let's not think. Let's not worry. Let's not go there for now, I told myself.

I felt moved by his ravenous hope and hunger for some happiness. Leaning toward him, I offered my lips to show him that I agreed, and we kissed softly. He brushed his hand through my hair and looked at me as if he wanted to remember every inch of my face. Then he seemed to snap out of his reverie and return to his sandwich, holding it up.

"Delicious."

He drank some water, and we ate in silence for a few moments before we finished and lay back on the blanket. He put his arm around my shoulders, and we stared up at the sky. A lonely cloud had somehow lost its way crossing from one horizon to another and appeared to be driven in two directions. The winds above eventually began to unravel it. It broke into gauzy wisps of itself and then moved in one direction more than the other.

"Clouds are slaves to the wind," Brayden said. "I wrote that in one of my poems."

"I like it," I said. "When will you let me read your poems?"

"When I'm finished," he said. He sat up and plucked a brownie out of the wrapped paper. "Now, this," he said, holding up another, "is a real poem."

"Right."

We turned when a peal of laughter sounded very close by. It came from our right.

"There's someone in the woods," I said.

He nodded. "Let's get out of the open."

We moved quickly to pick up our things and fold the blanket. He led me down behind some thick bushes, and we waited and listened. We heard their voices grow louder and moments later saw the Russell twins with one of their friends, a shorter, stouter, dark-haired girl. I didn't know who she was, but she stopped to complain about scratching herself on a low bush. They were all wearing shorts.

"There's no one here," the girl whined. "Let's go back. I want to go swimming, and your mother said we were going to have ice cream sundaes soon."

"I'm sure I saw some girl walking in the woods," one of the twins said. "It looked like Amber Taylor."

"Well, she's gone."

They stood there a moment, and then the twins relented and turned around.

"I wondered if they might have seen us when we were at the spring," I told Brayden.

He nodded. "Someone's always ruining it. Glad they didn't find the cabin though."

"Maybe we should return to your house," I said. "Or we could go to mine."

He thought a moment. "I like the idea of going to yours, maybe to your room."

"Yes, of course. There's no one home. It's a big day at the store, I'm sure."

"All right."

He helped me wrap up everything and get it all back into the bag. Then he paused and looked sharply at the woods again.

"Are they coming back?" I asked. He didn't answer. "Brayden?"

"What? Oh, no. They're gone."

"Good. Ready?"

He turned back to the woods. Maybe it was just my imagination, but despite the warm sunshine and the soft breeze coming over the lake, I felt a darkness, a chilling emptiness. For a few moments, all of the sounds around us, the monotonous hum of boat engines and the chirping birds, went silent.

"Brayden?"

I touched his arm. It felt like ice, so cold that I jerked my fingers off.

He turned slowly. His eyes looked different, more gray. "Tell you what," he said. "You head home first. I'll follow in a while. I want to check on my mother and my father and then get all my stuff together."

"I can wait."

"No," he said sharply. Then he smiled when he saw the look on my face. "It's better for now if no one sees us together coming out of the woods. You don't need more gossip about you, and people wouldn't understand about me, with my mother in a clinic seriously ill and all. Okay?"

"If you think that's best," I said.

"I do. For now," he added. He kissed me quickly. I felt no warmth in his lips. It was more like a period to a sentence, small, quick, and final. I suddenly felt something ominous, like a dark cloud on the horizon threatening the sunshine.

"You won't be long, will you?" I said.

"No, I won't be long."

I still hesitated. He smiled.

"I won't be long," he repeated.

"Okay."

I turned and started away. After a few yards, I looked back. He was still looking after me, but there was something final in the way he stood and gazed at me. He lifted his hand. I waved back and then continued on. I walked with my head down, plodding slowly because I felt a trembling in my body. Something wasn't right. All of a sudden, something wasn't right, I thought.

When I reached the Littlefield and Knotts houses, I heard someone call my name and looked up to see Angie Littlefield with Myra Kent, another girl from her class.

"Oh, hi," I said.

"Where are you coming from?" Angie asked.

"The lake," I said.

"You can't go to the lake through that property. It's posted. That's private property," she said, probably because her parents had forbidden it.

"There were lots of rabbits and birds, deer and raccoons."

"So?"

"They didn't pay attention to the signs, either," I said.

"Huh?" Angie said as if I were speaking in a foreign language.

"Why should they be able to do that and not me?" I added. It was definitely something Brayden would have said.

And, as he would have done, I left them standing there with their mouths wide open.

16

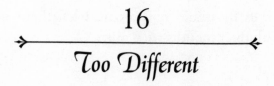

Too Different

He didn't come to my house.

Somehow I wasn't surprised, even though I was very disappointed. Fifteen minutes after I had arrived at the house, I stepped out onto the front porch and looked down the road, anticipating that I would see him coming. Some of the neighbors drove in and out of the street, and I saw Angie and Myra start out for town, but other than that, the street was very quiet. Nervous now, I pulled a chair up closer to the railing and sat watching for any sign of him. When minutes became close to an hour, I decided to call his cell phone. As before, it rang and rang. After nearly two minutes, I hung up and returned to the porch. When I heard the phone ringing inside a half hour later, I practically flew off the chair and nearly pulled off the screen door to get into the house quickly.

"What are you doing?" I heard my mother ask, and felt my heart sink with disappointment. Just on my "hello," she realized that I was out of breath and excited.

"Just sitting out front," I told her, fighting to calm myself.

"So, what have you done with yourself all day?"

I thought a moment and decided I was through with half truths.

"I went on a picnic with Brayden."

"Oh, how nice. Is he there now?"

"No. He was coming over, but he hasn't appeared yet."

"How is his mother?"

"There wasn't any change as far as I knew earlier, but maybe something's happened," I added, now thinking myself that this could be the reason he had not arrived. Perhaps he had gone right from the lake and either met his father or taken a bus or a taxi. "He's not here, and I can't reach him on his cell phone."

"Oh, well, then maybe something is going on. I'm sure he'll call you when he is able to. Why don't you come to the store around closing time? We'll go to Von's for some dinner tonight."

"Okay," I said. "Unless Brayden shows up," I added quickly. "I sorta promised I would make him dinner here. I'll call you."

She was quiet a moment, but she didn't hang up. I was about to say, "Mom?" to see if she was still there.

But then she said, "The other night, when you were out too long and said you fell asleep at the lake, Amber, were you with Brayden?"

For a moment, I couldn't swallow. "Yes," I said.

"You didn't have to keep it a secret, honey," she said. "You know that we trust you to do the right things."

I could feel the tears welling in my eyes.

"I know. I'm sorry," I said.

"We'll talk about it some other time," she promised in a softer voice. "For now, it's just between us, okay?"

"Okay," I said. That simply meant that Dad wasn't going to be informed, but I certainly didn't underestimate the significance.

My parents never lied to each other or kept secrets from each other. I knew that because too often either my mother or my father would tell about something that was guaranteed to upset the other, but hiding it was just not in their DNA, as they say.

"Women can have some secrets between them. It's the nature of our species," she told me, bringing a smile to my face. "Don't worry."

"Thanks, Mom."

"See you later, then," she said.

I returned to the front porch and looked out at the street. There was still no sign of him. I tried calling him again, and again the phone rang and rang until I gave up. Finally, I accepted that he wasn't going to appear for whatever reason, and I went up to change into something to wear to dinner with my parents. I was coming downstairs when the phone rang. I rushed to it.

"This story you're spreading about me is so ridiculous that it makes you look like someone very desperate," Shayne began after my hopeful "hello."

"Excuse me? What story?"

"You know exactly what story I mean."

"Most people know I don't spread stories and that I hate gossip. Maybe it's your sister's doing. You surely know she was spreading a story about me."

"She never would . . ."

"You mean the evil dwarf?" I interrupted. "Weren't those your words?"

"It had better stop," he said.

"I have no intention of talking about you anymore," I said. "I hope you and your sister reciprocate. Maybe you can threaten to expose something else about her to your parents to get her to stop."

"Yeah, I'll do that. I hope this new guy has better luck with you than I had."

"In his case, it won't be a matter of luck," I said. "I imagine, though, with most girls you date, it is."

"Right. Enjoy yourself," he quipped. I could hear the frustration building. He hung up before I could reply.

I wondered if I should call Ellie and pretend to be angry that she had betrayed my confidence but decided against it. Why stop her now? I thought. Brayden's plan was working. I smiled to myself and left the house. My parents and I would walk to the restaurant and walk home. I didn't need our car. As I went past Brayden's house, I wondered when he would get back to me. For whatever reason, he wasn't going to answer his cell phone, and I had no other way to get to him. I had no choice. I'd have to wait.

When my cell phone rang before I turned the corner at the end of the street, I scooped it out of my pocket quickly, hoping again that it would be Brayden, but it was Ellie.

"What are you doing tonight? Are you with the new guy?"

"No. I was going to have dinner with my parents in town."

"Boring," she sang. "A few of us are getting together and going for burgers and fries at the Coral. You know, the place on the other side of the lake. I'll come by and pick you up. Where are you going to be in, say, an hour? Home or at the store?" she followed, assuming that I would jump at the invitation.

I knew why these girls wanted me along. They all hoped to hear salacious details about my time with Shayne. I wasn't afraid of that, but I didn't want to do anything to prevent me from meeting Brayden if and when he should call. My parents would understand if I backed out at the last moment, especially my mother, but it would be more difficult to get away from the girls.

"I'll call you back and let you know," I said.

"Oh, c'mon. You haven't been out with us for a long time, Amber."

"I'll call you back," I insisted.

"Yeah, well, don't keep me waiting too long. I have to pick up Charlotte first. Her father took away her car."

"Glad he finally did something."

"She'll get it back sooner rather than later," Ellie assured me. "Her mother can't stand her moping around the house."

"I couldn't care less. By the way, Shayne Allan called me. He was very upset. He heard I was spreading stories about him and me."

"Did he? I heard his buddies were already teasing him and calling him Mr. Misfire." She laughed. "Don't be angry, Amber. It was too good to waste, and why shouldn't he suffer a little, too?"

"I'm not angry," I said. "You're right. It was too good

to waste. And I assure you, I'm not suffering because of Shayne Allan."

"You sound much better," she said. "I was telling everyone how you've changed, come alive. Everyone's happy for you, too. I know I am."

"Thanks. I'll call you," I said, and flipped the phone closed.

I have changed, I thought, and it wasn't simply because I'd had sex with someone. Even before Brayden and I embraced in that sleeping bag, I had begun to feel different. Suddenly, I was able to see and hear things as if I were above it all. I wasn't being condescending. I really felt older, wiser. Brayden had given me a sixth sense, an insight I had not possessed. After being with him, I couldn't help but see how silly, insignificant, and juvenile most of the other girls in my class were. I'd always had trouble participating in inane and catty conversations, but now it was going to be impossible. If the others in my school thought I was acting like a snob before, they'd now surely believe I had become a full-fledged one. Life in my small community was not going to get very much better for me. *He had better not leave,* I thought. *I'm going to need him beside me to get through it.*

I turned onto the main street and headed for our store. The village was in that late-afternoon, early-evening mode. Twilight was starting because of the height of the mountains in the west, and the soft, cool shadows of early summer were creeping in like fog. Some stores and restaurants had already turned on their lights, and if you looked carefully, you could see the first stars beginning to appear, looking like brilliant tiny bubbles rising to the surface of the darker blue sky. Was it just my imagination, or were shadows different in the summer from how they were in the winter? In the winter, they seemed to come faster and be deeper, harsher, seizing everything they touched as the temperatures dropped.

Pedestrians walked differently in early summer evenings from how they walked in early winter evenings, for sure. They had to be moving briskly in winter. They tightened their buttons, zipped up their jackets, closed their collars, and always seemed to be a step behind their visible breath. Getting somewhere was always more important than going there. You felt as if you were running a gauntlet when you went to the grocery or drugstore. At least, I did. However, I knew there were many residents who preferred our winters to our summers. They enjoyed the brisk air, the sharper evening skies, and, above all, the diminished traffic and noise.

People were really different in so many ways, and yet there was this terrible need, this urgency, to avoid being too different. This was especially true for kids my age. We dressed alike. We liked the same music, celebrities, even food, and when someone stepped away, disagreed, changed style, and stopped being a follower, he or she became distrusted and, more often than not, disliked. I was confident that despite his good looks and his brilliance, Brayden would fall into this category eventually at our school, as he probably had at every school he had attended. But I was determined to stand by him. If necessary, we would keep completely to ourselves, and we would never be unhappy about it.

I knew his staying here was very far from certain.

Right now, it even looked impossible, but that didn't prevent me from fantasizing more and more about it. We'd go to school together. Most of the time, we'd come home together. We'd study together. Jealous classmates would come up with all sorts of ridicule, claiming that we were joined at the hip like conjoined twins or something. But ironically, they would want us at their parties, and girls who recognized that we had something very sophisticated going on would want to be friends with me, would hover about, listening keenly in hopes that they would pick up some clue, some advice, some wisdom that would make them seem just as sophisticated. Of course, they would never admit that. They would even attack one another for trying to play up to me too hard.

Imagining it all brought a smile to my face. I could live very well in this picture, I thought as I entered the store. Dad was just wrapping up his tools and materials in the rear. Mrs. Williams was helping Mom finish their review of the day's receipts. There were no customers. Everyone looked up at me.

"Hey, Amber Light. We had a pretty good day," Dad said. "Mrs. Russell was just in here buying a birthday present for her husband, a pretty expensive watch. And she preferred the watchband I had created for it."

Mom looked at him and came around the corner of the counter. "That's his way of telling you that her daughters claimed they saw you in the woods down at the lake today," she told me in a voice just above a whisper. She brushed back some of my hair. "On private property. Is that where you went for your picnic with Brayden?"

302 V. C. Andrews

"Yes."

"Might be better if you avoided the lake properties. You know how uptight some of those people get."

I didn't say anything. The cabin, the area around it, had all become too magical for Brayden and me simply to give up so easily. I foresaw many more days and evenings there for us once his mother's situation eased up.

Mrs. Williams picked up her purse.

"Thank you, Millie," Mom told her as she started to leave.

"No, thank *you*," Mrs. Williams said. "You look very nice, Amber," she told me. "I like the way you're wearing your hair these days."

"Thank you," I said. Mom looked at me as if Mrs. Williams's compliment had pointed out some hidden changes. Her eyes twinkled with some delight but also with a woman's intuition about her daughter. It made me blush.

"See you next weekend," Mrs. Williams said. Dad called his good-bye to her, and we watched her leave.

"Let's get going, Gregory. We're hungry."

"Yes, boss," Dad said, and closed up his safe.

"I have to make a quick call," I said, and stepped out to do it.

I knew that if my mother heard that some of the girls wanted me to go out with them, she'd push me to do it, but I was determined now not to.

"I can't get out of dinner with my parents," I told Ellie. "We've got some family matters to discuss." It wasn't a total lie. Anything we discussed would in some way involve us as a family.

"Oh, too bad. Maybe tomorrow night."

"Maybe. If I'm free," I added.

"You promised we would double-date," she retorted quickly.

"We will," I said, sounding as casual as I could, even though I didn't know when, if ever, I would go out on a regular date with Brayden. "Later," I added, and hung up just as Mom and Dad came out of the store.

"Anything new?" Mom asked. It was clear that she thought I had gone out to speak privately to Brayden.

"I wasn't talking to him," I said. "I was talking to Ellie."

"Oh. You want to do something else?"

"No, this is perfect," I said.

Minutes later, we were walking through the village together. I could see that there were questions my mother wanted to ask me about Brayden Matthews and myself now, but she wanted to talk privately. If Dad noticed, he didn't let on. Just as whenever we ate dinner at his friend Von Richards's restaurant, we were inundated with greetings and small talk from local residents. Before the dinner ended, when Mom and Dad had coffee and I had a piece of peach pie, Von came over to sit with us.

Most of their conversation was about the economy and the improved summer business we were all experiencing. Von was sort of the informal mayor of Echo Lake because so many other businesspeople and residents were in his restaurant at one time or another during the week or the month. Complaints and general political debate filled the air. Because of whom he spoke to, Von usually had some insight others didn't and commanded more respect and attention. When Dad asked him if he knew anything about our new neighbors, I listened keenly. Mom looked at me to see how I would react.

Von sat back, folding his arms across his chest. He was a stout man, with thinning gray hair, who was aging faster than my father, who happened to be about the same age.

"That was the Sloans' property. They came close to being foreclosed on. Did you know that?"

"No," Dad said, looking at Mom. She shook her head.

"Yeah, well, that was one of those inside deals, in my opinion," Von continued. "Someone in the bank alerted this real estate hog in Portland, and he scooped it up. I didn't hear that he had sold or rented it," Von added, his eyes having widened with surprise.

"Well, they haven't been there that long, and apparently, the wife is not a well woman. We haven't seen hide nor hair of the couple," Dad continued. "Amber, however, has spent some time with the teenage son."

Von nodded, looking at me and smiling. "If I moved next door to her, I'd be spending some time with her, too. What are they like?" he asked me.

"Mr. Matthews works for a brain trust about economics," I said. "And Mrs. Matthews is a fairly well-known artist." I didn't want to say much more about them to him, certainly not about Brayden's mother's condition.

"I can't think of a brain I'd trust," Von joked. Dad laughed. Mom reached under the table and squeezed my hand. "Got to get back to the mine," Von added, rising. "Thanks for coming."

We watched him walk away, and Dad signaled for the check. The walk home was casual and delightful. Dad talked about the changes he had lived through growing up in Echo Lake, the things he had done with his father and his grandfather, and how important he thought it was to have a sense of place, somewhere you could always call home even if you left and never returned. As always when he reminisced, he became a little philosophical.

"Where you're brought up has something to do with shaping who you are," he said. "Even if you don't realize it, it does."

Mom agreed, and then Dad began to tease her about her Southern background. They went at each other play-fully for a while. I watched and listened to them and smiled. But of course, my thoughts went to Brayden, someone who, from what he had told me about himself, had never had a sense of home, a sense of belonging any-where. I thought he knew that and missed it. It was why I believed he really wanted to stay here, especially now.

But this dreamworld I was creating for myself exploded the moment we turned the corner to start down our street. I stopped walking at the sight of the truck pulling away from Brayden's house, followed by Brayden's father in his car. He was alone. For a moment, none of us spoke.

"Did they just move out?" Dad asked Mom.

"It looks like it. Amber? Did you know this was hap-pening?"

I shook my head, my eyes tearing over mostly from shock. "No," I managed. I watched the vehicles turn and disappear.

"That was the shortest rental in Echo Lake history," Dad said. "We didn't even get to meet them. Was it something I said?" he joked.

Mom just looked at him. She reached out for my hand, and we continued to our house. We paused at Brayden's.

"To tell you the truth," Dad said, "it doesn't look any different from when they were here, if they were here. Maybe we all imagined it."

"Mrs. Matthews was apparently very ill, Gregory. Perhaps something serious happened to her and they never got a chance to really settle in."

"Oh," Dad said, sorry he had made light of it.

"Why wouldn't he call me?" I asked my mother.

"If something happened to his mother, honey, he might not yet be in the state of mind to think of calling you, or anything else, for that matter."

"Maybe we can find out somehow."

"You don't know where she was taken, do you?" my mother asked. Dad was heading for the front door. I shook my head. "Then we'll just have to wait for him to phone you, honey. There's nothing else to do about it tonight, anyway." She started for the house and paused to look back at me. "Coming in?" she asked.

"Not right now," I said.

"There's no point in agonizing over it, Amber. There's nothing you can do right now."

"I'll be in soon," I said sharply.

Dad was standing in the open doorway, watching and listening. She looked at him and continued to the house. They both went in while I stood there, hoping that Brayden would suddenly appear to explain it all.

There was no light from his house, of course, and there
were no sounds coming from inside.

Out of nowhere, it seemed, a crow sailed onto the
roof. I was caught in a whirlpool of different emotions:
disappointment and sadness, of course, but also anger
and rage. Why did his father bring them to Echo Lake if
his mother was so unstable? And why did he leave them
alone like that? Poor Brayden, I thought, tossed about
so much. How did his father hope or expect him to have
any sort of normal life?

I dug my cell phone out of my pocket and tried to
reach him again, but his phone just rang and rang and
rang. I dropped mine back into my pocket and headed for
the house. My father was upstairs, but my mother was in
the kitchen, puttering around, I assumed, to wait for me.

"He still doesn't answer his cell phone," I told her.

"Obviously, it's something very serious, Amber.
You'll have to be patient."

"It doesn't make sense, Mom."

"These things seldom do," she said.

"No, I mean, I thought we had become very close, and
no matter what, he would want to talk to me, be with me."

She nodded. "No matter how good the time you've
spent with him has been, Amber, you can't expect to
know someone completely that quickly."

I shook my head. "That's not true. He's . . . special.
We were able to really get to know each other quickly."

She stared at me a moment. "How well?" she asked.

I knew what she was after. I shook my head. I
wouldn't talk about it now, maybe not ever if I never saw
him again, I thought.

Without replying, I turned and rushed out and up the stairs to my room. I threw myself down on my bed and buried my face in my pillow. What was going on? How could all of this be happening? I thought I would cry but suddenly had the urge to sit up instead. I turned to look out my window and across the way to what had been Brayden's bedroom. The window was dark, of course, but suddenly, I thought I saw his face in the glass, looking as it had that first time I saw him there, floating. I leaped up and went closer to my window. When I studied the dark bedroom window this time, I saw nothing.

Maybe he was there for just a few seconds, I thought. Maybe he had come back for something. Maybe he was still there. Without hesitation, I hurried out of my bedroom and down the stairs. My mother was just putting the lights out in the kitchen and going up herself when she heard me and saw me rush by.

"Amber! Where are you going?" she called.

I didn't pause to answer.

17

Puzzle Pieces

I ran down my driveway and across to Brayden's house. I knocked, waited, then tried the doorknob. It was unlocked. Every light was off downstairs, but I thought nothing of it. That was the way it was most of the time when his mother was there. I stepped in slowly and listened. I could hear something. It sounded like something or someone scratching on a wall or a floor. I thought it might be coming from the roof and realized that it might be a crow strutting over the shingles.

"Brayden?" I called. I waited, listened, and called once more. When there was no response, I felt my excitement begin to fade away. Perhaps I had wanted to see him so much that I had imagined it. I tried a light switch and was surprised to see the chandelier in the hallway illuminate. The electricity was still on, but that could just mean that the electric company had not gotten around to shutting it off. I went forward and looked into the living room. The boxes I had seen still packed on the floor were gone. Otherwise, it didn't look much different from before. There had been little done with it when they were living there. None of the downstairs area looked much different, in fact, except in the kitchen, because the boxes were gone, along with whatever dishes and plates and cups I had seen.

Of course, my thoughts went to Brayden's room and the attic. I had little hope of finding him, but I would not leave without looking in both of those places. Slowly, I made my way back to the foot of the stairway. The chandelier threw enough light for me to walk up easily, but at the top, when I flipped the switch that should have turned on the hallway light, nothing happened. Probably a dead bulb, I thought, and wondered if Brayden or his parents had ever noticed, since I had never seen the light on there through any of the windows. Despite the darkness, I continued, and when I reached what I knew was his parents' bedroom, I felt around the door frame and found a light switch.

A lamp on a side table went on. It was weak and cast a dim yellowish glow on the walls, unable to wash away the darkness and shadows totally. I looked for some sign to suggest that they weren't completely gone. However, the bed was stripped, and there was nothing on the old dressers and side tables except for the single small lamp. Of course, there was nothing on the walls, either. The emptiness made it seem so desolate and deserted. The walls reeked of depression, but it was Brayden's room I wanted to see most, so I moved quickly to it. My heart was thumping, because I was hoping to be shocked by the sight of him standing there.

He wasn't. There was nothing left in his room, either, and the bed had also been stripped. Of all of the rooms I had seen before, this one had had the most in it, with his computer and pictures and clothes, but packing away what was there wouldn't have taken much time.

Disappointed, I turned and headed for the attic. Halfway up the stairs to it, I paused. The sounds I had heard before had grown louder. My heart started thumping again. Why was I even going up there? If Brayden's father had taken away everything else, why would he have left anything up there? Even if he hated the artwork, he would surely have taken it and destroyed it, rather than left it there. Perhaps he needed it to show her therapist what sort of thing she had been doing.

But then, I thought, maybe it was Brayden I was hearing. Maybe he was doing something with the art material, something his father either had overlooked or wanted to ignore. Firming up my courage, I continued up the short stairway. The door was closed. I turned the knob and opened it in small, jerky motions at first before pushing forward and thrusting it fully open.

Instantly, at least four large crows leaped off the floor, flapping their wings madly. They screeched and rushed toward the open window, one of them coming very close to me before they all got out. I screamed and then shut the door so quickly and so hard that I lost my footing and fell back on the stairway, but I was able to seize the narrow banister and stop myself from tumbling. Why had they left the window open? Maybe it was an oversight, but for some reason, the crows had been drawn into the attic.

I hadn't seen much of the attic because of the darkness and the shock of the crows, but I thought it was empty. I was determined to be sure and straightened myself up. I pushed the door open again and looked at the attic, now somewhat illuminated by the night sky. There was nothing left. The portrait was gone, as were all of the art utensils and easels. I stood staring at the dark, empty space. As I tried to recall it all, it seemed more like struggling to remember the details of a nightmare.

"Amber," I heard, and turned. My name echoed through the empty house. "Amber, are you in here?" It was my mother.

"Yes," I called down.

"What are you doing in here?"

"I'm coming down," I said.

I descended the attic stairway and headed for the main stairs. At the bottom were my parents, both looking up with surprise, both in their robes and slippers.

"What the hell are you doing in here?" my father asked, now visibly annoyed. "Why did you run out of the house like that? You scared the hell out of us."

"I thought I saw Brayden," I said, continuing down.

"You thought you saw Brayden? Where?"

"In his bedroom."

"What? Why would he be here if they moved out? There's no car in the driveway, and the house is obviously empty. You can't just enter someone's property like this and go traipsing through it, especially after some renters just left. If something was broken or missing, you could get blamed. What were you thinking?" he demanded.

I stood there speechless. How could I even begin to explain it?

"I came in here once before. I thought Brayden was

here then, too, and I . . . shouldn't have, but I explored the house."

"You did what?" Dad asked, grimacing. He looked at my mother, who shook her head.

"None of the boxes were unpacked, and except for his room, nothing looked like anyone was living here. I knew his mother worked in the attic, that it was her studio, so I went up there."

"Spying and snooping?"

"Oh, Amber," my mother said, "this sort of behavior is so unlike you."

"I know. I'm sorry, but I went up there, and I saw the painting she was doing. It was a portrait of Brayden, and it was . . . horrible."

"So, now you're an art critic?" my father said without a note of humor.

"No, it was horrible because it was . . . horrible. It was a grotesque distortion, terrifying actually."

"The woman was not well," my mother said. "Regardless, you shouldn't have done that then, and you certainly shouldn't be doing it now."

"But . . ."

"What?" my father practically shouted. "What?"

"He hasn't called me. He said he would if something came up."

"First," my father said, "we never got to meet this boy, so we can't tell you our opinion of him and whether or not he was the sort of young man who would keep a promise. We have only your word for it, and it was pretty clear from the start that you were quite taken with him. Your judgment was obviously clouded."

"Gregory," my mother said, hoping to end it.

"No, Noreen. This is unacceptable. You get home, young lady," he said, pointing to the door. "We'll talk more about this. I'll go up and turn off the lights you left on. I can't believe this." He shot past me and hurried up the stairs.

"Let's go home," my mother said when he started back down the stairs.

I nodded, lowered my head, and walked out. They followed silently, Dad closing the door behind them.

"Was it unlocked?"

"Yes," I said.

"Terrific. Some tenants. Run off and leave the place wide open."

"Something terrible must have happened," I told him.

He mumbled something to himself as we crossed to our driveway and went up to our front door.

"You should have realized something was not right with these people, Amber," he continued when we entered the house. "You couldn't get the boy to come over to see us. He didn't want to meet any of your friends. His mother was probably heavily medicated most of the time. His father sounds like an idiot, not a genius, leaving them here like this. It's clear they're all gone, and you're disappointed because this boy didn't bother even to say good-bye. I guess that shows you what he really thought about your friendship. I'm sorry now that you had anything to do with him. For whatever reasons, he was obviously not as sincere as you believed. I should have been more involved. If I had, you wouldn't have been so taken in and . . ."

"No!" I screamed. "He was wonderful and made all the other boys in this town look like idiots."

"Amber," my mother said to calm me.

"No, he's unfair. You don't know anything!" I screamed at my father. "Go read another book on World War One, and leave me alone!" I pounded up the stairs. I slammed my door shut and stood there pouting and gasping. When I heard them coming up the stairs, I went into my bathroom and locked the door. I sat on the edge of the tub and sobbed silently. I heard my mother open my bedroom door. She stood for a moment and then left, closing the door again.

Why was this happening?

Was my father right? Was Brayden no different from any other self-centered boy, after all? *It can't be true. It just can't be,* I told myself. I embraced myself and rocked on the edge of the tub, chanting this hope. When I came out of the bathroom to go to bed, I heard my parents' muffled voices. They were arguing. It wasn't something they did very much, so I felt bad. After a while, they quieted down, and I cried myself to sleep, hoping that sometime during the night or early in the morning, Brayden would call me to explain everything.

He didn't.

I overslept the following morning. My mother came in, not to wake me but to tell me that she and my father had decided I should not go in to work.

"We think you should take the day to get over things, Amber."

"I can work."

"Let the air settle first," she said. It was one of her

favorite expressions, one she said her father had used. I did feel as if I was at the center of some whirlwind. "You know how your father feels about any of us putting on a down-in-the-dumps look to greet people coming in to spend a lot of money on some happy occasion. Later," she added, moving to leave, "you and I can have a heart-to-heart about all this, okay?"

I nodded.

She smiled, but I could see the tension in her face. She closed the door softly and went down to leave with my father. I lay there staring up at the ceiling and feeling sorry for myself for nearly another hour. I really wasn't hungry, but I rose and forced myself to have a little breakfast. While I was chewing lazily on a piece of toast and sipping some coffee, the phone rang. I forced myself not to hope that it was Brayden, and I was glad I had done so. It was Ellie.

"You missed a great time last night," she said. "I never realized how many girls and even guys disliked Shayne Allan. Everyone was taking pleasure in spreading the story about him and calling him Mr. Misfire. I guess the guys were always too jealous and the girls he ignored or belittled, like *moi,* are sucking up the revenge."

"I'm happy for you all," I said dryly.

"So, what's new with Brayden? Is his mother any better? Can we plan on something soon?"

"No."

"No?"

"They're gone," I said.

"Gone? What do you mean?"

"Gone, gone," I said, raising my voice. "They left, moved out of the house. They're gone. What's so hard to understand?"

"Already, but . . . oh," she said, finally understanding. "That's why you sound so upset. Was it a sad parting? Is he going to write or something? Visit in the future?"

"There was no parting. When we came home, they were already gone."

"He left without saying good-bye? I don't get it. I thought . . . I mean, you made me think you and him were getting to be a thing."

"Yeah, we were a thing. I'm not in the mood to talk about it, Ellie. Right now, I couldn't care less about any boy."

"Oh. Well, do you want me to come around? We could do something, go somewhere to help get your mind off it," she offered. I knew that what she really wanted was more detail. How much had I committed to this aborted relationship? How broken was my heart?

"No. Thank you. I just want to be alone for a while."

"That's not good. It's better if you get out, mix with people, do things. I know. I've been disappointed in love enough to know." She gave a short, hollow laugh.

"There's a difference."

"What?"

"You expected it."

"Huh?"

"It's hard to explain right now, Ellie. Please. I'll call you. 'Bye," I added quickly, and hung up.

I was sure that she was falling back into thinking the worst of me. I was even a snob about my romantic failures, and as a snob, I would not lower myself to share anything intimate with girls so far below me. She didn't understand; she couldn't understand. I really believed that teenagers in love were just in some strong version of like. In the backs of their minds, they had to anticipate breaking up. How many would actually expect to go on and marry their boyfriends from high school? There were enough examples of that being disastrous. You could go hot and heavy and say all sorts of intimate and promising things when you were in a teenage love affair, but it was more like reciting a script to me. Everyone was expected to say these things and do these things.

A mature romance was surely deeper and more substantial. That's what I had thought I was beginning to have with Brayden. We were both too bright and perceptive to play games with each other. More important, we recognized a need that each of us fulfilled for the other. That was more mature. That was real commitment. No, Ellie could never understand, and I could never explain it to her in a way that she would understand. I probably couldn't even explain it to my mother and certainly, I knew now, never to my father.

This realization didn't make me feel any better. In fact, it made me feel worse. There had to be a very serious and understandable reason for Brayden to leave without saying good-bye. Instead of resenting him for it, I should be sympathetic, I thought. I shouldn't be pouting and fighting with my parents. I should follow up and seek a way to help Brayden. I couldn't do that while wallowing in self-pity, and I couldn't do that if I settled for accepting that he was gone and that was that. No, I had to be more determined. Our feelings for each other called for me to be more determined.

Suddenly filled with energy and hope, I rose and went upstairs to put on a pair of jeans and a blouse. I slipped on my running shoes, brushed back my hair and pinned it into a ponytail, and then hurried out of the house. I had a plan, an idea. Not even glancing at the now depressingly empty house next door, I jogged into town, but not to go to my family's jewelry shop. When I reached Main Street, I stopped running so as not to attract any unnecessary attention and instead walked quickly to my father's friend Von Richards's restaurant. There were about a half-dozen early lunch customers. Von was not in sight. As soon as the hostess, whom I knew to be one of his daughters, approached me, I asked for him.

"He's in the kitchen," she said.

"Could I speak to him? It's important."

She looked at me suspiciously and then shrugged and went back to the kitchen. Almost immediately, Von came out behind her. He was wiping his hands on a dish towel and nodded at an empty booth on my right. I followed him to it.

"Hey, Amber," he said. "What's up? Something the matter with your parents?"

"No, they're fine, Mr. Richards."

"I think you can call me Von, Amber. What can I do for you? You want something to drink?"

"No, thank you. Remember when we were here for dinner, and my parents were talking about our new neighbors?"

"Oh, yeah. What about them?"

"Well, I got to know their son."

"I remember."

"Yesterday, they packed up and moved out."

He sat back. "They weren't there long. Maybe they had a hard time with the landlord. I hear he's a mean son of a bitch, you'll pardon my French. Ruthless guy. He's been trying to get his hands on some lake property recently. Stan Watts told me he's been making the sorts of offers that are hard to refuse, but Stan's holding his ground."

"Who is this man?"

Von scratched his head and looked at me as if he was deciding whether he should get up and call my father before talking to me any further.

"I thought maybe he would tell me why the Matthewses left and where they went."

"Oh. The young man never told you?"

"His mother's been very ill. I think it has to do with that," I said. "I feel bad about it."

"Young love," he said, nodding and smiling. "His name's Marcus Norton. He has a company out of Portland simply called Marcus Norton Investments. Stan tells me he's a man in his seventies. No question, he wants the property as an investment. I'm surprised he didn't find a way to unload that house next to your parents before this. Maybe that's it, Amber. Maybe we'll find out he sold it recently, and that was why the family left. I can find that out later today."

"No, I don't care about the house," I said, maybe too abruptly.

He pulled his head back. "Well, that's about all I know about it," he said. He smiled. "You're not going to lack for new boyfriends."

"I'm not worried about that, either, Mr. Richards. Thanks for the information." I rose and turned to leave.

"Hey," he called. I turned back. "If this guy left without telling you why or where he was going, he's not worth much more of your time and effort."

"You and my father sound alike."

"We have good reason to. We're both homegrown," he said, smiling.

"Thanks," I said, and hurried out, passing his very curious daughter, who looked as if she was about to pounce on her father to hear why I had wanted to speak to him.

I thought about stopping at the store to tell my parents what I intended to do, but I hesitated, because I knew that my father, especially, not only would try to talk me out of it but might forbid me from doing it. It was easier just to go home, get what I needed, write a note explaining, and leave. When I reached our street, I broke into a jog again. As I ran, I thought how interesting it was that this Marcus Norton was trying to buy the property that Brayden had discovered and that he and I had considered our own private wonderland. I had no idea why he would want to purchase it other than what Mr. Richards had suggested: another property to hold for investment reasons. But still, it lingered in my mind and seemed somehow to be a piece in this puzzle I was trying to solve.

When I reached home, I went on my computer and looked up Marcus Norton Investments in Portland. I found it listed on NW 5th Avenue. The description fit what Von Richards had described. I called and asked to speak with Mr. Norton.

"He's not in right now," his secretary said. "I expect him back in about three hours."

"That's perfect," I said.

"Perfect for what?" I could hear her surprise and the near laughter in her voice.

"I need to see him. It's urgent."

"What's it in regard to?"

"It's personal. I'll be there in around three hours. My name is Amber Taylor, and I live in Echo Lake."

"Well, he has a full schedule."

"Please, just fit me in for ten minutes," I begged.

The desperation in my voice softened her, and she said she would fit me in when I arrived.

As soon as I hung up, I ran up to my room and dug out the money I kept in a dresser drawer for special occasions or reasons. I made sure that my cell phone was charged, put a few other necessities into my purse, grabbed a light jacket, and went down to write the note.

Dear Mom and Dad,
I'm sorry I upset you both last night. It's very difficult to get someone else, even you two whom I love so much, to understand why I'm so involved with Brayden and disturbed about him after knowing him for so short a time. Maybe I'll find a way to do that later. In any case, I decided he was worth my making a little extra effort to understand and perhaps help in some way. Please don't worry about me.

I'm off to Portland to talk to someone who might know more about the Matthewses. I'll call if I'm going to be home late.

I love you both very much.

Amber

I almost wrote *Amber Light* for my father's sake, but just the thought of doing that brought tears to my eyes, and I didn't want to be some weepy girl right now.

Right now, I wanted to be a determined young woman who would get the answers to her questions and solve all of the mysteries herself.

There would be plenty of time to be weepy if that was where the journey led me.

I was soon to know.

18

Answers

When I saw that there was heavy traffic heading toward Portland, I was afraid that I would arrive after Mr. Norton's business hours and it would turn out to be a wasted trip. That was the only excuse I had for speeding and going through what must have been a radar trap. I was practically in tears when the highway patrolman signaled for me to pull over.

"In a rush?" he asked when he walked over to my car window.

I took a deep breath and said, "Yes. I'm afraid to miss an appointment."

"Imagine how many you'll miss if you crash," he said. "Let me have your license and registration, please."

I dug it out and handed it to him. He looked at it, started for his vehicle, and then suddenly stopped as if he had heard something or someone. I watched him stare at my picture for a long moment, turn slowly, and come back to my car. I was afraid there was something wrong with my license and I would be in even more trouble. Maybe he wouldn't let me drive on. But he surprised me.

"What guarantee do I have that you will slow down and stay within the speed limit?"

I looked at the traffic and then at him. "I'll try," I said. My honesty brought a smile to his face.

"Try harder, Amber Taylor," he replied, and handed my license and registration back.

"Thank you. I will."

"You'd better. We don't want you eternally late for an appointment."

He stepped back. Very slowly and carefully, I pulled back onto the highway.

"Someone's watching over you, Amber Light," I muttered, and shook my head, still amazed at my good luck. I couldn't even begin to imagine giving my father the news of my getting a speeding ticket on top of rushing off to Portland without first telling him and my mother. I did watch my speed. Staying within the limit didn't make all that much difference in my arrival time in Portland, either. I was well within the three hours I had arranged with Mr. Norton's secretary. The city was busy. I was close to rush hour, but I found a place to park close to the address of Marcus Norton Investments.

Earlier, I had feared that I would arrive in a rainstorm, but as if my urgency and enthusiasm had the power to control the wind, the clouds began to thin out and part, until blue sky was everywhere. For a moment, I stood looking at the busy traffic and the pedestrians streaming out of buildings and hurrying to their own vehicles. Now that I was there, I was very nervous. What if this Marcus Norton was a very mean, brusque man? Von Richards's comments suggested that he was that sort. What if he didn't feel it was proper to give out information about any of his tenants? I would be so embarrassed if he asked me to leave. I rehearsed how I was going to approach him and exactly what I would say to get him to be forthcoming and not think I was a total nutcase.

The Marcus Norton Investments offices were on the first floor of a building with a glazed version of architectural terra-cotta, which was basically an enriched molded clay brick. It was obviously one of the older buildings and not very tall. None of the buildings in Portland were, to protect the views of nearby Mount Hood. I knew a little about the city because Dad had told me that its economic and industrial boom had sunk at the start of the First World War. It was a shipping town, and business had been heavily damaged. Real estate and the lumber industry had brought it back and stimulated the expansion of the dock facilities. My father loved getting into conversations with old-timers about all this.

Despite my determination, when I entered the company's small lobby, I could feel myself trembling. The receptionist, a thin, dark-haired woman with hazel eyes and thin lips, looked up from her computer keyboard. I imagined that she was in her late fifties if not early sixties. Growing up around jewelry and colors made me more critical than most my age when it came to hair dye jobs, makeup, and clothing, I think. I thought her short hair looked as if it had been dipped in a pool of cheap ink. With her very fair complexion, the contrast made the poor coloring job even harsher.

"Yes," she said, as if I had asked a question. Her lips tightened like those of someone who didn't want to be disturbed. Whatever she was doing was challenging her, I imagined. Just my luck to be greeted by someone already in a bad mood, I thought.

"I called earlier today. My name is Amber Taylor."

"Oh. Yes. Well, Mr. Norton has an attorney in his office at the moment. I have no idea how long he'll be occupied. He didn't tell me about this meeting," she added, as if she had known me for years and I was someone who would give her great sympathy. "It's not unusual. I don't know why I keep a daybook anymore. I have no idea how long this meeting is supposed to go. You can wait or come back another day."

"Oh, no, I can't. I drove all the way from Echo Lake, remember?"

She shook her head. "No, I don't remember where you came from." She pushed some papers around and looked at what must be her notes. "Yes, I see it. Well, I can't rush him out of a meeting. You'll have to decide what to do."

"I'll wait," I said, and sat on the small settee that faced his office.

She looked at me askance. "I can't imagine what could possibly bring someone your age this far to see Mr. Norton."

"It's very important to me," I said. I knew she was expecting me to reveal it all, but I wasn't going to chance her deciding that it wasn't important enough to take up her boss's time. She waited for me to say more. Instead, I reached for one of the magazines. They were all about real estate or finance, nothing I would otherwise pick up. When I opened one, she smirked and returned to her work.

It was nearly twenty minutes before the door opened. There were two men stepping out, one very tall with styled light brown hair and a bronze tan. He wore a gray-black pin-striped suit and a black tie. I didn't think he could be more than in his mid-thirties. The man beside him was a good six inches shorter, stout, with thin, balding ash-gray hair in puffs over his temples and down the back of his head. His nose was a little wide, but he still had striking iceberg-blue eyes. Although he had what Mom would describe as a barrel chest and wide hips, his face was narrow, his cheeks even a bit sunken. He looked my way while he was shaking the other man's hand.

"Okay, Alex, let's close this thing by the end of the week. Good work," he said.

The younger man smiled. Then, when he turned and saw me sitting there, he paused and widened his smile.

"Things are looking up for you, Marcus," he told Mr. Norton, who shrugged and held his grin.

"So, what do we have here, Mrs. Douglas?" Mr. Norton asked the receptionist.

"Amber Taylor. She's come here from Echo Lake to see you on a personal matter."

"Oh." He widened his smile. "Well, come right in, Miss Taylor," he said. He looked toward the young man who was standing at the entrance. "Call me," he told him.

"Will do."

He stepped back for me to enter his office. It looked

twice as big as the lobby. There was a wall bookcase on the right, with a settee like the one in the lobby in front of it and a glass coffee table and two soft-cushioned chairs. There was another soft-cushioned chair off in the right corner. The office walls were covered in a dark pecan paneling. On the left was another, larger table with some blueprints spread over the top and a few chairs around it. The wall on the left had a number of plaques, framed letters, and pictures. There was a large bay-style window behind the oversized dark walnut desk. All of the papers on it were neatly stacked. In front of the desk were two more soft-cushioned chairs.

Mr. Norton closed the door and moved quickly to his desk, as if he needed to have it between him and anyone visiting. He nodded at one of the chairs. "So what can I do for you, Miss . . ."

"Amber Taylor," I said, taking the seat.

He sat. "Amber." He smiled, folded his hands together, and sat a little forward. "So?"

"I live next door to the property you rented recently in Echo Lake."

He didn't say anything immediately. He just looked at me for a moment. "Who told you I rented a property in Echo Lake?"

"Didn't you?"

"It wasn't rented."

"Oh."

"Why are you inquiring about that, anyway?" he asked, losing the softness of his smile quickly.

"The family, the Matthewses, moved out abruptly yesterday. I want to know where they went," I said.

He continued to stare at me, his eyes filling with impatience, waiting for me to continue. It was easy to see that he was the kind of man who disliked small talk. My father would call him a bottom-line man, the sort who wants you to get right to the point and not try to influence him first with conversation designed to set it up more attractively.

"Why?" he asked.

"Well, I know that Mrs. Matthews wasn't well, and just before they all had to move, she . . . got worse. Their son, Brayden, was supposed to come to my house that day, and when he didn't show up, I tried to reach him, but he never responded. On our way home from dinner at a local restaurant, we saw the small truck and Mr. Matthews leaving the house. Brayden never answered his phone. I called and called. I'm very worried about him, and I thought that if he was nearby, I could maybe speak to him and help him."

Mr. Norton just continued to stare at me, making me feel very uncomfortable.

"I mean . . . well, we were becoming very close. I was hoping that his family would stay in Echo Lake and he would finish his last year of high school in my school. It's very important to me to speak to him again," I added when he still didn't speak. I waited. The silence was very unnerving. "I know that it might not be legal or ethical for you to give out personal information, but I assure you, Brayden won't be upset."

"What did you say your name was?" he asked, picking up a pen.

"Amber Taylor. My family owns the Taylor Jewelry Store in Echo Lake. It's been there for years and years."

He wrote something, nodded, and looked up at me again.

"Did you talk to Mrs. or Mr. Matthews while they were living there?"

"Actually, no. I tried to talk to Mrs. Matthews once, but she . . . she was ill and getting worse. She never came out of the house, as far as I knew, and Mr. Matthews went away on an important meeting almost as soon as they had moved into the house.

"Look, I'm not after them to get money or anything," I added, thinking that he was suspicious of my intentions. "I knew that Mrs. Matthews was seeing a therapist and was suffering from a serious mental condition. Brayden explained all that to me." I paused. Maybe I was telling him too much, I thought, but what choice did I have?

"Brayden eventually revealed that she had tried to commit suicide and she was in a clinic somewhere near Portland. That's why I thought they had to move out, so he and his father would be closer. I guess she has to stay in the clinic for a long time. I would just like to get in touch with him. It's been hard for him to make friends his age. I don't know what you know about them, but because of the work his father does, his family has had to travel a lot."

I paused. I was talking too much, I thought. Mr. Norton was staring at me strangely again.

"Amber Taylor, Taylor Jewelry in Echo Lake?"

"Yes, sir. My parents don't know that I've come here," I added quickly.

"Is that so?"

"I just had to try to find him, and when Mr. Richards told me who owned the property . . ."

"Von Richards?"

"Yes. When he told me that you owned the property and told me about your company, I called to make this appointment."

He rose so quickly out of his seat that I actually pulled back in mine.

"Wait here," he said, and walked out of his office, closing the door behind him.

I imagined that he was going out to ask his secretary where the Matthews family had relocated. But why did he say that he hadn't rented the house to them? The way he looked at me while I was explaining everything gave me the feeling that I might even be in the wrong office. Maybe Von Richards had it wrong. Maybe Marcus Norton didn't own the house the Matthewses had been in. Maybe, however, he owned so many properties that he was going out to check with his secretary to see if the house in Echo Lake was one of them. I would certainly feel stupid if I were in the wrong office, and to top it off, I had driven all this way for nothing. The owner of the property might not even be in Portland.

I began to feel very uncomfortable. I glanced at my watch. Mr. Norton was out there talking to his secretary for nearly ten minutes. What was going on? I heard my cell phone go off and dug it out of my purse quickly, hoping and praying that it was Brayden finally calling, but the screen told me that it was my mother. She must have discovered that I wasn't home and was looking for me, but I didn't want to talk to her just yet. I didn't want her to know where I was until I found out where Brayden was. She might try to talk me into coming home. I let it go to voice mail and flipped it closed when Mr. Norton finally reentered his office.

Without speaking and looking very upset, even a little nervous himself, he went around his desk and sat facing me again. I felt someone else in the room and turned sharply to see Mrs. Douglas standing behind me. She looked absolutely terrified. She wasn't much taller than I was, and now that she was out from behind her desk, I saw that she couldn't weigh more than one hundred pounds. She had her thin arms folded across her small bosom, but tightly, like someone who was clinging to herself.

"Let's get this completely straight," Mr. Norton began. "You tell me that you've come here to find out where the Matthews family now is because you're concerned about Brayden Matthews, whom you met while the Matthewses were in the house next to yours. Is that correct?"

"Yes, sir."

"And you spoke and spent time with Brayden Matthews in Echo Lake recently?"

"I saw him yesterday, in fact," I said.

He looked at Mrs. Douglas when she gasped. I turned to look at her, too. She had brought her right hand up to press against her lips.

"Why do you ask me that?"

"Mrs. Matthews is my daughter," he replied.

"Oh."

"She is indeed in a clinic, and she is seriously emotionally ill. It's also true that she has gotten worse. I was hoping that a new location, a new environment, a beautiful small community, would help her, that maybe she would return to her artwork. She and Sanford have a beautiful home here in Portland, but it's become impossible for her to remain there. I have it up for sale."

I nodded. All of that made sense, even though I still didn't know the details.

"Do you know why she's so sick?" he asked me.

"No. Brayden never told me."

"Brayden never told you," he repeated. Then he leaned forward. "I hope you're a disturbed person, too, and this isn't some sick joke," he said.

"Pardon me?"

"She's sick because she was in a terrible automobile accident. She was hit by a lumber truck just north of Portland. It drove her car off the highway and down a steep embankment. She suffered a broken leg and cracked ribs. The window on her door shattered and ripped out some of her face on the left side."

"Oh!" I said, practically gasping it. So that was why she had kept her face covered the first day I had seen her and why she had been wearing that scarf around her face when I saw her in the doorway receiving her groceries. But why wouldn't Brayden have told me that?

"Yes. But she wasn't alone in the car," he continued. "My grandson Brayden was in the car."

"Brayden?" I held my breath. Had he suffered some brain damage? Was that why he behaved the way he had in Echo Lake? Was his situation worse now?

"Brayden Matthews died from severe trauma to his right temple occurring during the rollover," Mr. Norton recited as if he were reading from a news article. "My grandson has been dead a year yesterday, matter of fact, matter of cold fact, so I don't know what the hell you're saying or why in hell you came here," he added in a raised voice. His eyes turned steely cold and he clenched his teeth. "My daughter was driving and blamed herself for the accident and my grandson's death. That's why she is suffering so terribly emotionally and psychologically."

I couldn't speak, but what he was saying certainly explained the grotesque painting she had done of Brayden in the attic.

"I called your family's jewelry store and spoke to your mother. Apparently, your parents are very upset with you and have no explanation for your actions and behavior. I hope you know how much you've upset them."

I shook my head. "This isn't true," I said. "It can't be true. I was with Brayden."

"Really." He sat back and gazed at me a long moment, his anger calming. Then he took a deep breath. "Like I said, I don't know why you've come here and why you're doing this. Your mother claims you have not been mentally ill, but she did admit that neither she nor your father ever set eyes on anyone claiming to be Brayden Matthews, that all they knew about him came from you, so now they are concerned about your mental health."

I started to cry. "I did know him. I did," I insisted. "He was there. We spent a lot of time together."

He looked at Mrs. Douglas.

"My grandson lies next to my wife in the River View Cemetery, section one forty-three. Maybe you should go see for yourself. Mrs. Douglas, provide this young lady with directions, please."

"This can't . . ."

"I think I've given you enough of my time, Miss Taylor. As I said, I don't know your purpose or reasons for coming here. If you're not mentally ill yourself, then whoever put you up to it, some jealous competitor or some displeased customer, whoever he or she might be, they're a sick son of a bitch. Good day," he said firmly.

I tried to swallow but couldn't. Instead, I rose and hurried out of his office. Mrs. Douglas stood at her desk. She looked as if she wanted to scratch my eyes out. Without speaking, she reached into a file and handed me a printout of the directions to the cemetery and the cemetery map.

"Take it. You should go visit the grave and apologize to that poor boy's soul for what you have just done to his grandfather," she said.

I looked at the paper. I was afraid to take it, but she thrust it at me again and I took it.

"Now, please leave, or I'll call the police. And never come back here," she added.

"I'm not lying," I said.

She raised her eyes toward the ceiling as to avoid looking at me.

With my legs moving as if they had a mind of their own and wanted me out of there, I left the office. I stood outside on the sidewalk, dazed. The traffic went by;

pedestrians crossed in front of me and behind me. One man knocked into me gently. My cell phone rang again. It was my mother calling once more, and once more I didn't answer.

I walked quickly to my car and sat behind the wheel, staring out for a while. *This can't be happening,* I told myself. *How can this be true? There has to be some great mistake, but how could a grandfather and a father make such a mistake about his daughter and grandson?*

I looked at the directions to the cemetery. I didn't want to go there, but now there was no way not to. I could never go home without seeing if what Mr. Norton had told me was indeed the cold truth.

Fifteen minutes later, I drove in and found my way to the section he had described. It wasn't hard to find the grave sites. The tombstones were larger than any nearby. I walked up to the two, saw the one for Delores Norton and just to the left of hers a tombstone that read: "Brayden Mark Matthews, Beloved Son and Grandson."

The date of his death matched a year ago yesterday, just as Mr. Norton had said.

But that wasn't what convinced me that it was my Brayden's grave.

It was the quote on the monument: "I hear a different drummer."

It was part of a quote from Thoreau's *Walden.*

"If a man does not keep pace with his companions, perhaps it is because he hears a different drummer."

I read the words repeatedly, and then I felt my legs soften and the earth shift beneath my feet as it began to spin.

It was like a curtain coming down.

Darkness washed over me.

Other people visiting grave sites nearby found me sprawled on Brayden's grave. I was taken to Legacy Good Samaritan Hospital's emergency room, where the doctor checked my vitals and kept me resting. Hours went by. I fell in and out of sleep, dozing, more like someone still stunned. Finally, when I opened my eyes again one time, my parents were standing there, my mother holding my hand. They looked absolutely terrified. I started to cry.

"We don't understand what's happening, Amber," my mother said softly. She wiped away my tears.

"The boy you claimed you were with has been dead for a year?" my father asked.

"I was with him," I insisted.

My father shook his head and sat facing the wall. He looked more stunned than I felt.

"We want to take you home now, Amber," Mom said.

"I feel so strange," I said.

"The doctor says there's nothing physically wrong with you. They gave you something to calm you down for now."

"Nothing *physically*," my father emphasized.

"When we're home, we'll be able to sort this out better," she continued.

"I don't see how we're equipped to do that," my father followed.

"Gregory."

"For God's sake, Noreen, she's been talking about being with a boy who's been dead for a year and she's come all the way to Portland to find out where he is." He turned to me. "Your mother doesn't want to come out and say it, but we talked about it all the way here, Amber. You need professional help. We'll find someone really good, and you'll get over this." He forced a smile. "Your imagination ran away with you. I always told you that you were like your friends, living in your own movie. It's all right. You'll be fine."

I looked away. What was left for me to tell them? I couldn't be upset with them for what they were saying or thinking. I knew they were concerned and afraid for me.

"Let me get her dressed so we can be on our way home," my mother said.

Dad nodded and rose. "I'll finish up whatever paper-work there is and meet you in the lobby," he said.

The medicine I had been given was kicking in, and I felt as if I could drift away. They took me out in a wheel-chair and fixed me up with a small pillow and a blanket in the rear seat. I slept all the way home, and when I got there, Mom helped me upstairs to bed and brought me something to eat.

"I'm sorry," I told her while she sat watching me eat.

"Just finish. Get something into your stomach and rest, Amber. Tomorrow things will be better."

When I was finished eating, she took the tray and gave me another one of the pills I had been given in the hospital. I didn't want to take it.

"It will help you sleep," she told me.

I took it, and she fixed my blanket and kissed me good night.

I closed my eyes and drifted in and out of sleep. Once, when I awoke, I thought there was someone

V. C. Andrews

standing in my room, but when I turned on the night light, there was no one. Through the window, the house next door was in darkness as usual. Silhouetted against the purplish-black night sky was that familiar crow on the roof. I stared at it for a while and then closed my eyes again and drifted in a sea of clouds into morning.

Epilogue

Mostly to please my parents, I agreed to see a therapist. Of course, they wanted to keep it a secret. My mother spoke with Dr. Immerman, who recommended someone who had offices in Greenwood. This therapist, Debra Martinson, specialized in the problems of younger people, especially teenage girls. She was about forty, probably, but had a very young face and a sweet, even bubbly personality. I think she was successful with teenage girls because she seemed to be one herself, but with far more wisdom. We got to know each other well during the first session. She almost didn't even bring up the reason for my coming to see her. It was toward the end of the session when she asked me if I found myself fantasizing often.

"All of us do," she added, "right up to the day we die."

"Yes, but . . ."

"But you feel this was more right now. That's natural, Amber. You're invested in this far more than you've invested yourself in anything. We'll give it time. If anything else occurs between now and the next time we meet, please write it down as closely to what happened as you can, okay? Otherwise, don't change your life. I mean, do whatever you usually do."

"What if my friends ask me about him?"

"Just say he's gone. He is, isn't he?"

"Yes," I admitted reluctantly.

She smiled. "With time, it will all be less painful for you. Someday you'll meet someone else who will capture your affections, and this will all drift away like some dream."

I nodded, but I didn't believe her. Time passed. We met again and again, each time talking less and less about Brayden and more about other things girls my age agonized about, especially the future that was coming, my leaving for college, my plans for a career, and my maturing relationship with my parents.

"Believe me," she said, "it will be harder for them to let you go than for you to leave."

We hugged after that session. She told me that she was going to advise my parents that regular sessions with her weren't necessary anymore and that she should be on a call-as-needed basis. Even though I had been reluctant to see her and that reluctance had come from my fear that she would get me to believe that all that had happened was some fantasy of my own making, I was sorry to leave her. She was likable, understanding, and she never made me feel as though there was anything seriously wrong with me.

Whatever, it satisfied my parents.

I avoided Ellie and the other girls for as long as I could but finally decided to go out with them one night. Even though there was still lots of time left to the summer, everyone's thoughts were on the impending school year, the senior year for almost all of us. We talked about high school things such as the senior prom, but we also talked about the colleges most of us were going to attend. I was still planning on staying in Oregon. Others loudly voiced their desire to get "as far away from this place as possible."

My experience with Shayne Allan was no longer a hot topic of conversation. Some of the other girls were having their own summer romances and wanted to talk more about themselves. I was grateful for that. Ellie was the only one who asked me about Brayden, and I did what Debra Martinson had advised me to do. I simply said he was gone and I didn't know where his family had resettled.

"I guess it wasn't even enough of an affair to remember," Ellie said, and I laughed. "What?"

"My father would immediately say, 'Deborah Kerr and Cary Grant.'"

"Who?"

"That's what I would say, and he would howl. They were the stars in the movie."

"What movie?"

"Forget about it," I told her, and asked someone else a question to get off the topic.

By mid-August, I had gotten so that I could walk past the house next door without giving it a second look. I was back to the way I was about that house before the Matthewses had moved in, and once again it was just a deserted old house. And then, one day, a crew arrived to begin repainting it, repairing all that needed to be repaired and cleaning up the yard. Some landscaping was being done, too, and the sidewalk was replaced. Von Richards told us that it had been sold to a family with two young children, a boy of eight and a girl of ten. The husband was an attorney who was joining Dave Russell's firm.

I knew that my parents were happy about it. The dreary, dark structure would literally disappear under the paintbrushes and sprays. It was like bringing the curtain down on some malicious, wicked dream. Any lingering thoughts and visions I had would be washed away.

"This time, we're bringing a cake or something over to them the day they move in," Dad said at dinner one night. My mother agreed. They both looked to me for my reaction, but I just smiled softly and nodded. Our talk returned to the store, the expansion Mom was now agreeing to do, and, of course, the excitement of my college plans, which would grow and loom larger as my senior year progressed.

I knew that nothing seemed to make them both more nervous than my wish to go for a walk at night after dinner alone, so I avoided doing that for nearly the whole summer. But one night in late August, I did just that. This year, the geese were leaving earlier, and the old-timers were predicting a colder, longer winter.

When I set out, I was intending to walk to the beginning of Main Street and then turn back, but I felt an overwhelming calling and turned off the street to take that shortcut between the Littlefield and Knotts houses. It was a good night for it, because the moon was nearly full, and there was little cloud cover. For me, it was more like a spotlight illuminating the path through the woods and down to the lagoon.

It was as quiet as ever. The nights were much cooler already, so there were no boats to be seen on the lake, and it was even difficult to hear the voices of people outside their lakeside homes. There was, in fact, a cathedral stillness. The birds I saw were as unmoving as frescoes on a church wall. The breeze barely made a ripple in the surface of the water.

I probably wouldn't have done it if it were not so well lit a night, but I turned and trekked through the woods to the front of the old cabin. For a few moments, I stood there looking at it, feeling like someone who was revisiting a dream, someone who had fallen so deeply asleep that she couldn't keep herself from slipping through the darkness. I saw the owl on the roof. It, too, looked more like a carving, some stone icon drawn on the wall of night.

Unafraid, I walked on and opened the cabin door. The moonlight seeped through every crack and opening, providing a hazy glow. I stared into the darkness until my eyes, now used to it, focused on what looked like an old notebook on the floor. I entered very slowly and at first just stood there looking down at it. Then I knelt and picked it up. It *was* a notebook. I moved into more moonlight and opened the cover. There was a title page: "The Eyes Behind the Eyes, A book of poems by Brayden Matthews."

I looked around sharply, turning in every direction. Then I went outside and listened.

"Brayden," I called.

There was only silence.

But I didn't need to hear him call back. I knew he was there and had been.

I had his book of poems.

Years later, when the man I fell in love with and married would ask me about them, I would tell him that they were written by a young man who'd had a tragic death but was still able to give someone else the gifts of hope and love.

Of course, he wouldn't fully understand.

But when my oldest daughter was ready, I would tell her my story and give the book of poems to her, and I was sure she would understand.

Embracing the book, I walked home that night feeling as if I would always be protected in the darkness.